Retribution for Acts of Terrorism

A MYSTERY IN ASPEN, COLORADO

Joel Feiss

iUniverse, Inc.
New York   Bloomington

This is a work of fiction. All of the characters, names, incidents, organizations, and dialogue in this novel are either the products of the author's imagination or are used fictitiously.

iUniverse books may be ordered through booksellers or by contacting:

iUniverse
1663 Liberty Drive
Bloomington, IN 47403
www.iuniverse.com
1-800-Authors (1-800-288-4677)

Because of the dynamic nature of the Internet, any Web addresses or links contained in this book may have changed since publication and may no longer be valid. The views expressed in this work are solely those of the author and do not necessarily reflect the views of the publisher, and the publisher hereby disclaims any responsibility for them.

ISBN: 978-1-4401-7871-9 (sc)
ISBN: 978-1-4401-7873-3 (dj)
ISBN: 978-1-4401-7872-6 (ebook)

Printed in the United States of America

iUniverse rev. date: 12/07/09

This book could not have been written without the love, support, and encouragement of my wife, Pearl.

Prologue

THE PHONE WAS ringing when Tanya and Susie Ramsey entered their home in Basalt, Colorado, after spending the day at the annual Aspen Fourth of July Parade. Susie ran over to the phone, picked it up, and said, "Hello, this is the Ramsey home." After several seconds she shrugged her shoulders, shook her head, and handed the phone over to her mother, saying, "It's for you, Mommy."

Tanya said, "Hello, this is Tanya Ramsey. Can I help you?"

"Tanya, this is Ahmed, and as I'm sure you will recall you assisted my employer recently when you cared for his father, who had end-stage renal disease. We have another very important job for you to perform for which you will be very handsomely compensated. There is a patient presently hospitalized in the Aspen Valley Hospital intensive care unit who requires some attention, and since you work some weekends at that hospital as an agency nurse, we feel you would be perfect for the job." Tanya recognized that he spoke in excellent English with a slight British accent.

Tanya said, "What sort of attention does he require?"

Ahmed answered, "That will depend on his clinical condition when you take over his care tomorrow. You will report to me, and we will discuss things further at that time. I want you to understand that what you will be doing to the patient will be harmful to him and will from your standpoint be unethical. However, I also want you to clearly understand that your compensation will be significant, but more importantly we know where you live, we know how much you love your daughter Susie, and we know that you would not want any harm to come to her. I hope I am making myself clear."

Tanya became weak and sweaty, and in a tremulous voice she responded, "This sounds insane. I can't do something like this. I just cannot do this."

Ahmed remained silent for several seconds and then said, "Let me make this perfectly clear. You will do what I say. You will not contact the authorities. You do want to see your daughter grow up, don't you?"

With tears streaming down her face, she weakly replied, "I understand."

Ahmed then gave Tanya the name of the patient and informed her that the money would be wired to her bank the following week.

Over five months later, just before Christmas, the headlines of the *Aspen Times* read:

BASALT NURSE FOUND MURDERED IN HER HOME

Chapter 1

———◆◆◆◆———

September 2007

THE SKY WAS beginning to cloud over as Dr. Ed Harris hiked up Cathedral Lake Trail. He passed beyond the aspen trees and headed higher up the frequently traveled but narrow path into a forest of spruce and evergreen trees. The air was cool and crisp as he passed above 9700 feet. September, he thought, was a perfect time to be in Aspen since the leaves of the aspen trees turned golden, the temperature was perfect for hiking, and the sky was generally clear except for the occasional late afternoon showers. The quietness and solitude of hiking in the woods of Colorado had always given him the needed escape from the structured routine of his medical practice as well as giving him the chance to let his mind wander aimlessly from one topic to another.

As he hiked higher up the path, his mind turned to the stock and real estate markets. It was his belief that the utterly peaceful feeling pervasive in Aspen was hiding the ever-increasing realization that a bear market would occur in the near future that involved both the U.S. and foreign stock and real estate markets. The excuses of hedge fund strategy problems and sub-prime loan defaults secondary to the failing housing market had been at the forefront of the news. Property values in Aspen had held up so far, but they would surely begin to decline as the realization of a true Wall Street bear market significantly reduced wealth.

Dr. Harris had always considered the hike to Cathedral Lake a challenge but clearly worth the effort. He could hear the hushed but forceful sounds of Pine Creek as he passed above the conifer trees. He headed higher, approaching 10,400 feet.

Pine Creek tumbled down from Cathedral Lake and paralleled the trail to produce a welcome coolness to the air, which every hiker appreciated since the trail became very steep at this point. At 11,200 feet, the old mine openings were visible, and then as the incline became more gradual and the effort a little less intense, Dr. Harris passed through the shady forest.

Just as he exited the forest, he could see the rock field just ahead. After he passed through the narrow trail on the rock field, he approached the most difficult section of the hike, which was an area of very tight and steep switchbacks. The trail eventually ended at 12,000 feet, where nestled in a clearing was the serenely beautiful Cathedral Lake.

Dr. Harris looked above the lake and considered heading higher to Electric Pass. However, he knew this was a tough hike to 13,600 feet and would take another two hours, which would make him late for his lunch date with his close friends, Jack and Penny Simpson. Ed rested for a few minutes at the edge of the lake and then began the descent.

He knew the hike down from Cathedral Lake took half the time and allowed for a more relaxed and less intense effort. His mind began to wander back to his medical school days, over twenty years ago, when life was certainly more hectic, but at the same time less complex, and his goals were easily visualized. His close friend, Jack Simpson, was always considered the brightest student and the most likely to remain in the academic setting as a researcher and professor of cardiology. However, as things would have it, Jack fell in love with an intensive care nurse, moved to Aspen, and began practicing cardiology. Dr. Harris knew that they were happy living in Aspen, where they could enjoy both winter and summer sports together. He was also aware of the fact that they had been unable to have children, but despite this misfortune they seemed to maintain a fulfilling relationship together. Penny worked in the hospital as a nurse; Jack's cardiology practice flourished; and they had accumulated significant assets, including a large investment portfolio.

Dr. Harris knew that the main topic of conversation at lunch today would involve the potential lawsuit that Jack was going to face in the near future. Dr. Harris was also well aware of the fact that even though specialists like Jack practiced medicine in a meticulous and caring manner, it was not unusual for them get involved in a medical malpractice suit since patients' expectations of care were not always met, and even in the best of hands things could go wrong. Dr. Harris was anxious to find out what exactly had happened.

The Pine Creek Cookhouse was clearly the best place for lunch in the Aspen area, boasting a gourmet menu and meals large enough to satisfy the clientele of cyclists and hikers that frequented the restaurant. The restaurant was situated a short distance from the Cathedral Lake trailhead in the ghost town of Ashcroft. There were spectacular views of Hayden, Cathedral, and Castle peaks from the outside dining area as well as from the large picture windows. The restaurant was constructed with pine logs, and the interior had beautiful vaulted ceilings, highly varnished pine tables, and a modern wood-burning fireplace near the well-equipped bar.

Ashcroft, a Western ghost town that was founded in 1879 by mining pioneers, had reached a population of five hundred full-time inhabitants by 1881. Pack mules carried ore over the pass to the nearest railroad in Crested Butte, Colorado, and Ashcroft was serviced by a stage coach. Aspen became the more highly populated town after the decision to bring the Denver & Rio Grande Railroad into Aspen, and this caused the town of Ashcroft to dwindle in size and popularity.

Jack and Penny biked the twelve miles from their Victorian home in Aspen to the restaurant and arrived exactly at 2 PM. They were both in great physical shape, as was typical for most Aspen locals. They rode their bikes along the gradual but difficult uphill Castle Creek road to the restaurant. Ed also arrived at 2 PM, somewhat dusty from the hiking trail. After the usual hugs and kisses, they were seated at an outside table.

Penny had held her years well, maintaining an athletic body and an attractive face highlighted by blonde hair pulled back in a ponytail. Jack was also in great shape, though he was somewhat shorter than Penny and beginning to bald frontally. He had penetrating blue eyes that women always found extremely attractive.

Jack had decided to practice without malpractice insurance. Going bare made the most sense to a large portion of physicians harnessed with the extraordinary cost of purchasing this protective insurance. This of course meant that all their accumulated assets, except their home and IRA, were at risk in a lawsuit.

While they were waiting for the waiter to come over to the table, Penny leaned over to Ed and said, "We have always trusted your judgment on financial matters, so Jack and I are anxious to see what your thoughts are on the case. We also want to ask what we should do with our assets."

Ed responded, "I appreciate the vote of confidence. Tell me about the case."

Jack said, "The patient was a fifty-year-old white male accountant who was visiting from New York. He arrived at the emergency room with atrial fibrillation, congestive heart failure, and an elevated blood pressure. He was treated with diuretics, anticoagulants, and an ace inhibitor to improve cardiac and renal function. Lopressor was used to control his heart rate. His symptoms of an irregular heartbeat had been occurring for several weeks on an intermittent basis, but he never sought medical care. He did well, becoming asymptomatic within twenty-four hours, and was started on Coumadin to thin his blood while awaiting more definitive treatment of his atrial fibrillation when he returned home. He remained hospitalized under my care for several more days until his level of anticoagulation was in perfect range with an INR of 2.5."

Ed said, "It seems everything went well. So what the hell is the potential lawsuit all about?"

Jack sighed and said, "After being discharged, the patient, Mr. Kahn, returned to the emergency room two days later with left upper quadrant abdominal pain. His CAT scan in the emergency room showed a splenic infarct typical of embolic clots coming from his heart with some intra-abdominal bleeding. He was admitted for observation, and during the night he suffered a massive stroke. He is presently in a rehabilitation center. His speech is affected, and in addition he has right-sided weakness, limiting his ambulation and use of his right upper extremity."

Ed said, "It seems unusual to begin having embolic phenomenon after being well anticoagulated." They all agreed that this was the crux of the case, but this left more questions than answers.

Coffee and dessert came, and they relaxed while enjoying the scenic view. They finished off the homemade ice cream and thought in silence about the case at hand.

Ed finally said, "I will be here for the rest of the week, so maybe we could review the records tomorrow and rediscuss the case while we hike up American Lake Trail." They decided to meet the next day, Sunday, at the hospital to review the chart and discuss the case in more detail.

Penny said, "Let's get any early start to avoid the usual late afternoon thunderstorms."

They parted ways. Jack and Penny biked back downhill along Castle Creek Road. Ed drove back to Snowmass, where he had a town house on Owl Creek Road. The drive was beautiful along the winding Castle Creek Road, which ran parallel to the creek and afforded great views of the mountain ranges covered with golden-leafed aspen trees and large evergreens. This was one of his favorite drives in the area. He could see the many horse ranches along the roadside as well as the large estate homes nestled high in the mountains and the rustic fishing cabins along the creek. Since there was no traffic on the road, he followed behind Jack and Penny for awhile. They were certainly a great couple and knew how to enjoy their life in the Aspen area.

Ed approached the roundabout on Highway 82. He entered the outer lane along with the rest of the traffic heading down valley to Snowmass, Basalt, El Jebel, and Carbondale. The traffic was light this time of year as opposed to the winter ski season that attracted tourists from all over the country as well as abroad.

The ride toward Snowmass afforded views of Maroon Bells in the distance. Ed passed the Aspen Highlands and Buttermilk Ski mountains on his left. He then turned onto Owl Creek Road for the less traveled and more scenic approach to Snowmass. This area was particularly beautiful, and if he was lucky he would get a glimpse of the elk that migrated this time of year. The Aspen-area citizens had been very proactive in their efforts to protect the elk during their migration. The scenic Seven Star Ranch was purchased by Pitkin

County to preserve this very important elk migration corridor. As luck would have it, there were no elk to be seen today.

Ed pulled into his parking spot in front of his town house, stretched, and went inside for a shower. He was hoping that his review of Jack's chart tomorrow would turn up something that could put his friend at ease since a malpractice case could be devastating to the physician being sued. He could not help but wonder what the circumstances were back in July that contributed to the patient's subsequent illness.

Chapter 2

———◆·◆·◆———

June 2007

THE PATIENT'S NAME was Samuel Kahn. He was fifty years old, overweight, and obviously sedentary by nature. He was born in Brooklyn, New York, as the grandson of a Holocaust survivor. He graduated from public school and went directly to NYU, where he graduated at the top of his class in accounting. Evelyn, his childhood sweetheart, majored in education, and they married while they were both still in college. They started a family as soon as he began earning a living. He had several accounting jobs before he began working as an accountant for a hedge fund specializing in oil-related companies, crude oil futures, and their options. He and the partners he worked for were going to Aspen for the week of July fourth to attend the yearly conference of oil drillers, equipment manufacturers, and oil speculators.

Hedge fund operators attended this annual meeting each year to gain information, but more importantly to raise money for their hedge funds. The income of the partners depended to a large extent on the amount of money that was invested in their fund since they received 2 percent of the invested money and 20 percent of the profits that they made for the client.

Sam Kahn did not do any trading but worked in the back room, keeping track of the trades as well as preparing the profit-and-loss statements each month. During the week prior to the July meeting in Aspen, Sam's colleagues noticed he seemed depressed and was drinking heavily. In the early part of June he had noticed that the hedge fund had a progressive increase of profits over the previous six months. These profits had risen nearly 50 percent on an annualized basis. This was an extraordinary return for any hedge fund, and it was especially unusual for oil-related funds. In fact, many oil-related funds lost money each year because of the large swings in oil prices secondary to presumed manipulation of oil prices by OPEC. He began to investigate the trades and discovered that the partners seemed to always be on the right side of the oil fluctuations just ahead of the OPEC meetings. This meant that they were incredibly lucky or had inside information which could only be obtained illegally.

The fund's name was Capital Investors of America, and it was owned by Mitch Carsdale and Jonathan Salem. They had previously worked together at the oil trading desk for Prudential, and after ten years of low-level trading, they decided to go out on their own. Mitch was in his early forties, tall, thin, and with sandy-colored hair he combed straight back. He worked out daily at the club which was one block from their office. Jonathan, also in his forties, was short, had a dark complexion and a short-cropped beard, and was obviously of Middle Eastern descent. The first couple of years were difficult since they only averaged a 2 to 3 percent return, which made raising money difficult even with their prior contacts at Prudential.

Sam noticed in reviewing the accounting records that over the last six months they had improved their performance, and at the same time one particular family of investors had increased their stake in the fund. He was sure that there had to be a connection to this family and the fund's ability to get inside information. Sam considered going to the Securities and Exchange Commission or the Commodity Futures Trading Commission, but at this time he wasn't even sure that they were breaking the law, and doing this would also end up jeopardizing his own career. His ambivalence led to an all-consuming depression.

Sam's wife Evelyn had been worried about him, but she had lived with him long enough to understand that with his stubborn personality he would only share his concerns with her when he was good and ready. Sam did, however, discuss his concerns with his closest friend, an attorney named Gary Goldman.

Gary was in his early fifties, of medium build, and had light brown hair. He always dressed in a business suit at work and had a reputation for being an attorney of the highest integrity. He had worked for the Securities and Exchange Commission prior to going into private practice for a large law firm in Manhattan in the same office building as Capital Investors of America. He and Sam had lunch together on a regular basis.

During a lunch a few weeks before Sam's trip to Aspen, Gary said, "Why don't you try to acquire more information about the suspected clients prior to seeking intervention by the SEC or the CFTC? An accusation of this type would have profound implications not only on your hedge fund but on the hedge fund business in general."

Sam said, "My main concern is the progressive investment strategy of this single investor, which corresponds to the exponential rise in the fund's profits. They have been wiring funds in from Dubai, and they have become our largest investor. I feel that in some way there is a link between this investor and the fund's amazing track record."

Gary suggested, "Maybe you should confront the partners with the facts and see if they have a simple explanation."

"I was hoping you could use your contacts at the SEC to check on my suspicions," Sam said.

"I'll see what I can do," Gary responded.

It was one week before the meeting in Aspen and Sam's eventual hospitalization when he confronted Mitch and Jonathan during their weekly business meeting. Both partners acted surprised by Sam's concerns regarding their extraordinary profits. They insisted that it was purely good market timing and a new trading system that they had developed. Sam thought they both seemed a little on edge, so he asked about the family from Dubai and their progressive increase of investment money.

Mitch said, "We know for a fact that they have been investing in many other funds as well as ours, and I'm sure they just like our trading style. Why are you so concerned, anyway?"

Sam answered, "I don't know, Mitch, it just seems like more than a coincidence. I guess I'm overreacting."

The meeting ended on a cordial note after they reviewed the last week's profit-and-loss statements, balance sheets, and trading fills.

Mitch and Jonathan returned to their office after the meeting and discussed the problem that had arisen with Sam. They decided to discuss this with the Dubai investor prior to attending the Aspen Oil Conference. They completed their trades for the day, and after the oil futures pit closed on the NYMEX, they went into their meeting room to discuss what strategy they would follow to handle Sam and, more importantly, how they would present this problem to their Dubai investor.

Mitch said, "It is eight hours later here than in Dubai, so we need to have a plan by the morning."

Jonathan said, "I believe we should let the Dubai family handle the matter since their resources are obviously greater than ours, and they have as much to lose as we do if a leak occurs." They decided to call at 7 AM, which would be 3 PM United Arab Emirates time.

The call was answered by Ahmed, the personal aide and bodyguard for Al-Shamir, who was the head of the family and cousin of Mohammed bin Rashid Al-Maktounm, the prime minister of Dubai. Jonathan relayed the message to Ahmed pertaining to the problem with the accountant and their concerns about his prying into their relationship.

"I will alert Al-Shamir of the problem at once," Ahmed said. "Please call if you obtain any further information, and rest assured that we will take care of this problem if we find it necessary to do so." He hung up and left Mitch and Jonathan confident that Ahmed had the means to control the situation. They knew, however, that they had to continue to monitor Sam Kahn's activities.

It became obvious to Mitch and Jonathan over the next week that Sam continued to investigate the client list and monetary distributions. Mitch again tried to reassure Sam that everything was being done in a legal way. Just prior to the Aspen meeting, they were convinced that Sam was a loose cannon.

Sam eventually divulged his concerns to his wife Evelyn. "What if I come with you to Aspen next week?" she asked. "Maybe you are making too much of this. You have been working for them for five years, and they have never given you any reason to doubt their ethics."

"You are probably right as usual," Sam said, "but I have this gnawing feeling that something is not right." The next day they flew to Aspen and checked in at the St. Regis Hotel, where the meeting was to take place. His illness and hospitalization occurred only two days after their arrival.

Chapter 3

September 2007

ED ARRIVED AT the Aspen Valley Hospital a few minutes after 7 AM and found the Simpsons with the hospital administrator, Kathy Ellington. She was a good friend and was going to join them on the hike up American Trail. Kathy was tall and slender with short, light red hair that highlighted her faintly freckled face and emerald green eyes. She carried herself with the air of confidence of someone who had succeeded on their own. They were all dressed in shorts, T-shirts, and hiking boots.

It took a short time for Ed to review the patient record, and as he had expected, it was as Jack had described. He also could not understand how Mr. Kahn could have gone from a perfect state of anticoagulation, or blood thinning, during his first admission to a state of poor anticoagulation just two days after his hospital discharge, causing him to get so devastatingly sick. Ed was sure that this unexplainable fact held the key to the case.

They packed up some fruit, energy bars, and ample water for the four-hour hike. They drove to the trailhead, which was off Castle Creek Road. American Lake Trail was a hike popular with the Aspen locals since it had a steep initial climb for one mile, utilizing switchbacks through Aspen trees, and then the trail leveled off with a path through shady woods. The four of them slowly ascended through this area. At 10,500 feet, the trail entered a spruce forest and then gradually

11

ascended to 10,900 feet. They hiked in silence, taking in the natural beauty of the climb. Jack and Penny hiked ahead at a faster pace and began a whispered conversation.

Jack said, "What do you think of the two of them together?"

Penny answered, "I don't think he's dated anyone since Lynn passed away."

Jack said, "He never said anything to me about dating anyone, and I think it's about time he started."

Penny then responded, "By the same token, Kathy had a bitter divorce and has not been in a serious relationship since leaving Chicago. I think they would be great together. Let's see how things go this week." They both stopped for a drink of water while Ed and Kathy caught up.

Ed was a little winded and said, "I can't keep up with you Aspenites at this altitude. I know Kathy was hanging back just to be nice."

Kathy smiled and said, "Are you kidding me? These two are aerobic animals."

The remaining part of the hike took them through several meadows, and then there was a steady climb to the lake at 11,400 feet. They rested awhile, hydrated, and continued to climb above the lake to 12,000 feet, where spectacular views of the lake below and the summit of Electric Pass could be seen. After a brief rest and satisfying their hunger with the remaining fruit, the four of them began the two-hour hike back down to the trailhead. They discussed the potential lawsuit, and all concluded that the reason for Sam Kahn's complications related to his decrease in anticoagulation over the two-day period after his discharge.

Ed said, "Even if the patient did not take his Coumadin, his blood should have still shown signs of anticoagulation. There was no obvious reason for this complication. If this had not occurred, then he probably would have done well and returned home safely for definitive treatment of his atrial fibrillation."

As a hospital administrator, Kathy had a definite interest in the case since the hospital would likely be dragged into the lawsuit along with the physicians involved. Her background as a nurse prior to completing her MBA in hospital administration helped her understand the technical aspects of the case. She was also at a loss to explain the sequence of events, but she promised to review the chart from a nursing standpoint.

The sky began darkening as the clouds appeared overhead and threatened an early afternoon storm. They reached the bottom of the trail as a few drops of rain fell, causing them to hurry to their car. They all drove back to the hospital to get their own cars. Ed and Kathy exchanged cell phone numbers and promised to get together over the next few days to discuss the case.

Kathy's curiosity got the better of her, and she immediately went to the medical records department of the hospital to review the hospital chart. She spent over an hour reviewing the nursing details, particularly looking for something out of the ordinary. She found no evidence of nursing error or negligence. She did, however, discover that the night prior to the patient's discharge, there was an agency nurse on duty in the telemetry unit where Mr. Kahn was a patient. She had worked at the Aspen Valley Hospital on prior occasions over the last couple of months but was not a regular part of the nursing staff. There were no other irregularities that Kathy discovered. She wrote down the nurse's name, returned the chart to its proper place, and headed home.

When she arrived at her house, Kathy learned that her daughter Laura was out with friends and her mother Ruby was also out for the day playing bridge with her friends. Kathy showered and changed, and then she called Ed. "How about getting some coffee at the Main Street Bakery?" she suggested. "I may have found something interesting as it relates to the case."

Ed said, "Sounds good to me. I can be there in half an hour."

They sat outside on the patio, ordered a couple of freshly made muffins and coffee, and enjoyed the fresh, cool air that was pervasive in the valley after a rain storm had passed.

Kathy said, "I'm not sure if it's important, but there was a nurse taking care of Mr. Kahn who was not part of our regular staff."

Ed asked, "Were there any drugs ordered out of the ordinary that night?"

She answered, "Not according to the chart."

Ed then said, "In gastroenterology we often see patients with gastrointestinal bleeding on anticoagulants. In order to stop the bleeding we need to reverse the anticoagulant effect and usually use fresh frozen plasma if a rapid reversal is needed. Vitamin K can also be used, but this takes longer to work. So if we need rapid reversal the fresh frozen plasma is used."

"That could only have been gotten from the blood bank," Kathy said.

"That's right. There would have to be a paper trail in the chart for this. There is also a drug called Novo Seven, which can be given intravenously and has a rapid and long-lasting effect to reverse anticoagulation from Coumadin and thereby enhances clotting. It is very expensive and probably not on your hospital formulary."

Kathy said she would check for this drug but still felt this was unlikely since there was no order for any form of anticoagulation reversal.

Ed thought for a minute and then said, "Well, that leaves us with no clear-cut answer to the puzzle."

"You're right," Kathy said. They sat in silence for a while, relaxing in the coolness of the late afternoon. It was interesting to Ed that he didn't feel the need to have a forced conversation with Kathy and felt comfortable in their silence. She finally said, "I have to get home to get dinner ready for my daughter and mother."

Ed asked, "How old is your daughter?"

"Laura is ten and a really great kid. She is a good student and quite the athlete."

"That's great. I'd like to meet her while I'm here."

Kathy asked, "How long are you planning to be in Aspen?"

"I'll be in the area for the rest of the week attending the annual gastroenterology seminar at the Silvertree Hotel, but I'm staying at my town house in Meadow Ranch on Owl Creek Road."

They sat a while longer, and then Kathy said, "It was really nice seeing you again. I hope we can do something to help Jack work through this lawsuit. He doesn't deserve to be dragged into a lawsuit at this time in his life." They said good-bye somewhat reluctantly and walked in separate directions. Ed turned as he approached his car to get another look at Kathy and was surprised that she had done the same and was looking at him. He smiled, waved good-bye, and got into his car.

That night Kathy called Penny and Jack to thank them for introducing her to Ed. Kathy said, "He seems like such a nice man."

Penny responded, "He may have difficulty expressing himself, but I can assure you he is a genuine guy. He has been through hell with his wife's illness and death, but he has never allowed his grief to interfere with his relationships with his patients or his friends. Socializing is going to be difficult for him, so if you really like him I would suggest you be proactive."

Kathy said, "Thanks, Penny. Talk to you later this week." She hung up and thought to herself, *It sure has been a long time since I've met a man that I can see myself with.*

The next afternoon, Kathy decided to take a chance and call Ed on his cell phone. She dialed somewhat hesitantly.

"Hello," Ed answered.

"Hi, Ed, this is Kathy Ellington."

"Hi, Kathy, I'm glad you called. I just got out of my meeting at the Silvertree and was thinking of hiking the Rim Trail before it gets dark. Do you have time to join me?"

Kathy said, "No problem, just give me time to change and drive to Snowmass Village."

Ed said, "Call me on your cell when you get close, and we can meet on Sinclair Road. We can leave my car there and take yours to the trailhead." They met without a problem and hiked up the steep switchbacks to the top of the rim. The rest of the hike was easy since the trail followed across the rim over the palisades. The view from the trail was of the entire Snowmass ski area. The sun was beginning to set and cast shadows over the ski trails. They hiked for about two hours and ended up at the junction of the entrance to Wildcat Estates and Sinclair Road. It then took about fifteen minutes to walk down to Ed's car. The sun had almost completely set, casting a golden hue over the area. Ed could not help but notice how attractive Kathy looked to him. He drove her back to the trailhead to get her car.

As Kathy started to get out of the car, she turned and said, "I've really enjoyed spending time with you. I hope we can see each other again."

Ed responded somewhat hesitantly, "I really had fun as well. I'll be back in November for the opening of ski season during Thanksgiving. Maybe we can make plans to see each other again."

Kathy smiled and said, "That sounds great." She could not help but think to herself that as cordial as he appeared, he at the same time seemed somewhat reluctant.

Chapter 4

November 2007

IT WAS EARLY November when the initial complaint came by special messenger, naming Jack Simpson, MD, and Aspen Valley Hospital in a lawsuit claiming multiple counts of negligence that caused the resultant cerebral and splenic infarcts to Samuel Kahn. He apparently had not recovered his speech or the ability to ambulate and only had limited use of his right upper extremity. Fortunately, Jack had acquired legal insurance for the defense of any possible lawsuits when he decided not to obtain full malpractice insurance coverage. This type of insurance would at least provide him with legal representation at a minimal cost, but it provided no coverage for damages if he lost a case. He contacted the law firm of Kaufman and Brandon to alert them and set up an initial meeting to familiarize the attorneys with the facts of the case. Their office was in Denver, but they did a lot of work on the defense side in medical malpractice throughout Colorado. The senior partner was Abe Kaufman, who luckily was going to be in Vail for Thanksgiving and agreed to meet with Jack at his office during that week.

The lawsuit had progressed much faster than Jack had anticipated. The notice of intent and pre-suit investigation were completed by the plaintiff's attorney in October, and an expert witness had been obtained from Denver. The next steps toward a possible trial by jury would involve pretrial discovery by depositions of those involved in the case.

The plaintiff's attorney was Michael Sutton, a well-known and respected attorney from Denver. He was an intimidating and relentless litigator with a large staff of paralegals and nurses. He also had physicians who served as expert witnesses and who very often would be easily coerced into claiming malpractice when indeed it was very questionable. In this case he needed a cardiologist who would claim that Jack's management of the case was below the standard of care in a community hospital setting. For the right price he obtained a cardiologist from Boulder, Colorado. This physician was one of Sutton's favorite expert witnesses, and he had used him many times in the past to get litigation started. The medical community considered the cardiologist a gun for hire for plaintiff attorneys, but he was rarely utilized in court because it was obvious that he was biased against other, more successful physicians.

Abe Kaufman arrived at Jack's office at 5:00 PM on the day before Thanksgiving for their initial meeting. Jack was finishing up with his last patient before the long Thanksgiving weekend and was looking forward to meeting Mr. Kaufman to go over the details of the case. He hoped that Mr. Kaufman would alleviate some of his fears and anxiety over the lawsuit, but on the other hand he feared that Mr. Kaufman might feel that the plaintiff really had a case against him. He could feel his heart race, and it was clear to Jack that he was having difficulty suppressing his anxiety over this lawsuit.

Abe Kaufman was a stocky man in his late sixties with a short-cropped beard, ruddy complexion, and a serious demeanor, making it clear to Jack that he was a no-nonsense litigator. Abe began the meeting by explaining to Jack the necessity for him to know the records in the most thorough manner, especially since the next phase of the litigation would involve his deposition.

He said, "Jack, I know this is all new to you, so let me explain in simplistic terms what you need to know about the legal process that you will be facing."

Jack took a deep breath and said, "Okay."

Abe noticed that Jack was nervously rubbing his hands over his thighs. He began by explaining, "The deposition is an interrogation by the plaintiff's attorney. The purpose of the interrogation is not only fact-finding of the medical details but also to note your appearance and demeanor. The opposing attorney is Michael Sutton, and I hate to say this, but he is as smooth as they come. He will attempt to get you to make statements that he could use later to show your lack of knowledge. He will even try to get you to contradict yourself. The best way to avoid these pitfalls is to know the case down to the minutest detail."

Jack said, "I have gone over this case in my mind so many times that frankly I'm sick of the whole thing."

Abe responded, "I understand how you feel, but let me assure you that you have more medical knowledge at your fingertips than any of these attorneys, so if you know the case and stay calm, you will prevail."

Jack leaned back in his chair and said, "I'm sorry, Mr. Kaufman, please go on."

"The plaintiff's attorney will ask questions pertaining to your training and background, hoping to find any flaw that he can use to win the case. The deposition can be used in court and is, in fact, the most important pretrial event for you as the defending physician. The deposition also is important because the expert witnesses will be reading your responses and will be able to tell how you handle the pressure. I also want to make it clear that the opposing attorney will also try to get you to state that a text or publication is authoritative. You should be sure to avoid saying that any publication is authoritative since Sutton could use statements from a publication out of context to make his case."

Following the discussion about the nature of the deposition and its importance, they began the process of reviewing the hospital record and the events leading up to Mr. Kahn's complications. They finished just as snow began to fall, covering the street outside of Jack's office like a thick, white blanket. November could sometimes be a good month for significant snowfall in Aspen.

Abe was getting ready to leave and told Jack that his next meeting would be with Louis Reiner, the firm's youngest attorney, but he assured Jack that Louis was thorough and promised to be a top litigator. At that time they would do a mock deposition and would have accumulated all the records of Mr. Kahn's health prior to and following his hospitalization at Aspen Valley Hospital.

Abe said good-bye and drove west on Highway 82 toward Vail. He felt the meeting had gone well, and although Jack was nervous, he had confidence that Jack would present himself as a physician who was competent and, more importantly, not arrogant. He also had the feeling that the apparent facts of the case did not truly demonstrate negligence. He could not help but wonder what had happened to Mr. Kahn between the time of his hospitalization and the time of his readmission through the emergency room.

Jack finished with the last of his phone messages and phone calls, and he was looking forward to Thanksgiving and having a few days off to spend with Penny. He locked up the office and decided to walk the few blocks home through the light snowfall.

Penny was waiting for him as he arrived and immediately wanted to know how the meeting went. "What kind of guy is the attorney?" she asked.

Jack answered, "He appears very competent and clearly is a no-nonsense guy. My next meeting will be with a younger associate. I hope they are not treating me like a second-class citizen because I don't have insurance."

"I doubt they would do that, Jack. Give the new associate a chance and don't prejudge him. I'm sure things will work out as they always do."

"Yeah, I'm sure you're right. I'll be okay. Don't worry."

Penny smiled and gave Jack a hug, but she knew he wasn't doing well. She was concerned how he was going to handle this on-going lawsuit from an emotional standpoint.

Chapter 5

November 2007

ED HAD BEEN following the weather reports in Aspen from Fort Lauderdale. He had been planning to go back to Colorado for Thanksgiving if the skiing conditions were good. This year there was a good preseason snowfall, rendering a thirty-six-inch base. He made arrangements with his partners to cover his nights on call and booked a flight to the Eagle-Vail airport in Colorado. He called Jack and Penny to let them know he would be there for Thanksgiving.

Penny said, "That's great! You and the kids can come for Thanksgiving dinner."

Ed responded, "This year they made other plans, but they will be there for Christmas. Maybe we can all get together then."

The drive from Eagle to Snowmass took Ed through Glenwood Canyon, which was spectacular with snow covering the rocky ledges and mountaintops. The sun's brilliance reflected off the snow. The river running parallel to the highway was a deep green, with ice forming along the edges. Ed drove his rental car slowly through the canyon, taking in the beautiful sights. He was also careful because of the light snowfall. The drive to Snowmass usually took less than one and a half hours. He was looking forward to skiing with Jack and Penny, and to seeing Kathy as well. He was especially interested to see what progress had been made in the lawsuit.

The drive through the canyon reminded him of the many times he and his late wife had made the same trip, either by themselves or with their children. He reflected back to those times as well as the many other wonderful moments they had spent together right up until the time of her illness with acute leukemia. He realized that as difficult as it was to really believe that he would be living his life without her and as much of a dramatic life-changing event her death was, he had to continue to be productive and to live his life to its fullest potential. He understood that people utilized different psychological mechanisms to handle these life stresses, and he felt he was doing as well as he could to maintain some sort of stability. As saddened as he was, he seemed to have the psychic resilience to continue to practice and be as good a father as was possible with grown-up children living their own lives.

His interest in the stock market and technical analysis seemed to take up a lot of his spare time and thoughts. This was a particularly interesting time in the markets. The fundamental reasons for the stock market's decline was a very weak and worsening housing market, oil prices rising to levels of greater than ninety dollars a barrel, and financial institutions losing billions of dollars in sub-prime loans and hedge fund losses. The Fed had increased liquidity into the system by cutting the discount rate and federal funds rate, which along with some recent high-tech earnings above expectation kept the market in rally mode to the October top. The globalization of the markets, along with the rapid economic growth in China and India, was also buoying the U.S. stock market. Ed still felt the market was topping out, and this was a time to be safe and take profits in all areas with the exception of gold, bonds, and oil-related positions. He knew this was the right time to get Jack and Penny out of the stock market.

The snow began falling heavier as he drove past Glenwood Springs on Highway 82 East and entered the Aspen area. After a brief stop in El Jebel for groceries, he pulled off 82 onto Brush Creek Road, which led to Snowmass Village. The view of the Snowmass ski area was simply breathtaking as the late afternoon sun seemed to give the landscape a pastel pink and purple hue.

It was early in the evening before Ed got the groceries put away. He made himself a light dinner and watched the evening news on CNN. He called Jack and Penny's house to say hello and see what was going on with their case. Jack told him that he had just gotten home from his meeting with Abe Kaufman, the defense attorney. Jack was to be on call Thanksgiving Day and was going to miss the season opening of Snowmass Mountain. Penny then got on the phone and suggested that Ed call Kathy since she was off work the next day and wanted to see him again. He was somewhat nervous about calling her, but he got her number from Penny and said he would see them for dinner tomorrow night.

Ed hesitantly dialed Kathy's number and was somewhat relieved to get her voice mail. He left a brief message to call him back whenever she got a free moment. Then he got his computer hooked up and got online to get the stock market data for the day.

Kathy called back a short while later, and they eventually decided to ski together the next day.

"Let's get an early start. It was forecasted to continue to snow throughout the night, and tomorrow should be a great powder day," Ed said.

"Sounds good to me," Kathy said. She then asked, "Is it all right with you if I bring my ten-year-old daughter along?"

Ed answered, "That would be great." They said goodnight and hung up. He finished collecting the stock market closing data and went to bed.

Thanksgiving Day was beautiful. The snow stopped falling at 7 AM and the sun began to shine, illuminating the freshly fallen snow and giving the entire ski area a serene atmosphere. Ed caught the shuttle to the Two Creeks area ski lift and met Kathy and her daughter, Laura. They seemed as excited as Ed did for the mountain's opening. Laura was of course a snowboarder, as all the local kids were now utilizing snowboards rather than skis. Kathy was ready for a powder day with her short powder skis. She was more beautiful than Ed had recalled. They caught the first chairlift up and were in dry, knee-deep powder for first tracks by 9:15 in the morning.

The three of them had a great day, stopping only for a quick lunch and hot chocolate. Laura was a great snowboarder as expected, and Kathy was a great skier. They ended the day in Snowmass Village. Just prior to leaving, Kathy reminded Ed about the agency nurse who had been taking care of Mr. Kahn on the evening shift prior to his day of discharge. She mentioned that the nurse had not been seen at the hospital again and felt there may be a link to the case.

Ed thought for a minute and said, "We should contact her and see if she could add some information not evident in the chart."

Kathy said, "I'll pull her file to obtain her address and phone number. Perhaps we could visit her after skiing tomorrow."

Laura excitedly added, "We'll see you at the Simpsons' for Thanksgiving dinner." Ed smiled. He was excited to see them again. They parted their separate ways.

Once Ed was out of sight, Laura said, "I really liked Ed. I hope we can ski again during my Thanksgiving break."

Kathy gave her a hug and said, "I feel the same way."

Chapter 6

November 2007

THANKSGIVING DINNER AT the Simpson home was usually traditional with a turkey and all the fixings. Penny was known for her hospitality to friends and family at holiday time. Ed, Kathy, Laura, and Kathy's mother Ruby were the only guests at the Simpsons' this year. Ed found himself alone with Laura when all the women went directly into the kitchen to help Penny and Jack was still making hospital rounds.

Ed asked, "How are you doing in school?"

Laura smiled and said, "I do okay."

"Yeah, so what kind of grades do you get?"

"Mainly A's, except in English. I find it kind of boring."

Ed asked, "So you like the sciences?"

"I really like math the best. What about you, Dr. Harris? What subjects did you like the best when you went to school?"

Ed smiled and said, "Lunch." They both laughed and then Ed asked, "Are you interested in any other sports, or are you just a great snowboarder?"

Laura stood, smiled, and said, "I happen to be captain of the school speed skating team."

"That's great, Laura, I'm impressed."

Kathy walked into the room and said, "What are you two up to?"

They both smiled, and Laura said, "Dr. Harris was just trying to find out if I was smart enough to be a doctor." They all laughed and went into the dining room since Jack had arrived and everything was ready. The main topic of dinner conversation was the upcoming lawsuit. Jack was more concerned than the facts seemed to warrant, but this was not unusual for physicians since a lawsuit was a threat not only financially but also challenged their medical skills.

Jack said, "I have to tell you guys that I find this whole legal system very foreign. I have heard that Mr. Kahn's attorney is very aggressive and can be extremely intimidating and manipulative. Decisions in the medical arena are made in seconds, and when viewed at a later time with additional facts not evident at the moment, those decisions may seem negligent."

Ed said, "I know how you feel, Jack, but you and I have been over this case. It is clear that you were not negligent."

Ed could hardly finish what he was saying before Jack said, "You know as well as I that there are physicians in the system who make a significant income testifying for plaintiff attorneys, and they are very skilled in rendering depositions and court appearances. Since lawsuits develop slowly over months or even years, new studies may show that what was once a standard of care is now considered negligent. Also, retrospective analysis is always easier than judgments made during the care of a sick patient."

These thoughts had evidently been bothering Jack, and it definitely showed in his solemn demeanor. Jack had always been carefree and confident, but now it seemed to Ed that his friend had become more introspective and worried. Ed and Kathy tried to reassure him that there was no negligence on his part. They also told him they felt that surely some important information would come from the agency nurse caring for Mr. Kahn the night prior to his discharge.

After dinner, Ruby and Laura thanked the Simpsons for a great holiday dinner and headed home, leaving Kathy with Ed, Jack, and Penny. They had some after-dinner drinks and let the conversation drift from medicine to skiing and finally to the state of the economy and the markets. The topic of oil prices always came up in their discussions since oil had come close to one hundred dollars per barrel and was to blame for a sinking economy and a declining stock market.

Ed said, "I really believe that OPEC manipulates the oil markets. Let me tell you about the sequence of events that occurred this month just prior to the November option expiration of oil futures. As oil approached one hundred dollars a barrel, the hype on television and the financial news media helped set up a large premium on the November 100 call options. The traders for Saudi Arabia were net sellers of these calls, and that allowed them to bring in a large amount of cash from speculators who bought these call options in hopes of making money as the price of oil exceeded one hundred dollars. Then, during the week prior to expiration of those calls, OPEC announced that they were going to increase production, which caused the price of oil to drop and thereby rendered the calls worthless." Ed realized that he sounded like an old economics professor, and when he realized that their interest in the markets was not as serious as his own, he dropped the subject.

The evening was drawing to a close, and Kathy was helping Penny in the kitchen. She confided to Penny that she had an attraction to Ed and said he was so different than the men she had met in Aspen.

"I have to say that I'm tired of being hit on by married doctors and men who think just because I'm divorced I'm ready to hop in the sack at a moment's notice."

Penny said, "Ed is a terrific guy. He's a good, decent man and was a wonderful husband. For selfish reasons I would love to see the two of you get together."

"Penny, you are a true romantic. How do I know he is even interested in me in a romantic way?" Kathy asked.

Penny smiled and said, "We'll just have to see how things go this week." They finished cleaning up the kitchen and came out to the living room.

Ed and Jack were sitting in front of the fireplace when Penny and Kathy walked in. They both stood, and Jack went over to Penny and gave her a kiss and said, "Great dinner."

Ed and Kathy stood there silently feeling a little awkward. Ed finally volunteered to drive Kathy home. They all said goodnight, and Kathy and Ed stepped out into a beautiful evening with snow falling lightly around them.

Ed drove Kathy to her home in the north end of Aspen, near the music festival tent and associated campus. They made plans to ski in the morning and then drive out to Basalt to see the agency nurse, Tanya Ramsey, in the afternoon.

Kathy said, "Laura will be skiing with her friends tomorrow, so it will just be the two of us."

Ed said, "Great, maybe I will have time to catch my breath." They laughed, hugged, and said goodnight.

The snowfall picked up quite a bit as Ed drove back to his town house. The flakes were large and light since the air was dry, and the temperature was dropping fast. He could not get over his excitement each time he saw Kathy. A relationship with her presented a set of problems, however. He lived in Fort Lauderdale, and she had roots here in Aspen. He was certainly not ready to retire or move to Aspen to practice as Jack had done, especially since his children lived in South Florida. He also had no idea how they would react to him having a relationship at this time. As he pulled up to his town house, he shrugged and laughed to himself since he really didn't know how she felt about him.

Chapter 7

November 2007

KATHY CALLED TANYA Ramsey early the next morning and fortunately found her at home with her six-year-old daughter. Kathy began the conversation by saying, "This is Kathy Ellington, the administrator at Aspen Valley Hospital."

"I know who you are, Mrs. Ellington. What can I do for you?"

"I would like to speak to you about your nursing duties at the hospital."

"Why?" Tanya answered reluctantly.

"It involves a patient you took care of recently. There is a lawsuit against the hospital and Dr. Simpson," Kathy said.

"Well, only if it's essential," Tanya answered nervously.

"It is important, Tanya. Would this afternoon at around four o'clock be all right?"

Tanya didn't answer immediately, but she finally said, "Yes."

Kathy and Ed had another great day skiing together. After skiing until noon, they stopped at the base of the mountain for a quick lunch and then planned to meet again at 2:30 PM so they could drive to Basalt together.

Kathy picked Ed up at his town house in her Jeep Wrangler. It was an older model, but it was immaculate and drove perfectly, especially on the snow-packed roads of the Aspen area.

During the drive, Ed said, "It's been a long time since I've been in Basalt. The last time I was there, I had said to my late wife how rapidly it was developing."

Kathy said, "You will not believe how things have changed in the whole down-valley area."

Ed said, "Unfortunately we never got back to Basalt to see the changes together."

Kathy looked at him and said, "I'm sorry."

Ed said, "Don't be sorry. We had a good life together and a great marriage." He then added, "Maybe we could come here for dinner some night?"

Kathy smiled and said, "I'd like that, Ed." After a pause, Kathy said, "I took the liberty of asking around about Tanya. She is recently separated from her husband, Todd, who is a ski instructor at the Sunlight Ski Resort in Glenwood Springs during the winter and a river rafting guide during the summer. He has a reputation of heavy drinking and is known to be abusive to Tanya when he gets intoxicated. Tanya has a good reputation as a nurse and mother, but she is somewhat of a loner except for one close friend who works with her at their nursing agency."

They pulled off Brush Creek road and headed west toward Basalt. After driving for about fifteen minutes, they pulled off Highway 82 and entered the town of Basalt.

Kathy and Ed arrived at Tanya's home at four in the afternoon. Ed took a close look at Tanya when she opened the door and noticed that she was a petite, very attractive Latina and had her hair pulled back in a ponytail. She was dressed in jeans and a long-sleeved jersey. After introductions, they settled in her living room, where Kathy tried to develop the sequence of events during Tanya's shift at the hospital the evening before Sam Kahn was discharged from his first admission. Ed noticed that Tanya was obviously anxious about the events of that evening.

Tanya said somewhat nervously, "I heard about the lawsuit but could not see that there was any negligence on the part of Dr. Simpson." They went through the medicines that were given that night and any possible changes in the patient's behavior, but they could not discover anything unusual. They thanked her for her time, and then Kathy asked why Tanya hadn't been taking more shifts at the hospital.

Tanya responded, "I have been fortunate to get more hours with my home health agency recently, so I have not needed to take hospital shifts to supplement my income. This gives me more time to spend with my daughter."

Kathy gave Tanya her card, wrote her cell phone number on the back, and said, "Please call if you remember anything else that may help Dr. Simpson or the hospital. You know what a fine cardiologist he is, and he certainly does not deserve this lawsuit."

Tanya took the card and placed it on the dining room table. She was a bit tremulous, but said nothing.

Tanya's daughter Susie awoke from her nap just as Ed and Kathy were leaving. Susie was a cute little girl with dark brown hair and large, brown eyes. Susie waved good-bye as Kathy and Ed went out the door.

Ed noticed that Tanya owned a Lexus RX 350 SUV, fully loaded, and he wondered how she could afford such a vehicle with her salary and probably no support from her deadbeat husband.

They headed back to Snowmass, taking Highway 82 East. They drove in silence most of the way, enjoying the view of Woody Creek with ice and snow lying along its sides. The sun was low in the sky by this time and lent a golden hue to the rushing water. Just as she turned up Brush Creek Road toward Ed's town house, Kathy broke the silence and asked if he was doing anything that night for dinner.

Ed answered nervously, "I thought you would never ask." They both laughed and then decided to meet later for dinner. Ed said, "I'll call the Hotel Jerome for reservations."

Kathy responded, "Pretty fancy place, don't you think?"

Ed said, "We'll count it as our first date." They looked at each other and nodded in silence. He then said, "Is seven thirty a good time for you?"

She answered, "That would be perfect."

Ed said, "I'll pick you up at your house. This will give me a chance to see Laura and your mother one more time before I return to Fort Lauderdale tomorrow."

Ed had no trouble making the reservation. He also called Penny and Jack to let them know about his meeting with Tanya Ramsey. He mentioned that he felt Tanya knew more than she was saying, but it was unclear exactly what she could be hiding. He said he would be back for Christmas week since his practice in Fort Lauderdale usually slowed down significantly at that time of year. Jack told Ed to keep in touch over the next few weeks and that he would call if anything developed from a legal standpoint. Of course they all hoped that the lawsuit would be dropped and life would return to normal.

"By the way, Ed, I hear you're going to dinner with Kathy tonight," Jack said prior to hanging up the phone. "I'm glad you two are getting along so well. It's about time you decided to socialize a little."

"News travels fast around here," Ed commented. "Thanks for the encouragement, Jack. She's a great girl, and I'm really enjoying her company. I'll see you Christmas week."

The night was clear and crisp when Ed arrived at Kathy's home at seven o'clock. He said hello to Ruby and Laura, who greeted him at the door, and mentioned that he missed skiing with Laura that day but hoped when he came back in December they could spend the day together.

"I'm not used to skiing with the old folks," Laura said with a smirk on her face and laughter written in her eyes.

"I didn't think I slowed you down that much," Ed said jokingly. Just then Kathy came into the room and offered Ed and Ruby a glass of white wine, which they gladly accepted. They toasted a great ski day and a happy holiday along with Ruby, who had been studying Ed in a way only a mother could do. Ruby finally said that she hoped to see Ed again, finished her wine, and took Laura into the kitchen for dinner.

Ed helped Kathy with her coat, noticing the fragrance she was wearing. It was a moment of nervousness, anticipation, and excitement. He wondered if he should actually reveal the fact that this was his first date since his wife Lynn died.

They encountered very little traffic during the short drive to the Hotel Jerome. It was such a beautiful and brisk night. Ed pulled up to the entrance of the Jerome, where they were greeted by the ever-present valet in his black cape and cowboy hat. Kathy and Ed entered the magnificent lobby with its antique Western décor, huge wood-burning fireplace, and the feeling of being part of an era long gone. The maitre d' took their coats and seated them at a table near the fireplace.

They ordered Caesar salads, venison, and lamb chops. While the waiter was preparing the salad at the tableside, they each had a glass of chardonnay. Kathy asked Ed how he was so fortunate as to be able to come out to Aspen so often.

"I have a great relationship with my associates in our medical practice," he answered. "We share expenses equally, but since our income is based on individual production, they don't mind if I take off as much as I do. I have also done well in the stock market and real estate in South Florida. I came from a modest background and found it necessary to work since I was a teenager. I moonlighted my way through medical school and my residency, so when I finally started making a little money I decided that as soon as I could afford it I would bring balance to my life."

"How long have you been coming to this area?" Kathy asked.

"Lynn and I began skiing after the first three years of my beginning private practice. We were introduced to skiing by one of the surgeons in town who had a condominium in Snowmass. We both fell in love with the sport and vowed to ski at least once a year. Each year we would try a different ski area with our friends. We went to Lake Tahoe, Snowbird, Alta, and even Switzerland one year. We started out our two boys skiing at the age of six. We found skiing in the winter and hiking in the summer a great way to share vacations as a family."

Kathy then said, "Tell me about your boys."

"I have been so lucky. Everett is twenty-six, lives in South Beach, and works as a real estate attorney. Luke is twenty-four and married his high school sweetheart last year. He is a stockbroker for Morgan Stanley, and they live not far from me in Fort Lauderdale. No grandchildren yet, but I'm hopeful."

Kathy then asked if Everett was married. Ed responded that Everett was gay but has had a life partner, Chad, for five years.

The waiter completed his preparation of the salad, and after placing the dishes on the table, said, "Enjoy."

Kathy waited for him to leave and then said, "If it's not too presumptuous of me, tell me about Lynn."

Ed was silent for a few minutes. Then he said, "We met while I was in medical school. Mutual friends were responsible for getting us together. She was the head of medical records at the teaching hospital where I trained. We immediately got along great. She came from a nice family who accepted me without noticeable reluctance, and before we knew it we were engaged. "After I was secure in my internship at

Jackson Memorial Hospital, we got married and had Chad during my residency. Times were tough at first, but I was able to find moonlighting jobs easily in emergency rooms in the Fort Lauderdale area. Luke was born as I was beginning my gastroenterology fellowship. We moved to Fort Lauderdale after I finished my fellowship, and then life really became full and rewarding for both of us. The medical community was just beginning in that area of Fort Lauderdale, and I was able to practice the kind of aggressive medicine that I was trained to do.

"Our love for each other grew stronger through the years, and I must tell you that I never knew life could be so wonderful. The boys did well in school, went to the University of Florida, and eventually joined the work force. They became independent, moved out of the house, and left us as happy empty nesters. Two years ago, Lynn began to fatigue easily and began having nosebleeds. She was diagnosed with an unusual and unfortunately untreatable form of acute Leukemia and died rather soon after the diagnosis. There are no words to explain the emotional upheaval one goes through. The entire period of time surrounding her death truly seems like it never really happened."

Kathy could sense Ed's emotional distress and placed her hand on his and asked, "Would you rather talk about something else?"

Ed answered in a choked-up voice, "Actually, this is the first time I have felt comfortable talking about the events surrounding her death." They sat in silence, sipping their wine for several minutes. Then Ed said, "Enough about me. Tell me what brought you to Aspen."

Kathy sighed and said, "I met Rob while I was a nurse in the ICU at Northwestern Medical Center. We were also introduced by friends. He was a bond trader on the floor at the Chicago Board of Trade. He was quite charming and wealthy. We had a whirlwind romance and were married in six months. We lived lavishly on his income, taking many vacations, especially to this area. Laura was born after two years of marriage.

"Things changed rather suddenly after her birth. He was not the father I had hoped he would be, and he apparently was playing around, even during my pregnancy. I found out the rumors about him and the young floor clerks at the CBOT were true. In fact, he readily admitted as much during the divorce proceedings. My mother was a widow by this time, and she was a great help with Laura. I took advantage of a large divorce settlement and went back to school at Northwestern to get an MBA in hospital administration. Fortunately, after I completed an internship in Chicago, a job opportunity opened up here in Aspen. My mother, Laura, and I moved out here, and we have been here ever since. My ex-husband has very little interest in seeing Laura, so everything has worked out well. Laura sees him only during summer break, which at the present seems to satisfy both their needs."

Dinner was served and, as usual, in an elegant style. Ed ordered a couple of glasses of Merlot to go with their venison and lamb chops. They stole looks at each other during dinner and had light conversations about skiing and the pleasures of living in a small tourist town with all the usual comforts.

"I have to admit that this is as close to a date as I have been since my wife died. In fact, this is my first date." They both laughed.

"I'm honored," she said.

Ed drove Kathy home. He walked her to the door.

Kathy said, "Ed, this was really a lovely evening. Thank you so much." She kissed him on the cheek. "I'll see you when you come back for Christmas."

Kathy and Ed both left each other knowing this was only the beginning.

Chapter 8

December 2007

I T WAS 3 PM on the Friday before Christmas vacation when Susie's teacher, Christina Gregory, was concerned that Tanya had not picked Susie up from school. She knew this was unusual because Tanya was one of the most reliable mothers in the class. If she could not be there because of a home health visit, then her friend Eloise was always there right on time. They never depended on Susie's father to be there because he was known to everyone in town as an unreliable drunk.

While Susie was busy coloring in a book, Mrs. Gregory went to the principal's office to discuss the problem with her. The principal, Dr. Tiffany Mathews, immediately called Tanya at home. When there was no answer, she then tried her cell phone. When there was no answer on her cell phone, Dr. Mathews called Eloise. Eloise said she had not spoken to Tanya all day. The principal then called the chief of police to let him know she had a gut feeling that something was terribly wrong, and could he please indulge an old friend and send a patrolman by Tanya's house to see if everything was all right.

Chief Owens radioed patrolman Gully and instructed him to stop by the Ramsey home and see if Tanya was there. Patrolman Gully was in the area, so it only took a couple of minutes for him to arrive at the house. He knocked on the door several times, and when no one answered he tried the front door. It was unlocked. He stuck his head in the door and called Tanya's name. There was still no answer, so he slowly entered the house and found Tanya's lifeless body on the living room floor. She was obviously dead, and beside the body was a bloody rafting oar. Her head was severely injured, and there was a telephone cord wrapped tightly around her neck. Patrolman Gully was only a rookie, but he knew enough not to touch anything and immediately radioed the chief. He established a crime scene area around the property.

Chief Owens called the Sunlight Ski Resort in an attempt to locate Todd Ramsey. They informed the chief that Todd was done for the day and could probably locate him on his cell phone. Chief Owens reached him after several attempts and told him to come down to the police station since Susie was there and he had some information that he would only discuss in person. The chief then called the school and asked Dr. Mathews to bring Susie over to the station. He informed the principal about the murder and thanked her for all her help.

Chief Owens summoned Harry McNally to his office. Harry, a fifty-year-old, prior-NYPD detective, had short, partially graying hair. He was well built, and his thin face showed the lines of a man who had experienced the tragedies of life, but he also had a certain look of warmth and kindness.

"We have a murder case on our hands, and I really need you to take the lead on this investigation," Chief Owens said when Harry sat down.

Harry responded, "I appreciate all you have done for me since I have been here, Chief, and I just want you to know that I will be more than happy to help out. The horrors of 9/11 are behind me now, and it's about time I began using the skills I gained as an NYPD detective." Chief Owens informed Harry of the imminent arrival of the murder victim's ex-husband, who would probably be the main suspect. Harry suggested they interview him together, but he wanted to run out to the crime scene first to get an initial impression.

Harry immediately drove over to the crime scene to assure it was secured properly and to briefly examine the murder victim. He wore latex gloves so as not to leave inadvertent fingerprints. It appeared to him that the time of death was probably midmorning and the cause of death was a crushed skull or asphyxiation secondary to the telephone cord wrapped around her neck. They would need the assistance of the Pitkin County Sheriff Department to gather the evidence at the crime scene. Then they would transfer the evidence to the Colorado Bureau of Investigation to perform the actual laboratory crime scene investigation. Harry would have liked to spend more time there, but he wanted to be present when Chief Owens interviewed Todd Ramsey. Before leaving, he noticed that the house was not terribly disheveled, as was usually the case in a domestic disturbance that was violent enough to result in death. He also noticed that the oar, which was presumably the murder weapon, was left at the crime scene and had too much blood on the flat part of the oar. He would have also expected more of the victim's hair on the oar. He obviously needed to return to the crime scene for a more detailed investigation, and he hoped that the crime scene would be kept secure until he could return.

Just as Harry was pulling up to the station, he saw the social service worker, Sheryl Lindsay, was also just arriving with Susie Ramsey. He knew this was going to be a difficult time for all involved.

Chief Owens was also notably anxious about the events but knew they must proceed as soon as possible with the interview. They decided to first privately inform Todd Ramsey of the murder without Susie being present to get his initial response. Then they would observe Todd as he informed Susie of her mother's death. Todd Ramsey showed up somewhat disheveled and reeking of bourbon. He was dressed in jeans, a turtleneck shirt, and his ski instructor jacket. Chief Owens escorted him into the interview room, offered him some coffee, and introduced Harry. Ramsey declined the coffee and said, "So what's going on, Chief?"

"I'm afraid we have some bad news for you, Todd. We're sorry to tell you this, but this afternoon we found Tanya at home, apparently beaten to death."

After a long silence, Ramsey broke down, and with his head in his hands he began to sob. "How did it happen? Who did it? What are you guys going to do about it? What about Susie, does she know? Oh, god, what am I going to do? What about Tanya's parents in California, do they know?"

Harry observed his reaction and quietly asked where he was all day. Ramsey looked up and slowly looked into Harry's eyes. Then he looked at Chief Owens and through gritted teeth said, "What business is it of yours? Do you guys think I'm responsible? I loved Tanya, and just because we were separated doesn't mean I would kill her. We had our differences and recently I have been living at my mother's house in Glenwood Springs, but I could never harm Tanya."

Harry asked, "How long have you been living out of the house?"

Ramsey answered, "Since the end of the summer tourist season." He then quickly added, "How about her new boyfriend? Have you considered him as a suspect?"

Chief Owens then said, "What new boyfriend are you talking about, Todd?"

"I don't know who he is, Chief, but recently Tanya has gotten new and expensive wheels and some new clothes for herself and Susie. I don't know how she could afford these things, especially since I have not been great about helping out. You know as well as I do that working as a river guide in the summer and a ski instructor at Sunlight I have not been of any help financially."

Harry then asked again where he was all day, and Todd said he was running some errands after working in the morning and then had a few drinks and lunch in Aspen. "Can anybody corroborate your whereabouts?" Harry asked.

"Possibly the waitress at La Cantina Mexican restaurant," Todd responded.

"Were you alone?" Harry asked. Ramsey started to get up as if he was going to leave, but Harry shoved him back into his seat and said, "Listen up. You are the prime suspect in Tanya's murder since you had motive, your oar was found at the scene with blood all over it, and you have been known to abuse her when you have been drinking. So answer the questions, or we will be here all night."

Todd looked at them both and said, "I was with a married woman, Chief, and her husband is the jealous type, if you know what I mean. I would prefer not to divulge her name or get her involved."

Harry then said, "We will be discrete when questioning her, but it is essential to clear you as the prime perpetrator."

Ramsey suddenly became agitated and again rose from his chair, fists balled up as if he was about to take a swing at Harry. Chief Owens grabbed him from behind and wrestled him back into his chair.

"Okay, enough questions for now, Harry," Owens said. "We need to talk to Susie together and make decisions in regards to her care."

"What do you mean? I'll take care of my daughter," Ramsey said.

Chief Owens thought to himself that he had known the Ramsey family for a long time, and he was confident that Stella Ramsey would make sure that Susie was well taken care of even if her son was guilty of this crime. If they did not arrest him tonight, it made the most sense now for Susie to stay with Todd and his mother in Glenwood Springs during Christmas break. They could then move back to Basalt after the crime scene investigation was completed so Susie could be close to her school and friends in the neighborhood. His mom could help with her care and still keep her job at the Wal-Mart in Glenwood Springs.

"Todd, I want you to calm yourself down so we can speak to Susie in a manner that will not frighten her," Owens said.

"I think I'll have that coffee now," Ramsey said. Harry and the chief stepped out of the interrogation room.

"What do you think?" Owens said.

"I'm not sure if he is telling the truth, but his demeanor is more of a depressed and angry man rather than a guilty one," Harry said.

Chief Owens said, "Well, he has had a hard time. He grew up in this area and was an Olympic candidate in the downhill. He sustained a knee injury during the tryouts and could never fulfill his Olympic dream. Since then he has been a ski instructor in the Aspen area, but because of his drinking and flippant attitude he couldn't maintain his job in Aspen and ended up at Sunlight, which is a smaller mountain mainly for locals, and there's not much opportunity for an adult ski instructor. He does pretty well with the kids, but the opportunities are limited. He has been known to have some bar brawls and minor domestic problems with Tanya, but nothing to this degree. I'm not sure if he is capable of this crime. Let's get him some coffee and give him a few minutes to compose himself before bringing in Susie."

Todd was sitting quietly in the interrogation room drinking his coffee when Susie ran up to him and began crying. "Where is mommy?"

Todd calmly said, "Mommy went away for awhile. You're going to stay with me and Grandma."

Susie looked around at the social service worker from school, Harry, and Chief Owens, and she asked again where her mother was.

Todd looked at his daughter and said, "Come here, kitten." She sat on his lap; he kissed her and began to explain, "Kitten, Mommy had a very bad accident. She's up in heaven now. Do you understand what I'm saying?"

"Yes, Daddy, but why did she have to die?" She quietly started to cry, her head on his chest.

"I don't know, but these good people are going to find out. We're going to stay at Grandma's for a few nights." He then looked up at Chief Owens and said, "Chief, can we leave now?"

Chief Owens looked at Harry and then said, "Yes, but Todd, don't leave the area. We'll be in touch."

Chapter 9

━◆━◆◆◆◆━◆━

December 2007

HARRY PULLED UP to the crime scene just as the team from the sheriff's department was getting their gear out of their van. The older member of the group was obviously the leader. There was a photographer, a photographic log recorder, and an evidence recorder. Harry introduced himself to the team leader, an attractive woman in her fifties dressed in jeans, turtleneck shirt, and a blue jacket with "C.S.I." printed on the back. She mentioned that they had already obtained a search warrant from the district attorney and were ready to begin their investigation. He couldn't help but notice that all of the other team members were young and wondered to himself how much crime scene experience they actually had between them.

Harry entered through the front door. Patrolman Gully was still there, maintaining a secure crime scene. Harry told him to head on home and thanked him for securing the core area of the crime scene. He again viewed the body and the presumed murder weapons. Photographs were taken by the team, and the body was placed in a black body bag to be transported to the morgue for autopsy and determination of the actual cause of death and time of death. Fingerprints were searched for by the investigative team, and photographs were taken of the living room. The oar was tagged and bagged. The telephone cord was also tagged and bagged.

Harry pointed out that there was some blood and hair on the corner of the coffee table. The investigative team took samples of the blood and hair to test back in the CSI lab by the forensic scientists.

Harry then commented that there was no sign of forced entrance, which would indicate that Tanya possibly knew the perpetrator or perpetrators. Harry walked through the rest of the house and found it to be well maintained, neat, and showing no signs of theft or destruction. After photographs of the master bedroom were taken, Harry went through Tanya's address book, which she had near the telephone on her night table. He noticed the card that Kathy had left with her and wrote down Kathy's phone number in his notepad.

While the investigative team continued to work the crime scene, Harry decided to talk to some of the neighbors. Since this was a working-class neighborhood, most of the neighbors had not been at home during the day when the murder took place. He did, however, find out that a type of utility truck had been parked outside the Ramsey home around noon. The neighbor across the street noticed two workmen entering the home but didn't pay much attention to them and did not know how long they were in the house. Nobody in the area noticed if Todd Ramsey was at the house today, but they all commented on his hot temper and heavy drinking.

It was getting late, and a light snowfall had begun. After Harry finished interviewing the neighbors, he returned to the crime scene, thanked the crew, and asked if they could call him with any information as soon as it became available.

Harry called his wife Grace to let her know that he was on his way home. He then called Kathy Ellington's number. Kathy picked up the call and sounded surprised to be called by the police.

Harry asked, "Why did you visit with Tanya Ramsey?"

Kathy explained, "Tanya was a nurse in the ICU and was caring for a patient who has brought a lawsuit against the hospital and one of the cardiologists on staff."

Harry informed Kathy of the murder and asked if he could meet with her at the hospital. Kathy agreed and said she would make time whenever it was convenient for him. They decided on 10:00 AM the next day.

Kathy immediately called Jack at his office to let him know about the nurse's involvement with Mr. Kahn and that the suspicions she and Ed had now seemed a definite possibility.

"I don't see any immediate connection to my malpractice case," he said.

"Jack, there may be none, but it just seems odd that she was on duty the night prior to his discharge from the hospital. It is also strange that he had an unusual outcome with his anticoagulation. And now she ends up dead!"

Jack said, "I'll be meeting with my attorney over the next few weeks and will be sure to let him know about these events."

"Sounds like a good idea, and I think I'll call Ed to let him know after I meet with the detective tomorrow." Kathy had the feeling that Jack's mind was in a different place, and the fact that he showed little interest in the information she was providing was somewhat puzzling to her. She had also been concerned with his noticeable mood change.

Harry was up early as usual. It was as if he never got used to the time change from New York to Colorado. He checked in at the station prior to driving to the Aspen area. He asked the chief if one of the other officers could possibly track down Tanya's credit card use and phone call records to see what workmen could have been at the house at the approximate time of the murder. Chief Owens was very accommodating and assigned Drew Trestle to help Harry with the investigation. He thought maybe the workmen had seen something or noticed if Todd Ramsey was in the area, as Ramsey was still the main suspect in the case. Harry and Drew worked the phones together for a couple of hours, but they drew a blank.

Harry left the station at 10:00 AM in his Ford Bronco. He drove east along Highway 82. It was a clear, crisp day, and a pre-Christmas high pressure zone was sitting over Colorado. As Harry drove, he thought about how good it felt to be back on an important case again, and maybe this was just what he needed to go forward and leave the horrors of 9/11 behind him. Not a day had gone by since 9/11 that he hadn't thought back to the event that caused such a senseless loss of life.

He lost a lot of close friends that day and couldn't understand the attitude of the terrorists and their utter disregard for life. The killing of noncombatants to create terror with little or no goal other than the creation of that terror was still an unimaginable concept for Harry to grasp. These terrorists lived among innocent Muslims, who seemed helpless to stop these acts of terrorism. This helplessness allowed these terrorists to behave as they did, just like a bully on the block. Harry also had difficulty understanding the Muslims funding these terrorists and assumed that it was done out of fear for their own lives or for protection of their wealth, but there was always the nagging possibility that they were acting in a passive-aggressive manner and really desired global conversion to Islam.

Harry pulled up to Aspen Valley Hospital at 10:30 AM. He went directly to the administrator's office. Kathy's secretary, Prudence Harding, asked Harry to take a seat.

"Kathy will be just a moment," she said.

Just as Harry was settling down in a large leather chair, Kathy came out of her office with the director of nursing. Prudence introduced Harry to Kathy and Monika Evans. Harry and Kathy then went into her office. Harry noticed that her office was small but well appointed with photographs of the Aspen area in each of its seasons. Her desk was neat. There were no loose papers around, and Harry thought to himself that this was a very organized woman who was young but probably very efficient.

"I'll get right to the point," Harry said. "I am investigating the murder of Tanya Ramsey, and I am here because I found your business card in her address book. I need to know what business you had with her and if you can in some way shed light as to who may have caused her death."

Kathy said, "I visited her last week because she was an agency nurse that the hospital employed for a week in the ICU. She happened to be caring for a patient that has brought a medical malpractice lawsuit against the hospital and one of our cardiologists. I was trying to see if she had any helpful information that might clarify the patient's complications, which resulted in a life-threatening stroke."

"And did you come up with anything constructive?"

"No, but she did seem very anxious during my visit. She seemed in a hurry to get me out of the house. There is one other thing that could possibly mean something. She was the nurse caring for the patient that brought this lawsuit, and in our opinion something happened to him that evening to reverse his anticoagulation." Harry looked puzzled, so Kathy explained that anticoagulation referred to blood thinning. "His INR, a measure of his blood thinning, was in perfect range the afternoon prior to his discharge. So, he had to have had either fresh, frozen plasma or some drug to reverse his anticoagulation the night she was on duty."

"Why do you think that?" Harry said.

"Because when he returned to the hospital only two days later, his blood showed no signs of anticoagulation, and his wife was insistent that she had given him his Coumadin—the oral medication to keep his blood thin."

"So it is your belief that Tanya may have been the one responsible for his problem? What would be her motive to do this?" Harry asked.

Kathy answered, "I have no idea. However, I did notice that she was driving a very expensive car that seemed out of place considering her income."

Harry stood up, handed her his card, and said, "Please call if you think of anything else."

Kathy escorted him out of her office and said, "Please keep me informed, Detective, if you think of any information that may help with our lawsuit."

Harry then drove over to the La Cantina restaurant in Aspen to see if he could confirm Ramsey's alibi. The manager on duty, Matt Singleton, was just arriving as Harry walked into the restaurant. Harry introduced himself and asked Matt if he knew Todd Ramsey. The manager said he knew him well and in fact went to high school with Todd down valley. He said that he saw Ramsey often when he was a ski instructor on Aspen Mountain but that he had gotten fired from the ski school because of his rudeness and heavy drinking.

Harry then asked, "Has Todd been in the restaurant lately? In particular, yesterday around noon?"

"Not that I am aware of," the manager answered.

"Could you have missed seeing him?" Harry asked.

Matt responded, "That is doubtful since we haven't been that busy. We are still in pre-Christmas mode."

Harry then asked to go through the receipts from yesterday, but he came up without any charges by Ramsey. As far as he could determine, Ramsey was lying about his whereabouts at the approximate time of the murder. "Would you please ask the employees who were present on the day shift if they saw Mr. Ramsey yesterday? He also claimed to be with a woman at that time."

"That seems typical of Ramsey."

Harry thanked the manager, handed him his card, and headed down valley to the morgue to view the autopsy with the state forensic pathologist who was driving in from Denver.

Since this was a forensic autopsy, family permission was not needed. The pathologist had already completed the external examination before Harry arrived. He was middle-aged, bald, very thin, and dressed in scrubs. He was dictating his findings into an overhead recorder. Harry noticed that he had a Southern accent. Harry introduced himself and asked what progress had been made.

"I have just completed my external exam, sir. I took photographs and viewed the body with my naked eye, and then I used an ultraviolet light to be sure that her body surface was not hiding any evidence. I recorded the obvious head trauma and the apparent marks left by the telephone cord around her neck. I was just about to start the internal exam when you entered."

Harry stepped a little closer to the autopsy table when the pathologist started to saw the skull to allow a close look at the brain to determine if there was brain damage from the head trauma. He told Harry that the skull injury looked more like one would see from a sharp object rather than blunt trauma from the supposed murder weapon. The brain did show an epidural hemorrhage from trauma to the temporal area of the skull. The pathologist felt this was probably the cause of her demise, but he wanted to examine the lungs to determine if asphyxiation from the telephone cord could have contributed to her death.

He then made a deep, Y-shaped incision to view the neck and chest cavity. Even before the microscopic examination, he concluded that it was doubtful that asphyxiation in any way contributed to her death. Harry couldn't understand why the cord was even placed around Tanya's neck if it did not cause asphyxiation. Hopefully, the microscopic examination would tell them if it was done after she had already expired.

The pathologist finished the autopsy and told Harry he would call as soon as he finished the microscopic exam. Harry thanked him in advance for his promptness, since the family was anxious to have the funeral before Christmas.

Harry left the morgue and headed back to his office. He checked with Drew Trestle to see if any information had been obtained about the utility truck that was seen outside of Tanya's house. There were apparently no calls made from Tanya's home to any utility or repair company. Drew also checked her credit cards to see if any recent charges were made to repair companies, but he drew a blank there also.

Harry felt that all the data up to this point was pointing to a domestic argument that ended in the death of Tanya Ramsey. The most likely scenario was that Todd struck her in the head with the oar, and she then fell against the corner of the table, which caused the head injury. Todd probably then tried to strangle her with the telephone cord to be sure she was dead.

The only problem Harry had with this scenario was his gut feeling that Todd was not the type of man who would commit a murder. He was clearly lying about something, but Harry doubted it was the murder. If Todd had lost his temper and pushed her so her head hit the table, why would he try to strangle her? If he did commit the murder by hitting her with the oar, then why did he leave it at the crime scene? Harry thought that so far there were more questions than answers.

Harry stepped outside the station to get some fresh air. He noticed Drew was outside smoking a cigarette.

"Drew, what do you think of the case?" Harry asked, walking over to him.

"Harry, we hardly ever see any domestic crimes resulting in death in this area. I'm sure your experience in New York leads you to Ramsey as the murderer, but I have known him since I've been on the force here, and I doubt he is capable of this crime."

"The statistics of violent crimes against female spouses in the United States resulting in death are staggering," Harry said. "Did you know that four women are murdered by their spouses every day? Statistics show that greater than one third of female murders are committed by their spouses or boyfriends. In Manhattan we saw this at an even higher rate, but this may have reflected a larger indigent population and drug-related domestic crimes. At any rate, Ramsey seems to be the prime suspect at this point in time."

"Harry, you know I will give you as much support on this case as I can, so don't hesitate to ask."

"Thanks, Drew, I appreciate your input." Harry and Drew stepped back into the station.

Chapter 10

December 2007

KATHY CALLED ED's office first thing in the morning to let him know about Tanya's death. Sohlia, Ed's office assistant, answered the private line, saying, "Gastroenterology Associates, can I help you?"

Kathy replied, "Yes, I'm Kathy Ellington from Aspen. May I speak to Dr. Harris, please?"

"He is making hospital rounds this morning—may I take your number?"

Kathy replied, "He has my number, and let him know that I'll be in my office all morning."

When Ed got to the office, all four of the front office girls were smirking and wanted to know who Kathy Ellington was.

He quietly responded, "Now, girls, don't get nosey!" He went into his office and closed the door. All four girls smiled and rolled their eyes.

Ed called Kathy on her cell phone and was surprised to hear about Tanya's presumed murder. Kathy then told him that the lead detective had been at her office because he found the business card she left for Tanya when they were at her house.

Ed said, "It sure seems to be quite a coincidence that the murder occurred right after our visit."

Kathy replied, "I agree with you, but apparently everybody in town seems to think that the husband is the prime suspect."

"Did you tell Jack about the coincidence?"

"Yes, I did, but he doesn't see how it relates to the malpractice case. He also seems a little distant."

"Well, it does seem like a stretch to link the two. Jack is probably right."

"So, are you still planning to come to Aspen during Christmas? We have had almost seven feet of snowfall already, and there is one week to go before Christmas."

"Yes, I'll be there through New Year's Day. In fact, all my kids will be coming for the holidays as well."

"That's great. I'm not sure if you have plans, but we are having Jack and Penny over for Christmas dinner, and you and your family are certainly welcome to join us."

"I'm sure that will work for us, and it will be nice to see Laura and Ruby again. Keep me informed as to the case, and I'll call when we arrive. I've been thinking about you a lot, Kathy." "Me too, Ed. I'll see you soon. Call me at home in the evening if you get a chance."

Ed began seeing his office patients. There was the usual array of gastrointestinal illnesses, such as refractory reflux esophagitis, Crohn's disease, ulcerative colitis, end-stage liver disease, and a large number of cases of irritable bowel syndrome. As he worked his way through the list of the morning patients, he was thankful for the newer medications that had changed the management and outcome of so many of the gastrointestinal illnesses as compared to when he first started to practice.

He had just finished the last of his morning patients when his medical assistant, Nancy, announced that a new drug representative was bringing in lunch and wanted to discuss a new medication for hepatitis. As much as most doctors disliked wasting time with drug reps, Ed always appreciated how difficult their job was and believed that very often, if given a chance, they could really be helpful by introducing new forms of therapy.

During lunch, Ed sat with his office staff and listened to their complaints, which focused mainly on the burden private insurance companies had placed upon them. It was apparent to Ed that the industry's need to cut costs caused so much wasted time and office manpower just to get approvals for needed diagnostic tests and medications. They came to the conclusion that the solution to the health care problem may best be obtained by a gradual change. There would be finite yearly goals that would need to be met until a fully integrated single-payer system was accomplished, eliminating the insurance companies and their profits. The goals would be to broaden the population that would be covered and expand the number of primary healthcare providers and specialists. There would always be those that would demand special attention and were able to afford to pay extra for this kind of care. That void would certainly be supplied by entrepreneurial physicians, hospital corporations, and home healthcare agencies that would be available at a cost premium. This would leave a two-tiered healthcare system.

As they finished lunch, Ed said, "Now that we have solved America's biggest problem, let's get back to work." They all laughed, thanked Lisa, the drug rep, and left the lunchroom.

Ed was happy to be busy and still enjoyed the challenges of medical practice, but most of all he enjoyed the relationships he had developed with his patients and his office and hospital staff. It had recently become very clear to him that he was fortunate to be able to make the best of his life even after the loss of his wife. If he had not had the passion for medicine and the challenges of trying to master the stock and financial markets, he doubted that he could have maintained emotional stability. The children were a help, but they had their own demons to overcome and their own lives to lead.

Chapter 11

December 2007

THE VIGIL TOOK place at a funeral home for the family and friends to gather for the purpose of praying for Tanya's soul, consoling each other, and viewing the open casket. There were candles at both ends of the casket. Flowers were present in the room, and a rosary was placed in Tanya's hand. Todd Ramsey took care of all the arrangements with the funeral home and the church which Tanya and Susie had attended on a regular basis. Tanya was a devout Catholic and attended church every Sunday, unless she had a nursing assignment. Tanya's parents came in from Sacramento. They knew that her husband was a suspect in her murder. They also had distinctly distrusted Todd from the very first time they met him. They could not look him in the eye the whole time they were at the vigil.

Susie was quiet, obviously sad, but well behaved during the vigil and stuck pretty close to Grandma Ramsey. Most of Tanya's friends were nurses who worked down valley in the towns from Basalt to Glenwood Springs. They signed the visitor sign-in book, viewed the body in the open casket, and paid their respects to the family. The vigil lasted several hours. It was evident to everyone that attended the vigil that none of Todd Ramsey's friends or associate ski instructors were present, and he basically sat by himself the entire time as an outcast.

The Requiem Mass took place in the church the following day. The priest was sixty years old, of Latin descent, and short, and he

51

had a ruddy complexion. He was dressed in black and was obviously saddened by the event since he was close to Tanya and Susie. He greeted the casket at the door of the church, sprinkled it with holy water, and then recited Psalm 129 and Psalm 50. The service took about an hour. Afterward, the priest stood at the foot of the coffin and granted the departed absolution.

After the Requiem Mass, the coffin was taken to the cemetery at the edge of Basalt. The priest performed a traditional graveside service. He again sprinkled the casket with holy water, asked that her soul rest in peace, and ended with the sign of the cross over her body.

The mourners then returned to Todd Ramsey's mother's home in Glenwood Springs. Neighbors brought over food, liquor, and soft drinks. Many of Susie's friends from school came over with their parents to pay their respects and console Susie. The atmosphere was somewhat subdued. Everybody had mixed feelings about Todd and whether or not he was guilty. Most everyone there knew about his drinking and occasional abuse. The rumors of infidelity were also on people's minds.

Tanya's mother waited for an opportunity to say something to Todd. Her moment came when he walked out onto the front porch to smoke a cigarette. She followed him. She was seething, but she knew she couldn't make a scene for fear that Susie might hear her.

She came up behind Todd and said, "You lying, cheating bastard. You had to kill my baby. You took everything from her. You took her dignity, her security, and now finally her life. You should burn in hell. I will never forgive you."

"Betty, I didn't do it. I swear. I may not have been a good husband, but I loved Tanya. I would never hurt her."

"You are nothing but a lowlife drunk. I told her not to marry you."

"Betty, I will give up alcohol, I promise. I will do it for Susie. I was framed. Please believe me."

She looked at him in disgust and said, "Who would kill Tanya?"

"Betty, on Susie's life, I swear it wasn't me." Betty huffed off, leaving Todd by himself again.

He was just finishing his cigarette when Susie came out onto the porch and said, "Daddy, you look so sad. Don't worry, you will be okay. I will take care of you."

Todd gave her a hug, held back his tears, and said, "I know, sweetheart."

Harry revisited the crime scene while everybody was at the funeral. He noticed that the other oar was located on the porch and was readily visible as he walked up the steps to the front porch. The house seemed smaller than when he was there on the day of the murder. It needed a coat of paint, and the exterior was obviously in some disrepair. Todd certainly was negligent in maintaining the house for Tanya and Susie.

Harry put on a pair of latex gloves and entered the house as the sun streamed in the front windows. He was trying to visualize the events that could have occurred seconds prior to Tanya's death. Harry then noticed that the room had two smoke detectors, and oddly enough they were different in design. Also, it seemed odd to him that a room this small had two smoke detectors. Harry checked the other rooms in the house and noticed that all the other detectors were of similar brand except the one that was different in the living room. He got a chair from the dining room and climbed up on it to detach the odd smoke detector. On closer inspection, he saw that it was a fake smoke detector hiding a GSM listening device. Harry placed it in an evidence bag to bring back to the forensic lab to look for fingerprints and possibly track the buyer. He thought Todd was possibly spying on Tanya to see if she was having an affair. Harry then inspected the rest of the house, checking for other spy devices. Finding none, he made a quick call to the station to ask Chief Owens if they could obtain Tanya's banking records at Alpine Bank.

Chief Owens said, "Why is that important?"

Harry answered, "It just seems curious that Tanya could afford an expensive SUV. I also want to get Tanya's work record to see if she may have worked for somebody in her home health job that may have funded her in some way."

Chief Owens then said, "It seems to me that all the evidence points to Todd as the murderer."

Harry said, "I don't think things are as clear cut as they appear." Harry then said, "Chief, please try to get me those bank records and her work schedule as soon as possible."

Chief Owens responded, "We are already on it, Harry."

Harry then said, "I'm bringing Todd back in for questioning again. His alibi didn't check out, and I have the feeling he has been hiding something."

It began snowing again as Harry drove back to the police station. It had snowed almost every day in December with an accumulation of nine feet in the mountains. As Harry pulled up to the station, he hoped the autopsy and forensic lab reports would be completed for his review. He also needed the forensics lab at the sheriff's office to evaluate the fake smoke detector/listening device.

It was the Friday before Christmas, and the Basalt Police Department was in the process of celebrating their annual Christmas party. Harry had completely forgotten about the party. He was happy to see the entire staff present and sharing a closeness that reminded him of his precinct in Manhattan. He got himself an eggnog and joined the party. The party broke up early since the staff was anxious to get on with their Christmas shopping.

Harry went to his desk and reviewed the autopsy report, which was in an enclosed envelope in his in basket. The cause of death was an epidural hemorrhage secondary to sharp trauma to the skull. There were no signs of asphyxiation as one would expect if the telephone cord around her neck caused her death. The autopsy also showed no other signs of bodily trauma. Harry thought this was unusual since Tanya would have had other signs of trauma if she and Todd were having a domestic fight. More importantly, however, was the fact that there was no trauma on the other side of Tanya's head that would have occurred if she was struck by the oar.

So, what were the oar and the telephone cord doing there if they were not the cause of any bodily harm? The autopsy showed no unforeseen medical diseases present. There was no evidence of rape or recent sexual intercourse. The report summary stated that Tanya Ramsey died from a single sharp blow to the right temporal area of the skull, causing an epidural hemorrhage with subsequent herniation of the brain.

Harry then turned his attention to the crime scene investigation report. The report was typical of most CSI reports. There were only the facts stated without opinions or conclusions. The report was divided into five categories. The categories included a summary, scene, processing, evidence collected, and pending information. The most important facts that Harry could glean from the report involved the sketches of the crime scene, the presence of Tanya's hair and skin on the coffee table where she struck her head, and the fingerprints present in the house. The fingerprints were not limited to the family. The CSI team stated that additional prints were found, and they were in the process of establishing identities. These were in the pending part of the report. There were also latent footwear impressions that were found on the tile entranceway. These did not match anybody in the family either and were placed in the pending part of the report as well.

Harry was also expecting to find Tanya's bank statements and home health client list, but these were not present on his desk. He called Chief Owens on his cell phone to find out what progress was being made on these important parts of his investigation. Chief Owens informed Harry that the home health agency needed to get an opinion from their attorney because of HIPAA laws of patient confidentiality, but if need be a court order could be obtained after Christmas. He apologized that they had not obtained Tanya's banking records, but the bank had closed early to allow their employees time off for last-minute Christmas shopping. They would be open Monday morning, and the Chief felt they could obtain those records at that time.

"Go home, Harry," Chief Owens said.

"Okay, Chief, but I want to let you know that there is more to this case than is present on the surface."

It was already dark when Harry left the station. He didn't realize it was so late and was grateful that his wife was always so understanding. He wasn't sure he deserved a woman this wonderful, who never complained if he was late because of a stakeout or an investigation that took longer than anticipated. While he was driving home, he thought back to the early days of their marriage when they lived in a small studio apartment in Manhattan. She worked in the secretarial pool while he was completing the police academy and working his way up to detective with its improved pay grade. She was always there for him, and she was especially helpful in getting him through the post-9/11 stress and associated depression. He appreciated her more than he could ever express in words, and he knew that she was the type of woman who knew how he felt even though he seldom verbalized his feelings. Harry was happy to have a couple of days off for Christmas, but he knew that he was also anxious to get back to work on this case on Monday.

Chapter 12

December 2007

ED WAS THE first to arrive at the town house in Snowmass on the Sunday before Christmas. He always liked to get the place ready for the kids before they arrived, so he got his shopping list together and headed to the village market just as a light snowfall began. He was especially excited as well as apprehensive about this family ski vacation because it was the first time since Lynn's death that he and the kids had vacationed together. Ed realized that they were all carrying on with their lives by this time, but he also knew that this vacation would bring back many bittersweet memories for all of them.

Ed called Jack and Penny to touch base and let them know that he would see them at Kathy's house for Christmas Eve dinner. Next he called Kathy to let her know he was in town.

She said, "I'm so glad you called. The skiing has been wonderful, and I am not working tomorrow, so how about getting an early start?"

Ed responded, "Sounds like a plan. My kids will be arriving in the late afternoon, so we can ski all day together. Can we meet at Two Creeks in Snowmass at nine in the morning?"

Kathy answered, "It's a date, and I must tell you that there has been nine feet of snowfall in the month of December. It has been years since the snow has been this good in Aspen so early in the season."

"I'm really looking forward to seeing you," he said.

"Me too," she responded. As she hung up the phone, Kathy thought to herself how much she enjoyed being with Ed. Here she was acting like a teenager over this tall, good-looking guy with salt-and-pepper hair and a very calm demeanor. He did seem a little quiet and reserved, but she thought that possibly added to his charm. And what a great smile.

Ed was waiting on the benches at Two Creeks Lodge when he saw Kathy leave the parking area. She was carrying her skis over one shoulder and her poles in the opposite hand as she made her way along the snow-covered crosswalk. He sat there watching her and was mystified as to how she could look so cute and so athletic at the same time. He finally jumped up to help her with her skis as she approached. They hugged and briefly kissed.

Ed said, "Boy, I missed you." She smiled and kissed him again. They walked over to the lift area, stepped into the bindings of their skis, and caught the first lift up at nine in the morning. It was colder than usual for Christmas week, but luckily no wind was present to add to the drop in temperature, which was already down to five degrees Fahrenheit.

They were sitting nestled together on the lift when Ed said, "Where is global warming when you need it?"

Kathy said, "I know. It is really freezing today. You know that while the politicians are debating what to do about global warming, we in Aspen have been taking it seriously, and in fact the city of Aspen adopted a plan to reduce greenhouse emissions that are responsible for trapping heat in the atmosphere. The plan, launched in March 2005, is called the "Canary Initiative." The plan utilizes a combination of alliances with other cities, sharing of scientific knowledge, and reduction of greenhouse gas emission by using fuel-efficient and hybrid vehicles. Even the busses in Aspen are hybrids now."

Ed said, "I didn't expect a lecture on global warming." They both laughed and got ready to hop off the lift.

As the lift approached the top of Elk Camp, they caught a breathtaking view of Maroon Bells. They skied off and headed down Bull Run. The weather stayed cold, but the sky was clear.

As late morning arrived, the sky turned a deep blue color which served as a backdrop for the beautiful snow-covered mountain ranges, evergreen trees, and bare aspen trees. They skied the morning hours away without stopping until lunchtime. They took a break at noon to have a bowl of soup and some fruit at Brothers Grill on Fanny Hill.

While they ate, Ed asked, "Why do you think skiing is so much fun?"

Kathy didn't answer right away, but she finally said, "That's not an easy question. I think the answer would be different depending on who you asked. Some people really dislike the sport. I personally like the feeling of controlled speed. There is also a little danger and risk to skiing. You can let as much of that risk in as you are comfortable with, but you must always have control. Of course, this is also a sport done in the beauty of the outdoors and surrounded by spectacular views."

Ed had trouble keeping his eyes off her as she spoke. She was not only physically beautiful, but he sensed a true honesty in every word she spoke. He was almost embarrassed by his feelings since he had known her for such a short time.

She interrupted his thoughts when she said, "Enough talk about skiing—let's go back out and enjoy the day." Ed paid the bill, and they stepped outside into the cold and took off downhill to the Elk Camp gondola.

Ed's family arrived at the Aspen airport at 6 PM. The Aspen area had been their favorite vacation spot since they were children. Luke and his wife Amy departed from the plane first, followed by Everett and his partner Chad. They happily breathed in the fresh air and views of Buttermilk Mountain. As they came through the glass doors and entered the terminal, they couldn't help the feeling of excitement that always encompassed them when they arrived in Aspen.

Ed was waiting for them in the terminal. They all hugged and kissed Ed and headed for Ed's four-wheel drive Ford Explorer. As they pulled out of the airport, the conversation immediately turned to the ski conditions.

"So, Dad, what is the base now, and are all the lifts open?" Everett asked.

Ed said, "The base is seventy-two inches already, all lifts are open, and it's the best skiing ever."

They all laughed and said in unison, "You say that every time we go skiing."

"You guys will see," Ed said.

Amy asked, "Am I cooking dinner tonight, or are we going out?"

Ed said, "No, tonight we are going to have Christmas Eve dinner with Jack and Penny at my friend Kathy's house."

Everett said, "So, Dad, who is Kathy?"

Ed answered, "She is the administrator at the hospital and a friend of Jack and Penny. I skied with her and her daughter my last trip out, and she and I have been trying to help Jack with his lawsuit. She's really nice. I think you'll like her."

Amy and Luke looked at each other and smiled.

"Sounds like a fun Christmas Eve," Chad said. Ed pulled up to the town house just as it began to snow.

After everybody got freshened up, they sat around the fireplace as the conversation centered on the stock market.

"This Christmas rally is probably the last chance to get my clients out of the equity market and into bonds and cash," Luke said.

"Well, from a technical standpoint, if the October ninth top cannot be taken out, then I feel we will be in a real secular bear market. That could easily result in a 25 to 35 percent drop in equity prices," Ed said.

Chad added, "I can tell you from a real estate standpoint that there has been the highest number of loan defaults I have ever seen. Also, the bankruptcy attorneys I have talked to say they have never been this busy. The sub-prime problem is running deeper than anyone ever imagined. Some observers are saying that the whole problem of easy lending started as a political movement when President Clinton, Congress, and the Fed decided that all Americans should own their own home. They put pressure on lending institutions to provide easy and innovative lending policies. When the speculation bubble reached extremes, the house of cards came tumbling down."

Amy stood and said, "All right, guys, enough doom and gloom for one night. Let's head over to Dad's friend's home for Christmas Eve dinner." Amy then suggested that they stop at the village market on the way to pick up a few things so they would not arrive empty-handed.

They arrived at Kathy's home just as the sun was setting. Their arms were filled with candy, flowers, wine, and a gift for Laura to put under the tree. Ed warmly greeted Kathy with a hug and a kiss on the cheek. Ed introduced his kids to Kathy, Ruby, and Laura. Ruby was delighted at what she was seeing. Jack and Penny ran in to see everyone.

"Gosh, it's good to see you all!" Penny said. Upon entering, one could not help but notice the warm atmosphere of this old, Victorian home.

"You must show us around. I love the antiques and charm of the home," Amy said.

While Kathy took them on a tour, Ed and Jack stepped into the kitchen to discuss the lawsuit in private. Jack still seemed anxious about the case.

"There is something unusual about this case, Jack," Ed insisted. "Are you aware that the nurse who was caring for your patient in the ICU the night before discharge was murdered? The murder came shortly after Kathy and I visited her during my last trip out here."

Jack responded, "Yes, Kathy mentioned it to me, but the rumors around town are that the husband is the main suspect."

Ed said, "Well, that may be, but it sure is a strange set of coincidences, and I know you, Jack, and I am confident that you treated this patient perfectly."

Jack was silent for several minutes and then said, "Thanks for your confidence, Ed, but it hasn't been easy coming to grips with this whole mess. I would prefer not to discuss it any further. Let's try to have a good time this week while you guys are out here."

"Sounds good, Jack. Let's drink to that."

Between Ruby, Kathy, and Penny, dinner was perfect. Conversation went from the environment to real estate and ended up on the presidential candidates from both parties. This group was open-minded. They all seemed to agree on change, but they wanted the person that was best for the country. For once this wasn't about sticking to party lines, and they agreed that for the Democrats Hilary was a strong candidate but Barack Obama offered a change and a new approach though he was not the most experienced. As far as the Republican Party was concerned, they had to overcome all the negative sentiment that George Bush had acquired. Mitt Romney's Mormonism bothered some people, and Huckabee was clearly too far right for this group, so they unanimously felt John McCain seemed the most experienced and would probably be the Republican candidate.

Finally after everything was put away, Laura excused herself, saying she was ready for bed. She said goodnight to everyone. Ed's kids wanted to go for a little night life, and they politely invited the others, who declined. Kathy told Ed she would drive him home.

"Okay then," Ed said, "you young people better not complain tomorrow when I wake you for skiing!"

"Dad, it's Christmas. Maybe we want to sleep in."

"That will never happen; you know the best skiing is early in the morning."

"Yeah, yeah, yeah." With that, Luke, Amy, Chad, and Everett took off. Jack and Penny also left, telling them they'd see them tomorrow.

Kathy drove to Ed's. He invited her up. They had a glass of cognac. Ed then gave her a wrapped gift box.

"I thought you might like this," he said as Kathy untied the bow. She opened the box. It was a beautiful Burberry scarf in shades of pink and brown that matched her jacket.

"Oh, Ed, how thoughtful, I love it." She kissed him briefly on the lips, but then the kiss became more passionate as their bodies came in intimate contact. They could both sense the other's desire as they continued to kiss and caress each other.

After several minutes, Ed said, "Kathy, I'm a little out of practice." She put her fingers on his lips and led him slowly to his bedroom. He dimmed the lights, and they slowly undressed each other. They got into bed and kissed tenderly. They made love with a passion and hunger that neither of them had known for a long time.

As they lay close together, Ed said, "God, I think I've wanted you since the first day I met you. You are so beautiful."

"Ed, I had hoped this would happen too. Actually, I feel like a teenager!" They laughed, kissed again, and continued to make love passionately until they were both physically exhausted and satisfied. Before they knew it, it was nearly 2 AM.

Kathy said, "Listen, we don't know what time your kids will return. I really shouldn't be here."

"I know. I wish you didn't have to go. The kids are leaving on the thirtieth. Will you be my date New Year's Eve?"

"I would love to!" They both laughed. They were both thrilled at how great the evening had gone.

Ed walked Kathy to the car, kissed her goodnight, and said, "I know this sounds silly, but please call me when you get home." She put her hand on his cheek and said she would.

Chapter 13

December 2007

IT WAS THE Thursday following Christmas Day when Louis Reiner, the attorney for Dr. Jack Simpson, arrived at the Down Valley Rehabilitation Center to take the deposition of the plaintiff's wife, Mrs. Kahn. Louis, a nice-looking young man in his early thirties with short, blonde hair, was dressed in a suit, carried a brand-new briefcase, and gave the impression that this was his very first case. Unfortunately, Mr. Kahn had been in the rehabilitation center since his discharge from Aspen Valley Hospital. He had made minimal progress from a neurological standpoint since he was still paralyzed on the right side of his body. The main issue they faced for the deposition was the fact that Mr. Kahn was still not able to speak other than to say yes or no when asked a question. Louis had therefore arranged for the deposition to actually be taken from Mrs. Kahn in the presence of Sam Kahn and his attorney.

Evelyn Kahn, a pleasant-looking brunette of medium stature, was dressed in a velour outfit and had been with her husband on a daily basis since he had been admitted to the rehabilitation center. The rehabilitation center arranged for her to stay in a nearby Ramada Inn in Glenwood Springs. Their two children had visited several times since he had been there, but only briefly whenever they could get away from work and school. Their son Josh was working toward his MBA at New York University, and their daughter Tammy was a school teacher in

Westchester County, New York. She had recently gotten married and had been able to visit her parents in Colorado during the Thanksgiving and Christmas school breaks.

Evelyn and Sam had a good marriage. She had always been a no-nonsense woman and knew full well she needed to be strong for Sam and their children. She came to the rehabilitation center first thing each morning and turned out to be a perfect caregiver. She had a calm demeanor and seemed to understand Sam's poor communication better than anyone at the center. Sam was shaven and dressed for the deposition, and he was seated in a wheelchair at the end of the conference table. He was a bit nervous and kept looking to Evelyn for reassurance.

The lawyer for the Kahns, Michael Sutton, was dressed in jeans, a turtleneck shirt, and a blue blazer. He was tall, handsome, and carried himself with an air of confidence. Will Kitch was the attorney for the hospital. He was middle-aged, tall, thin, and wore thick glasses. He had a very tentative demeanor, but his firm from Denver had a reputation for toughness, having rarely found it necessary to settle a case. They represented most of the Colorado hospitals and nursing homes.

The court reporter was setting up her Stenograph Smartwriter as the attorneys entered the room. Everybody introduced themselves to Sam and Evelyn and handed their business cards to each other. Louis Reiner began the questioning since he had set the deposition. Mrs. Kahn answered the questions in a straightforward manner, and Louis was able to establish that Mr. Kahn was in good health prior to the onset of atrial fibrillation, hypertension, and the congestive heart failure that prompted his emergency room visit. When asked about prior physician visits, Evelyn answered that it had been a long time since his last regular exam.

Louis then asked, "Could Mr. Kahn have had high blood pressure or, for that matter, atrial fibrillation for quite some time?"

Sam and Evelyn looked at each other, and then Evelyn said, "It's possible, but Sam gave blood regularly since he has "Group O" blood type, which is the universal donor. They routinely checked his blood pressure and cholesterol before each donation. They would have also noticed if his pulse was abnormal, so I would say that it was unlikely that he had atrial fibrillation or hypertension."

Louis then asked, "Did Sam ever use cocaine, alcohol, or excessive caffeine?"

Sam said, "No."

Evelyn then said, "To be honest, sir, Sam was drinking quite heavily for a couple of months prior to his visit to Aspen. It didn't affect his work or our relationship."

Louis thought for several minutes and then asked, "Why was he drinking so much?" Sam looked at Evelyn, and Louis noticed they both had an unexpected look in their eyes. Not a look of embarrassment or guilt as he had expected, but one of fear. Louis thought to himself that their expression was out of place. He wondered if the other attorneys had the same impression. He then asked, "Was the drinking related to difficulties at work or with your personal life?"

Michael Sutton interrupted and said, "I object to this line of questioning!"

Louis knew that he must have hit upon a sensitive issue. He then said, "Please, Mr. Sutton, we are not in court now. I'm only trying to get an impression of his physical and mental health prior to his illness."

Evelyn then responded, "Unfortunately, only my husband can answer that question." She then folded her arms across her chest.

Louis said, "I understand that Mr. Kahn was an accountant and worked for a hedge fund. Was he a trader, or did he handle the profit-and-loss statements?"

Evelyn answered, "He did the accounting and checked the trades against their positions." Louis then asked, "Was there hypertension, atrial fibrillation, or alcoholism in Mr. Kahn's family?"

Sam responded with a definite, "No," before Evelyn could answer.

Louis then said, "Mr. Kahn, did you take the medicines that Dr. Simpson prescribed for you upon your discharge from the hospital? Also, why didn't you return to New York as planned?"

Mrs. Kahn responded, "I was with my husband at the time, and I can assure you he took his medicines as prescribed. We did not return to New York immediately because the oil conference was not completed yet, and that gave us a few days more to stay in Aspen."

Louis then asked, "What is the name of your employer, and can you supply me with his address and phone number, please?" Mr. and

Mrs. Kahn again looked at each other with the same look of fear Louis had noted before.

They hesitated in their answer, so Mr. Sutton promptly answered for them, saying, "We'll certainly supply that information for you."

"I have one last question." Louis looked directly at Mr. Kahn and said, "Are you in pain?"

Evelyn then said, "Look at him, Mr. Reiner. Does he look happy to you? Does he look like he will ever recover and be able to work again? Please, sir, I think we've answered enough questions for now."

Michael Sutton asked the attorney for the hospital if he had any questions. Mr. Kitch asked for any information they might have in regards to prior hospitalizations and physician visits. Mr. Sutton said they would supply him and Mr. Reiner with that information and also give them standard "release of information" forms that had been signed by Mr. Kahn so they could obtain any medical information they may need in addition to what they had already received in the pre-deposition discovery. Louis thanked the Kahns for their cooperation.

Louis and Will Kitch, the attorney for the hospital, decided to have lunch together to discuss possible defense strategies. They were both heading back to Denver, so they decided to stop in Frisco, which was about halfway to Denver.

Louis said, "Follow me, but if we get separated we'll meet at the Frisco Diner. It's a small restaurant on the right just as you exit I-70."

They ordered soup, sandwiches, and coffee. They both thought that after their expert witnesses reviewed the case there would probably be no negligence for either the hospital or Dr. Simpson. The major problem, of course, was the devastating physical and psychological injuries to Mr. Kahn. Even though no malpractice had been committed, the appearance of the plaintiff and his family could influence the jury to award a significant amount of financial compensation to them. There was still one fact that neither of them could figure out. Why, if Mr. Kahn was well anticoagulated on the evening prior to discharge, did the effect of that anticoagulation disappear and cause him to develop the thrombotic emboli that caused his subsequent complications?

Louis then asked, "Did you notice the fear in their eyes when they responded to the questions about his recent heavy alcohol intake and difficulties at work?"

Mr. Kitch said, "No, I didn't notice anything unusual in their expression. What are you thinking?"

Louis said, "I'm not sure what to make of it, but it just seemed out of place." They finished lunch, split the bill, and headed back to Denver.

The remaining drive took Louis about an hour and a half. He could not get the look in the Kahns' eyes out of his mind. He felt that there was something important that linked Mr. Kahn's heavy alcohol ingestion, his job, and some critical unknown fact that caused him to be fearful. How did all of this relate to his illness? Louis decided that he must follow his instincts and take a deposition from Mr. Kahn's employer.

As evening approached and the sky was glowing pastel pink and purple, Louis drove down from the foothills into Denver. The town of Genesee brought back memories of his childhood, when he had visited the herds of buffalo and visited the gravesite of Buffalo Bill. As he passed the Mother Cabrini Shrine perched on top of the last peak of the foothills, he could see the glow of the city lights of Denver, giving him the feeling that he was leaving the frontier and approaching civilization.

Chapter 14

December 2007

I⟀ was the Friday following Christmas when Harry decided it was time to reinterrogate Todd Ramsey. He was still the lead suspect in Tanya Ramsey's murder. Harry had arranged to meet Todd at the station after Ramsey finished with his ski lessons. Todd showed up at four o'clock sharp. He was sober, clean shaven, and had a much different demeanor than when Harry had seen him last. He came without an attorney even though Harry had advised him to do so. Harry escorted him to an interrogation room, offered him some coffee, and then sat down across from him. Ramsey declined the coffee and seemed very calm.

Harry said, "Let's pick up where we left off. I want you to know that I could not verify your alibi at La Cantina. So, you need to tell me where you were on the day of the murder."

Todd was silent for several minutes. Harry knew Todd could sense his impatience, but Todd was still apparently hesitant to divulge his whereabouts or the identity of the person he had spent the afternoon with. Todd looked around the room, and Harry realized that he was concerned with the two-way mirror.

Harry said, "Let's take a walk outside and get some fresh air." They got up, put on their jackets, and walked outside.

Todd said, "I will tell you where I was that afternoon, but you must understand that this must be kept quiet since it will affect an important family in Basalt."

Harry responded, "I will do my best to secure your privacy if you can just be honest with me. It appears that you are trying to straighten out your life and take charge of the care of your daughter."

Todd responded, "I have stopped drinking, and I make sure I am home every night with Susie. I get up early every morning to fix her breakfast and get her off to school. The truth is that I was with the mayor's niece the day of the murder. She was visiting from Atlanta and wanted to learn how to ski. The mayor set her up at the ski school, and since I was available that morning, she was assigned to me for four hours of lessons. She is a graduate student at Emory, finishing her PhD in art history. The day started out as usual, with the basics of speed control, parallel skiing, and balance. This girl was quite the athlete, however, and by the end of the lesson she was parallel skiing down all the beginner runs and wanted to try the intermediate trails. The lesson went real well, and she asked me to join her for lunch. She wanted to go to a local hangout rather than eat the usual fare on the mountain. I took her to Doc Holliday's in Glenwood Springs. It's a bar I used to frequent, and it has great sandwiches. I had no intention of anything but having lunch and a beer. She was quite the looker, however, and after a few drinks she came on to me. One thing led to another, and I took her back to my mom's apartment, where we spent the rest of the day in bed. She went back to Atlanta a few days later, and I haven't heard from her since. I have the phone number to her apartment in Atlanta. I know the mayor would really be pissed if he found out about this. I think he's hoping she'll meet a lawyer or doctor, not a ski bum like me. Besides, he's old fashioned and thinks she's never had sex! Believe me, Detective, she's been around."

Harry said, "What is her name? Will she back up your story?"

"Her name is Tiffany Anderson. I'm not sure she will back up my story and tell you the truth, but I think she might be truthful if she was confident her uncle would not find out."

Harry asked, "What about the boyfriend you thought Tanya may have had?"

"I don't know who he is. Susie hasn't mentioned anyone, but I can't explain how Tanya could afford the new car, clothes for her and Susie, and her recent attitude of independence." The sun was beginning to set and they were beginning to feel the cold, so they returned to the interrogation room at the station.

After they were both seated, Harry said, "I will ask you for the last time, Todd. Did you kill your wife or have anything to do with her murder in any way?"

Todd responded, "No, sir, I did not."

"Is there anybody you know of who would possibly consider killing her?"

"She was liked by everybody, and I can't think of anyone who would want to harm her." Harry got up and motioned to the door. "Todd, stay in touch. I will contact your alibi in Atlanta, and she'd better back up your story. Oh, and Todd, I have one last question. Did you install a listening device in the house to possibly spy on your wife?"

He looked at Harry as if he was crazy and answered, "Of course not. Why would I do that?"

"Well, some men get jealous or overly possessive and can't stand not knowing what their wives are doing when they are separated."

Todd smirked and said, "That's not my nature, Detective."

Harry said, "All right, Todd, you can go for now. I'll call you if we need to talk again." Todd walked out of the station as the sun finally set.

Harry dialed the number in Atlanta, and a young woman answered. Harry introduced himself and asked if she was Tiffany Anderson.

She said, "Yes, I am, sir. What's this all about? It's not about my uncle, is it? Did something happen to him?"

Harry answered, "No, this is about Todd Ramsey. I need to know if you were with him during your vacation in Basalt during Christmas break."

"Yes, sir, I took a private lesson with him at the Sunlight Ski Resort."

Harry then asked, "Do you remember the date and how much time you spent with him?" "I had a four-hour lesson which began sometime in the morning, but I don't remember the exact time. It was the Friday before Christmas." She paused and then said, "I need to know why you are asking me all these questions."

"I know this is personal, but I want you to understand that whatever you tell me will be held in the strictest confidence, and this includes your aunt and uncle."

"Well, Detective, what exactly do you want to know?"

"I need to know exactly what transpired after your ski lesson."

"How important is this information, sir?"

"I must tell you that a life depends on your answer, young lady, so please be truthful with me."

"Well, we went to lunch at this bar in Glenwood Springs, had a few drinks, and to be honest I got pretty toasted. I made some sexual advances toward him, and one thing led to another. We went to his place and spent several hours in bed. What's wrong with that?"

"If need be, would you testify to this if it was kept confidential?"

"Yes, I would, sir."

Harry then said, "Please do not discuss this matter with anyone since it involves a pending murder case and nobody has been charged as yet. Well, you have been very helpful, Tiffany, and I appreciate your honesty." Harry hung up the phone and realized that he no longer had a murder suspect.

Harry was sitting in his office when Chief Owens walked in. "Harry, what's wrong? You look like you have been hit by a truck."

"Chief, I believe Todd Ramsey did not murder his wife. He has an alibi for the time of the murder, and I have just confirmed his story. I have every reason to believe the woman he was with at the presumed time of the murder."

"Who is this person providing his alibi?"

"Chief, I hate to tell you this, but it was the mayor's niece. She had a private lesson with Todd, and following the lesson they spent the afternoon together. That is why the school couldn't find him to let him know to pick Susie up from school."

"Oh shit, I know that girl. I had dinner at the mayor's house while she was in town. She really is a beautiful girl. I can see how Todd was attracted to her."

"Chief, I promised her that we would keep this confidential if possible."

"I understand, and believe me; I would prefer not to tell the mayor about this."

Harry asked, "Did Drew get the banking records and the list of prior home care patients that Tanya worked for?"

"Yes, and he said it would be on your desk first thing in the morning."

Harry was also waiting for the pending reports from the crime lab, in particular the foot impressions and fingerprints that were found. He also needed the information on the listening device disguised as a smoke detector. Hopefully these would lead to other suspects.

Harry tossed and turned all night, bothered by the fact that he had no suspect. He somehow felt that the utility truck seen that day at Tanya's home was an important piece of information. It seemed to take forever for the morning to come. He was up as the first light streamed through his window. He arrived at the station hoping the reports were on his desk from the CBI and Drew Trestle.

The pending reports from the Colorado Bureau of Investigation were on his desk. The shoe impressions were identified as European made. The smoke detector listening device was not traceable because the identifying stock numbers had been filed off. The report also confirmed Harry's suspicion that it could have been easily bought over the Internet. The fingerprints taken in the house had no known criminal matches. Harry had been hopeful that there would be some match to link her murder to a prior criminal. He knew that the problem with fingerprinting was that it was not universal. If somebody was not fingerprinted as a criminal, at work, or when applying for a gun permit, they would not show up in the fingerprint files of the Criminal Record Center. It was also difficult to attempt matches of foreigners since they were not in the U.S. system.

Drew Trestle came into the station at 9 AM and immediately updated Harry on his investigation of Tanya's phone records, bank deposits, and credit card activity.

"Harry, I believe we may have uncovered some helpful information. It appears that Tanya's bank record shows a fifty-thousand-dollar deposit in September. She withdrew twenty-five thousand dollars and placed the money in an educational trust for her daughter Susie. She also bought the SUV that was parked outside her home. Her charge cards showed some large purchases at Wal-Mart."

"What about her phone records from Qwest and her cell phone records from Verizon?"

"I wasn't sure how far back to investigate the phone records," Drew said.

Harry suggested, "I would recommend six months of records. That way you can identify any patterns that developed and also see if any unusual numbers show up."

"Thanks, Harry. Give me a few hours and I'll get you that information."

Harry made a call to Tanya's home health agency. He asked for the director of nursing and was put through.

"This is Briana Sheridan," a woman's voice said. "Can I help you?"

"I'm Harry McNally, a detective with the Basalt Police Department. I'm investigating the murder of Tanya Ramsey, and it would be helpful to have a list of the patients that she cared for over the last year since there may be some link to her murder."

"I am so sorry, but I can't help you, sir, since the HIPAA laws prevent us from giving that information without the consent of the patient involved. HIPAA stands for the Health Insurance Portability and Accountability Act, and it basically assures the privacy of the patient's medical records."

"I know what HIPPA stands for," Harry said in somewhat of a harsh tone to his voice.

"There are significant financial penalties and potential jail time for offenders," Briana responded.

Harry was frustrated by her attitude. He said, "Does that mean I need a court order to get that list of patients and their demographic information?"

"If you get a subpoena, I can comply without the usual twenty-day waiting period."

Harry said, "Go ahead and get the list ready. I'll have the subpoena by lunchtime."

"You have been very understanding, Detective. I will get right on it." Harry had no problem getting the subpoena from Judge Thompson, a good friend of Chief Owens.

The patient list from the home health agency showed that Tanya had cared for a great variety of patients over the last year. Most were elderly and were recently discharged from the hospital or several of the local rehabilitation centers in the Glenwood Springs area. Most of the time she saw the patients once or twice a week. There were a couple of instances, however, where she did private-duty nursing for a single patient for one or two weeks. She and her friend Eloise each took a twelve-hour shift. Tanya usually worked the day shift so she could be home with Susie in the evening.

Drew came over to Harry's desk while Harry was reviewing the patient list. He had the phone lists and had compiled the calls in columns. Most of the calls were to and from her friends, her parents, and the home health agency. There were a few random calls notable from sales people for cable companies, political calls for the Democratic and Republican parties, and the usual calls to support the public TV station. When they cross-referenced the two lists, they found calls from a phone number in Aspen that corresponded to a nursing assignment she had last February. The patient was a chronic renal failure patient on home dialysis who visited the Aspen area with his family. Tanya worked with this patient for two weeks, assisting him with his dialysis and nursing needs. He was from Dubai, and the family was quite wealthy as evidenced by the house they rented in the Horse Ranch Estates in Snowmass Village. Following her assignment there, Tanya received several long distance calls from Dubai in early July of 2007.

Harry needed to know who sent Tanya the fifty thousand dollars that she received in early July. He reexamined the bank records and found that the money came in via a wire from a branch of Northern Trust Bank in Manhattan. He was going to need a court order to get the name of the sender. He called the assistant DA assigned to the Ramsey case and convinced him to get the court order. Harry next called Tanya's friend and co-worker, Eloise Cruse. He asked if he could meet with her to discuss their work schedule and see if she knew anything about Tanya's private life that might shed light on the case. There was still the possibility that Tanya had a boyfriend who helped her financially and could have been responsible for her death.

It was late in the afternoon when Harry met with Eloise Cruse. She was in her mid-fifties, moderately overweight, and had graying hair. She had a very pleasant manner. Her home was small but neat. There was only one bedroom and a den. She drove a late-model Ford Explorer. Harry introduced himself at the door, and they went into the living room.

Eloise offered him a cup of coffee, but Harry declined the coffee and then asked, "Who lives here with you?"

"My husband. Our kids have all gotten married and are scattered throughout the United States. They visit during holidays mostly, especially if the skiing is good. My husband works construction for a company that does renovations in Aspen. It keeps him busy, and my home health schedule also keeps me on the run."

"The reason I needed to speak with you, Mrs. Cruse, pertains to Tanya's murder. It seems that Todd has a good alibi, and although we haven't ruled him out entirely, I am exploring other possibilities. I understand that you and Tanya worked closely together, and I thought perhaps you could answer some questions."

"Of course. I would do anything to help you solve Tanya's murder case. She was a wonderful mother, nurse, and friend. I can't imagine who would want to kill her."

"Did she have any enemies that you are aware of, perhaps a nursing job that didn't go well?"

Eloise answered, "Definitely not. This is a small town, and I would know if she had a bad result."

"How about a boyfriend? She had been separated from Todd since last summer."

"There was no new boyfriend. Tanya devoted herself to Susie."

"How would you explain the new SUV she purchased?"

"I'm not sure how to explain that, Detective. Her work schedule and mine are similar, and I'm sure Todd didn't help out much with the bills. I was kind of curious about the SUV myself."

"I have one last question, Eloise. You both worked for an Arab family back in the summer. Do you remember the name of the family, and was there a special relationship that Tanya may have had with them?"

"The patient was the grandfather of a wealthy Dubai family named Al-Shamir. They were very nice and very generous. We mainly dealt with a bodyguard named Ahmed. I was not aware of any special relationship they may have had with Tanya."

Harry rose to his feet, thanked Eloise for her time and honesty, and said, "If you can think of anything else, please don't hesitate to call."

It was getting dark when Harry returned to the station. The court order was on his desk that would give him the name of the person who wired Tanya the fifty thousand dollars. He would call the bank first thing in the morning. Harry then remembered that Grace was making a special dinner and he had to go to the grocery store on his way home.

Harry pulled into the mini-mart as the temperature was dropping. He threw his coat on and headed into the store on his search for lemons, anchovies, and grated parmesan cheese for the Caesar salad. He was sure Grace had all the other ingredients at home. He was excited about a romantic dinner at home after a tough few days on the Ramsey case. As he was wandering around in the back of the store, a teenager approached the cashier, pulled out a handgun, and pointed to the cash register.

He said, "Don't make a sound, and just hand over the cash." Harry could see the teen through the aisles without being seen. He was of high school age, medium build, and obviously not from a poor family. Harry wondered what the hell the kid was doing. Harry pulled his .38 caliber pistol out of his shoulder holster and clicked off the safety. He gradually worked his way up toward the front of the store. Just as he approached, the store clerk glanced toward Harry. The teenager noticed his eyes move in Harry's direction, and he wheeled around, pointing his gun in Harry's direction. Harry fired first, hitting the kid in his gun-holding shoulder and causing him to drop his gun and fall to the floor.

Harry calmly told the clerk to call 9–1–1. "Instruct them to send paramedics and to alert the Basalt Police Department to send two uniformed policemen to the mini-mart to follow the kid to the hospital." Harry applied first aid to the boy's shoulder and asked his name.

"Jeffrey Cunningham," he answered. "I never intended to use my gun, sir. I just needed some extra cash. My parents are going to kill me."

"Where do you live, son?"

"Aspen, sir." Jeffrey became pale and sweaty but remained alert. Harry stayed at his side, elevated his legs on several cases of Pepsi, and kept talking to him to keep him awake.

The paramedics and police officers arrived at the same time. Harry knew the uniformed officers and filled them in on the case. They read the boy his Miranda Rights and followed the ambulance to the Glenwood Springs General Hospital. Harry called Grace to let her know what was going on and that he would be home soon. He thought to himself that the paperwork could wait until the morning.

Grace had dinner ready when Harry finally got home.

She said, "Tell me about this shooting at the mini-mart."

"It was a clean shoot, but what's so disturbing is that I was forced to shoot a teenager. He was from Aspen and appeared to come from an affluent family. He probably needed the money for drugs. I can't imagine any other reason for this type of crime. I hope we will not be seeing more of these teen crimes in this area."

Grace gave Harry a hug and said, "I'll fix you a scotch while you take a shower. Then we'll sit down to dinner."

Chapter 15

———————

New Year's Eve

ED'S FAMILY LEFT Aspen to spend New Year's Eve with their friends. Ed felt that this vacation was the best time they had spent together in the last two years. He was certainly grateful that they accepted Kathy and her family so easily. He knew they probably spent a lot of private time discussing the possibility that he was appearing to finally move on with his social life and whether they were ready for this to happen. Obviously they accepted his decision.

Kathy and Ed decided to spend the evening alone at his town house. Ed was planning to do the cooking, so after skiing with Jack and Penny, he spent the late afternoon buying last-minute items for the dinner he was going to prepare for Kathy.

Kathy arrived at 7 PM just as a light snow was beginning to fall. She was carrying a shopping bag containing a bottle of champagne and chocolate-covered strawberries. She also had an overnight bag.

Jack and Penny decided to attend a New Year's Eve party at the Snowmass Club with their friends from the medical community. This was a tradition that started just after the Aspen Valley Hospital opened. It was always a good party, and this year Penny was in charge of all the arrangements.

Harry and his wife always spent New Year's Eve alone. Even when they lived in Manhattan they preferred to be alone and were always thankful to have the time together in the safety of their home. Chief Owens had invited them over for a party that he and the mayor of Basalt gave each year for their respective staff members. Harry felt bad about declining the invitation, but he knew the Chief would understand.

Sam Kahn and his wife were fortunate to have their children fly in for New Year's. They all decided to make the best of a tragic time and try to bring a little joy into Sam's life. He still couldn't speak, but they all knew he was grateful for their company. The rehabilitation center made special arrangements for a little party and a turkey dinner for the entire family.

Todd and Susie Ramsey spent New Year's Eve together. This was the first New Year's Eve in a long time that Todd spent sober. He and Susie were back in their home and cooked spaghetti and meatballs for dinner since it was Susie's favorite.

Louis Reiner arrived in Manhattan two days after the New Year. He was there to take the deposition of Mr. Kahn's employers, Mitch Carsdale and Jonathan Salem. He checked into the Hilton near their office. The deposition was set for 3:30 PM after the oil market closed at the NYMEX. Louis arrived early and was ushered into their conference room by the receptionist.

While waiting, he went over the questions he intended to ask to establish Mr. Kahn's state of mind and health prior to his illness in Aspen. He needed to know why Mr. Kahn began drinking so heavily prior to the Aspen oil conference and what all the stress was about. He also needed to understand why he and his wife had a look of fear in their eyes when asked about work. The court reporter and Michael Sutton arrived a few minutes before three thirty.

When Mitch and Jonathan entered the conference room, Louis stood and said, "I'm Louis Reiner. I hope this isn't too inconvenient, gentlemen. I don't think this will take too long." Michael Sutton also introduced himself. The attorney for the hospital, Will Kitch, had chosen not to attend.

Mitch and Jonathan were sworn in by the court reporter. Louis asked the usual questions regarding the official name of the company, the actual job description of Mr. Kahn, and the nature of his health and disability insurance packages. Louis noticed that Mitch and Jonathan seemed relaxed and at ease with the questions so far, and he knew that they were letting their guard down. So just when they thought things were going well, Louis said, "It has become obvious from prior depositions that Mr. Kahn was under a lot of stress and was drinking heavily just prior to the Aspen conference. I was wondering, Mitch, if you have an explanation for this change in his behavior, since excess alcohol consumption is a contributor to atrial fibrillation."

Mitch responded, "Nothing was going on that I am aware of. In fact, our profits have been soaring recently."

"Would he have gotten a bonus?"

"Yes," Jonathan replied.

"His wife was confident that there was nothing wrong with their marriage or children," Louis said. "Could he have been worried about his job security?"

"There has never been a question as to his job security," Mitch quickly said.

Jonathan then added, "Maybe you should speak to Sam's friend Gary Goldman. They had lunch together almost daily, and he may know something about Sam's marriage or personal life that his wife was not aware of or not discussing." Louis noticed that Mitch looked at Jonathan in disbelief as if to say, how could you have divulged the name of this close friend? Louis immediately knew he had hit upon a sensitive matter.

He wanted to press on with more questions about Kahn's job security, but Michael Sutton interrupted and said, "I don't see how this relates to the case."

Louis ignored Sutton and then asked, "Who is replacing Mr. Kahn at this time?"

Mitch said, "We were fortunate to get a young man who recently graduated from NYU Business School. His uncle and his family are our biggest investor group to date."

Louis then asked, "What's this young man's name?"

Mitch said, "Allam Yaseen."

"Do you expect him to be a permanent employee?"

Jonathan answered, "The way things are going with Sam, we doubt he will be coming back. If he does make a recovery, we believe there will be room for both of them."

Louis took several minutes to review his notes and then said, "I have no further questions, gentlemen, but I would appreciate it if you could give me Gary Goldman's phone number."

Mitch said, "Sorry, we don't have his number, but he works in the law firm of Castleman, Gaines, and Brenner."

Louis said, "Thank you, gentlemen." They all stood and began to exit the room when Louis turned to Jonathan and asked, "Where were you guys during 9/11?"

They looked at each other and Mitch replied, "We were lucky."

Louis looked them booth in the eyes and said, "I bet you were."

Louis went to the law firm where Gary Goldman worked. He introduced himself to the receptionist and asked her, "Is Mr. Goldman available for a moment to discuss his friend Sam Kahn?"

She asked if he had an appointment, and when he said that he did not, she asked him to take a seat and she would check to see if Mr. Goldman was available. After a few minutes, Mr. Goldman came out of the back offices.

Louis said, "I apologize for not calling earlier, but I just completed a deposition with Mr. Kahn's employers, and they said you were his close friend."

He shook Louis's hand and said, "How about a quick lunch?"

Louis said, "Sure, I have time before my flight back to Denver." They caught the elevator down to the ground level and walked the few blocks to the Star Diner on the Avenue of the Americas. They were seated immediately and ordered coffee and sandwiches.

Louis began by saying, "I am the defense attorney for the physician in Aspen that the Kahn family is suing for malpractice. I understand that Sam and you are good friends, and my intention is not to jeopardize that relationship. However, I get the feeling that his illness was caused by anxiety and excess alcohol intake just prior to the conference in Aspen. I also have the feeling that in some way it was related to stress at work, although his employers denied this in the deposition that I just completed with them. Finally, I have the distinct feeling that the Kahns and Sam's employers are hiding something. I know that's a mouthful, and I don't want to burden you with my gut feelings, but if you have any information off the record it may help Sam in the long run."

Gary Goldman listened intently, and after a long pause said, "You are obviously a very bright young attorney, but I have to tell you that you are way off base trying to discuss this with me, even if it is off the record. Sam was in good health until he came under the care of your physician and that Aspen hospital. I'll be damned if I'm going to help his opposing attorney in this lawsuit."

Louis said, "I understand how you feel, Mr. Goldman, but Mitch and Jonathan just don't seem truly interested in Sam. In fact, they hired a nephew of one of their foreign investors to replace Sam."

Gary responded, "I plan to visit with Sam as soon as he returns, or I will fly out to Colorado to see him. I will think about what you said."

"Thank you for your consideration, Mr. Goldman. Lunch is on me." They got up from the table, and Louis paid the cashier. They walked out into the noise of New York City. They shook hands, and then Louis walked over to the Hilton to get his overnight bag. He caught a cab to LaGuardia Airport. As his plane flew over Manhattan, he could not help but notice the void left by the destruction of the Twin Towers.

Gary Goldman walked slowly through midtown Manhattan. He reflected back on the conversation that he and Sam had prior to Sam's departure to Aspen. He realized that Sam's concerns about the connection between the profits of Capital Investors of America and the Dubai family could in some way be related to their extraordinary surge in profits. Abuse of inside information of this sort carried large penalties. He didn't know how all this related to Sam's illness, but he hoped he could sort all this out after visiting with Sam and Evelyn. He decided that he would follow through with Sam's earlier request and contact some of his friends who still worked at the SEC and see if they had any information relating to recent use of inside information in oil-related trading.

Chapter 16

January 2008

HARRY ARRIVED AT the station to find the uniformed policemen from last evening with Chief Owens in his office. Harry had already prepared his report of the mini-mart incident with a detailed account of the shooting for Chief Owens.

Chief Owens said, "Harry, we have a big problem. I know you are having a rough time with the Ramsey murder, but I received a phone call from the Aspen police informing me that they have had a significant increase in teenage crime. We have also had a similar rise here in Basalt, and I know you are not aware of the fact that approximately eight years ago there was a gang of Aspen high school kids from affluent families performing break-ins for the purpose of stealing jewelry and electronic equipment. It turned out that they needed the money for drugs. We all fear the same problem is starting again.

"Fortunately the incident last night went well and nobody got killed, thanks to you. The boy came clean on the events of last night, and I'm sure his story will coincide with yours. This was his first offense, and the district attorney will probably let him plea bargain the case for a minimal punishment. I would appreciate it if you could meet with the Aspen police chief and get a feel for what's going on in Aspen."

Harry said without hesitation, "I will be happy to help if you can just get me the list of crimes and details from Aspen as well as here in Basalt."

Chief Owens said, "Consider it done. Thanks, Harry."

Harry sat down at his desk and immediately called the bank to get the name of the person who wired Tanya the fifty thousand dollars. The first vice president informed Harry that the wire came from an account in Manhattan. The bank was Northern Trust, and the account that the funds originated from belonged to a man named Al-Shamir. Harry realized that this was the family Tanya had worked for earlier in the year, but he knew that normally they would have paid the home health agency rather than Tanya. He immediately called the home health agency and found out that the Al-Shamir family did pay in full to them and would not have paid Tanya for those particular services. So why was the fifty thousand dollars wired to Tanya?

At this point in time Harry felt secure believing that Todd did not kill his wife. He also had no reason to believe that she had a boyfriend who may have committed the crime. There was no evidence pointing to a robbery that may have gone bad. This left Harry with the possibility that there was a relationship between the Al-Shamir family and Tanya's murder. He wondered if in some way her murder could be related to the visit from the hospital administrator. He decided to revisit Kathy Ellington at Aspen Valley Hospital. He called Kathy Ellington's office and spoke to her secretary, Prudence Harding. She arranged for Harry to meet with Kathy the following day at noon.

Chief Owens placed copies of newspaper clippings on Harry's desk that related to the prior teenage spree of robberies for drug money. Harry perused the articles and decided to visit the teenage boy he shot and arrested last night. He drove over to the Glenwood Springs hospital and parked in the visitor section of the parking lot. He entered through the main entrance, went over to the reception desk, and asked to get a visitor pass for Jeffrey Cunningham. He was directed to the surgical wing and found the boy's room without much difficulty.

Jeffrey was there with his right arm in a sling, and his left hand was handcuffed to the bed. There was a uniformed policeman sitting in a chair by the door. Jeffrey's mother was at his bedside. Harry introduced himself and was surprised to find them very hospitable, rather than angry as he had expected. Mrs. Cunningham had the intelligence to realize that things could have gone differently if Harry had panicked and shot to kill rather than disarm her son.

"I hope you're feeling better, Jeffrey," Harry said.

"Yes, sir, I feel pretty good considering that my stupidity almost got me killed. I am hoping to go home tonight if my attorney can get me released into the custody of my parents." Harry walked a little closer to the bed and said, "I need to ask you some questions, Jeffrey. I'm glad your mother is here, but if you would like to wait for your father or an attorney I can return another time."

Mrs. Cunningham said, "Go ahead, Detective, we might as well get to the bottom of this now."

Harry leaned closer to Jeffrey and in a soft voice asked, "Was this robbery a prank or a dare, or did you truly need the money?"

"I did it for the cash, sir."

"What did you need the cash for, Jeffrey?" Mrs. Cunningham asked, leaning forward in her seat and anxiously awaiting the answer.

Jeffrey hesitated. He looked at his mother and then at Harry. "I have been using cocaine for the past year. I began using recreationally with my friends. Since there were no withdrawal symptoms we all felt safe in trying it again, mainly at parties on weekends. However, as time went on I couldn't get the desired feeling out of my mind. All I thought about was coke and when I could use it again. I needed that rush of energy and feeling of being superhuman. I needed to have that feeling. With each use, however, I could never get the same feeling I had the first few times, and this led to my need for higher quantities of cocaine."

Mrs. Cunningham was obviously shaken by her son's story. She appeared speechless and somewhat embarrassed that she had no idea of the trouble her son had gotten himself into.

Harry could sense her dismay and said, "This is so typical of what's happening today. Parents have difficulty in knowing that their children are in this kind of trouble until they reach the point of personality change, decrease in school performance, or some medical problem."

Harry looked at Jeffrey and continued, "Consider yourself lucky in a way—you were caught prior to having a cardiac arrest, heart attack, or severe psychiatric illness. Since you have been straight with the police and if you can be straight with the district attorney, there is a good chance your sentence may only involve a rehabilitation center to serve your time and get yourself straightened out. It has always been my belief that strength of character comes from overcoming and learning from adversity. This certainly qualifies as that kind of adversity."

They were obviously grateful for his attitude and understanding. Mrs. Cunningham said, "Detective, I can't thank you enough for your straightforward attitude. I believe I can speak for my son when I tell you that he will definitely turn this problem around. He has always been an honor student and an athlete in high school with the eventual goal of becoming a sports medicine physician. I hope we can get this incident expunged from his record so he can attain his goals."

"I hope so as well, Mrs. Cunningham. Jeffrey, you need to know that there has been a rise in teenage crime in the Aspen and Basalt areas. Apparently several years ago, prior to my arrival from New York, there was a similar outbreak of teenage crime. These crimes were related to the need for drug money, and the kids who were involved were from wealthy families. From what I was told, the drugs were being sold by an employee of one of the oldest restaurants in Aspen."

Mrs. Cunningham said, "We have been living in Aspen for twenty years, and I do remember that crime spree. They were breaking into multimillion-dollar homes and stealing jewelry and electronic equipment. Jeffrey was only in elementary school at the time, and his sister was only in kindergarten. The names of the teenagers involved were withheld from the news, but in a small town word gets around pretty fast. We could not believe the families that were involved. Now we are one of those families." She began to break down and cry.

Harry stood there silently and then finally said, "I'm going to leave you two alone for now."

Harry sat down in the hospital cafeteria with a cup of coffee. He flipped open his cell phone and called Chief Owens. "Chief, I think it's time to bring the district attorney over to interview the Cunningham kid. In my opinion he is ready to talk, and he possibly has some information that will help bring the drug dealers down. Could you have the DA call his attorney? I'll arrange to have the parents present this afternoon."

"I hope you're right, Harry. I'm sure the DA will be willing to make a deal for information that will lead to some arrests. However, this kid did commit an armed felony. I'll call you back with the time the lawyers can be there. Good job, Harry." They hung up, and Harry sat for awhile drinking his coffee.

His mind wandered back to his life in New York City prior to September 11, 2001. He was always under pressure to solve crimes and had a huge backlog of cases which never seemed to decrease in size. Somehow he was able to maintain a happy marriage, probably because his wife was so understanding. He remembered the huge spike in crime that occurred in the 1980s and early 1990s, when the crack epidemic hit the city. There were 2262 murders in 1990, the peak year for murder in the city. Murder continued at a high level until 1994–1995, when there was a progressive decline in the rate of murder which had actually continued to the present. Harry was at a loss to explain this decline, but most police officers had attributed it to several key factors. The first was the development of Compstat, which reorganized the police department and utilized statistical analysis of precinct-related crimes to better serve the community in crime reduction. Second, at the same time five thousand new and better-educated police officers were trained and placed in the field. Third, Mayor Giuliani initiated a zero-tolerance campaign against petty crime and antisocial behavior. Fourth, there were programs that moved over five hundred thousand people into jobs from welfare, and housing vouchers were distributed that enabled poor families to move to better neighborhoods. Fifth, and probably most important, was the end of the crack epidemic.

September 11, 2001, however, brought a whole new set of physical and psychological problems to New York City as well as to himself. There were the physical problems of sleep deprivation, continued sinusitis, and chronic coughing that were related to the persistent air pollutants. Worse, however, was the psychological impact of the loss of friends and fellow officers in such a senseless and tragic manner. Equally painful were the visits to the families to try to console them when he himself had not reconciled with his own dismay. Each day the sights and smells of the area surrounding Ground Zero hampered his own ability to repress his feelings and move forward. His usual rational and controlled way of thinking could not overcome his feelings of hatred toward all those who even remotely appeared to be of Arab descent.

Harry was brought out of his reverie by the ring of his cell phone. He said, "Hello, Chief, what's up?"

"It's all set for this afternoon at 2 PM. Please inform the mother to arrange for the father to be present. The kid's attorney will be there at 1:30 PM to discuss their strategy. I don't think you need to be present for this interview since the assistant DA has been brought up to speed on the case. I'll see you back at the station later."

Harry went back up to Jeffrey's room to inform them of the meeting. He said, "The meeting with the assistant district attorney is set for 2 PM today. I would suggest you have your husband present. Your attorney has already been notified and will be here at one thirty to discuss your options. I wish you the best of luck, Jeffrey."

Jeffrey said, "I never thought I would thank the man who shot me, but I know that if it was not for your skill and calmness I could have been killed. Thank you very much, Detective." Jeffrey's mother was obviously pleased with her son's attitude. She also thanked Harry. Harry left the hospital and headed back to the station.

Chapter 17

January 2008

IT WAS LATE in the afternoon when Mitch and Jonathan decided it was time to call Ahmed in Dubai to discuss the recent events in regards to their deposition. They were concerned by the line of questioning and attitude of Louis Reiner. Ahmed took the call and tried to reassure them that everything was under control.

He said, "We have a couple of our most loyal employees in Colorado keeping a close eye on the situation, and they are in constant contact with Mr. Kahn and his wife. I will contact them to be sure that all is well. I want you to know that we will do everything possible to assure that our relationship remains secure and nothing interferes with our profits." Mitch and Jonathan thanked Ahmed and hung up, but they still had a sense that all was not as it seemed.

Ahmed immediately called Abdul Rahman and Pete Jensen. In his usual low and calm voice he said, "I haven't heard from you in a while. Is everything going as planned?"

"Well, sir, we have had a little trouble here," Pete said.

"What kind of trouble?"

"There was an unexpected accidental death of the nurse who was coerced to administer the drug to Mr. Kahn."

"How did that happen?"

Abdul broke in and said, "We picked up a conversation she had with the hospital administrator. We went over there to scare her and to reinforce the fact that if she told anybody about what she did we would harm her daughter. She panicked while we were in her house. She slipped and hit her head on a coffee table. She immediately became unconscious and died shortly thereafter." Ahmed was silent for a long time, contemplating what he had just heard.

Pete then said, "It was purely an accident. We covered it up to make it look like the husband committed the murder. We were dressed like utility workers and had a typical utility-type truck parked out front. I don't think anybody will be able to identify us."

Abdul then said, "In addition to our cover-up, this is a small town, and I doubt they have the ability to figure out what actually happened or to link her death to Mr. Kahn. We left no fingerprints at the scene and got rid of the utility truck."

Ahmed asked, "Are you sure that Mr. Kahn will remain silent?"

Abdul answered, "They are frightened of us. We are in constant contact with the wife. We are confident that we have control of the situation here."

Ahmed then said, "Abdul, you were assigned to work on this project because of your loyalty to the jihad. Pete is a mercenary employed to assist you. I must inform both of you that this project is an important part of a larger plan to raise funds for our attack on all those who desire to put a stop to Islamic Fundamentalism. I want you to keep me informed of any developments. Stay there and keep a close watch on the Kahns. We cannot afford any leaks at this point. We would prefer not to eliminate Mr. Kahn, but I'm sure you are aware that possibility does exist." Ahmed hung up the phone and immediately reported to Al-Shamir.

Harry pulled up to the hospital at noon for his meeting with Kathy. He made his way to her office and said hello to Prudence, who remembered him from his last visit.

She said, "Have a seat, Detective. Kathy will be with you in a minute." Harry took a seat. He pulled out his notepad and began to review his notes on the case. He had forgotten about the smoke detector listening device that he had found in Tanya's home. This and the utility truck seen at the house by a neighbor at the approximate time of Tanya's death made Harry realize that this was probably a professional murder.

Just then Kathy appeared in front of him and said, "Hello, Detective. What's on your mind?"

"Well, Kathy, I have come to the conclusion that there may be some connection between Tanya's murder and her ICU care of the patient you were concerned about."

"You are referring to Mr. Kahn," Kathy said.

"That's right."

"Come into my office, Detective."

Harry sat across from Kathy's desk. "I must ask you again, Kathy. Why did you visit with Tanya?"

"Well, Detective, as I mentioned before I was speaking with her because she was on duty the night before Mr. Kahn was discharged, and I was trying to see if there was something she might have seen that would explain his complications."

"Did you come up with anything?"

"Not really. I did, however, notice that Tanya was very anxious. I also noticed that she seemed to have a more expensive SUV than one would have expected for her income. Otherwise we could not relate her care to his complications. She could have given him a medication that would reverse his anticoagulation, but if she didn't chart the medication we would have no way of knowing it was given. However, I have no reason to believe she would do this."

Harry then asked, "What if she was paid by someone who also supplied the medication?" "Of course this would explain exactly what happened. But who would do this, and why?" Harry then responded, "I don't know. Had she been working at the hospital for a long time?"

"I actually checked on that. She began working at the hospital the day after he was admitted. She coincidentally asked to have some ICU time when he was admitted to that unit." "Do you have the dates of that ICU duty?"

"Of course, Detective. It was the first week of July."

Harry realized that was the approximate time the money was wired to Tanya. *This is all coming together now,* he thought.

"Well, you have been very helpful, Kathy. Thank you very much, and I will keep in touch."

Harry got up and was about to leave when Kathy said, "Please don't hesitate to call with any information that may help the hospital and Dr. Simpson in the pending lawsuit."

"I understand." Harry left the hospital and headed back to Basalt.

He began to connect the dots. This was a professional murder and was set up to look like the husband did it. This was in some way related to the Al-Shamir family and their relationship to Tanya Ramsey. The puzzling part of this connection was why anybody would want to medically injure Mr. Kahn. Was there a relationship between Samuel Kahn and Al-Shamir? He realized that a visit to Mr. Kahn was needed.

Chapter 18

————◆◈◆————

February 2008

GARY GOLDMAN TOOK off from the Newark Airport at 10 AM on
Saturday for his direct flight to the Eagle-Vail airport in Colorado on
his way to visit Sam Kahn. Gary had promised Sam that he would
visit at the earliest time his work schedule allowed. He had hoped that
Sam would be back in New York to continue his rehabilitation, but
each time Sam was ready for the transfer, some medical complication
occurred. He developed pneumonia in early November, which
prompted a three-week hospital stay in Glenwood Springs General.
This set his rehabilitation back tremendously from both a physical as
well as a psychological standpoint. He lost twenty pounds of weight
and lost a lot of muscle mass with its associated loss of strength. He
eventually improved with the care that his wife and the hospital staff
gave him.

He returned to the rehabilitation facility and began the long and
arduous process of rebuilding muscle strength, regaining the desire to
live, and restarting speech therapy. His next complication occurred
just after his children left. He developed an episode of prostatitis,
which was treated with a prolonged course of antibiotics. Just as he was
recovering from this urinary infection, he developed severe diarrhea
associated with fever and abdominal pain. He was diagnosed with
pseudomembranous colitis caused by the Clostridia Difficile toxin,
which formed because of an overgrowth of an opportunistic bacteria

uncovered when the normal intestinal flora were wiped out by the use of certain antibiotics. He was treated for this and finally recovered just one week before Gary arrived.

Gary decided to stay in the Hotel Colorado in Glenwood Springs. This was the oldest hotel in the area and boasted Teddy Roosevelt as one of its most famous guests. The hotel had a large collection of teddy bears in the lobby since the teddy bear was named after Teddy Roosevelt.

The drive to the rehabilitation center only took Gary a few minutes. Gary found the rehabilitation center without difficulty and went right up to Sam's room, where he found Evelyn at her usual position at Sam's bedside. She greeted Gary with a hug and a kiss. Sam was obviously happy to see Gary and smiled for the first time since his family had all been there for New Year's. Gary hugged Sam and could not hide his emotional dismay at seeing the physical deterioration that his friend had endured. Tears came to his eyes, and when Evelyn noticed his reaction she also let herself become tearful. It took several minutes for them to regain their composure.

Gary finally said, "New York sure misses you guys. When are you busting out of here?"

Evelyn spoke for Sam and said, "It won't be soon enough. As soon as he can ambulate with his walker and the speech therapist feels he can be treated at home. We are hoping it will be soon." Sam shook his head to signal that he agreed. He then tried to smile, but because of the stroke only the left part of his face moved, forming a partial smile.

Gary asked, "Have you been keeping up with the Democratic and Republican campaigns?"

Sam nodded yes, smiled, and with difficulty tried to say something.

Evelyn broke in and said, "This has been the most interesting and competitive race for the nominations we have seen in a long time. Sam has been following the race closely and was amazed at the popularity of Barack Obama. The country desires a change, and this young man certainly has the speaking ability and charisma to get the nomination. However, the degree of mud-slinging between Barack Obama and Hilary Clinton may ruin any chances the Democrats have in the general election against John McCain."

Gary shook his head in agreement and said, "The Republicans may get reelected even after the Iraq fiasco. These fools have run up a huge deficit, and with all their use of fear to justify the Iraq war they have not put a dent in the threat of terrorism all over the world as the Islamic extremists continue their quest for world dominance."

Evelyn piped in and said, "What about the problem of globalization which has wiped out large portions of the working middle class in Europe and the States, leaving them with no sources of income?"

"I know what you mean, Evelyn. Well, Sam, that catches us up on our usual lunch conversations. Let's get you out of here for a couple of hours. I rented a large enough car for you, Evelyn, and a wheelchair. Let's take a drive into Aspen and have lunch at the St. Regis Hotel. I'm sure they have wheelchair access." Sam nodded yes, and Evelyn was thrilled to get Sam out for a few hours. With the help of the physical therapist and Sam's usual nurse's aide, they got Sam settled into the car and took off for Aspen.

Five minutes later, the assistant to the physical therapist flipped open his cell phone and made a quick call. Soon after, a black SUV left from the rental apartment complex across the street from the rehabilitation center.

The temperature was five degrees Fahrenheit outside, and the sky was clear as Gary drove east on Highway 82. As they passed Mount Sopris, Gary noticed Evelyn was on edge and was continuously looking out the side-view mirror.

Gary said, "Evelyn, what's wrong? You seem nervous."

Evelyn turned and looked at Sam in the backseat. "Gary, we have to tell you something very important, but the information could potentially put you in danger." When neither Sam nor Gary objected, she continued, "Our lives have been threatened, and we are in constant fear." "Evelyn, what the hell are you talking about?"

"Sam's illness was a deliberate act to serve as a warning to keep Sam quiet about the inside information that Mitch Carsdale and Jonathan Salem have been using to obtain their extraordinary profits. There are two men here that seem to be keeping us under surveillance. They stop by Sam's room frequently, and they seem to know what we are doing all the time. One of them is of Arab descent, and the other looks like a military type with short-cropped hair and a muscular build. Frankly, they scare the shit out of us."

"Sam, do you recognize them from New York? Have they been to the trading group offices?" Sam shook his head no.

"I have to tell you something," Gary said reluctantly. "I had a visit in New York from an attorney. His name is Louis Reiner, and he represents Dr. Simpson in your lawsuit. He became very suspicious of foul play after taking the deposition of Mitch and Jonathan in New York. He also mentioned to me that you both appeared more nervous than the situation called for during your deposition. He seems like an attorney with a lot of integrity, but when push comes to shove he will do everything he can to defend his client." Sam and Evelyn did not respond, but it was clear to Gary that they were thinking seriously about his comments.

They passed the turnoff to Snowmass Village Ski Resort and continued east to Aspen. The sky remained clear, and just past the airport and Buttermilk Mountain they could see the majestic peaks of Maroon Bells. As they made their way around the turnabout and Aspen Highlands Ski Resort, they could see the beginning of the town of Aspen and Aspen Mountain.

Sam remembered that the St. Regis was situated at the base of Aspen Mountain, so he motioned for Pete to turn right at the Main Street Bakery and Café. They arrived at the St. Regis and got Sam loaded into a wheelchair without much difficulty. They did not notice the black SUV pulling into a parking space one block away.

The lunch was difficult for Sam, but Evelyn was terrific. She made it easy for Sam by ordering for him and cutting his food so nonchalantly it appeared normal. They talked without reservation, but Evelyn still constantly looked around and appeared anxious. Sam and Evelyn attempted to come up with a plan, but their thoughts seemed to be hampered by fear. Gary attempted to present a positive picture of the future, with Sam making continued physical progress as well as a successful financial plan that included winning the lawsuit and returning to work in a timely manner.

As they left the St. Regis Hotel, Evelyn spotted the black SUV pulling out of its parking space and could not help but notice that it was clearly following them.

Chapter 19

February 2008

IT HAD BEEN snowing almost daily for the whole month of February, producing the deepest snow base in the last ten years. Ed had made arrangements after his last trip to fly directly into Aspen on United Express so he could be in Snowmass for Valentine's Day to enjoy the great skiing and to see Kathy again. This was also the week that Jack and Kathy were supposed to meet with their respective attorneys for a defense strategy session. The meeting was scheduled to take place at the hospital after Jack finished office hours. Ed decided to attend, hoping he could contribute in some way to the meeting.

Louis Reiner and Will Kitch arrived at the hospital a little early and waited in Kathy's office until Jack and Ed arrived. Kathy introduced Ed to Louis and Will and then offered coffee to Ed and the two attorneys. They declined the coffee, thanked Kathy, and then all went to the conference room. Jack arrived at five o'clock and apologized for being late. Will started the meeting by stating that he believed the hospital had no culpability in the case if the plaintiff's attorney could only use facts derived solely from the hospital record and testimony from hospital employees.

Mr. Kitch said, "Michael Sutton called with an offer to settle for the limits of the hospital's insurance policy. This of course was his first offer, and I believe the hospital can get rid of the case for less, possibly one million dollars."

Louis said, "You realize this will give them enough funds to proceed with the case against Dr. Simpson with their hopes of a much larger settlement from us. The other problem with the hospital settling is the negative impact of the empty chair effect."

Jack asked, "What's the empty chair effect?"

Louis explained, "If a case goes to trial and one of the defendants is dropped from the lawsuit and leaves the other defendant standing alone, then the jury assumes the settling defendant is not culpable and therefore assumes the remaining defendant must be responsible for the plaintiff's injuries. This makes the defense of the remaining defendant more difficult. Personally I feel they have a weak case, and we should proceed together to defend Dr. Simpson and the hospital."

"So far we have spent very little money on our defense," Kathy said. "I'm not sure if you two attorneys are aware that one of the nurses at the hospital was apparently murdered. She was caring for the plaintiff for several days during his first admission to the hospital, which preceded his subsequent embolic stroke and splenic infarct. Ed and I met with her prior to her murder and felt she was hiding something."

"In addition, she seemed to be living a little beyond her means," Ed said.

Louis then added, "I had a suspicion that there was something unusual in the behavior of Mr. and Mrs. Kahn as well as his employers when I took their depositions. I couldn't put my finger on it, but it was as if they were afraid of something."

Jack Simpson's facial expression gradually changed from one who was listening intently to one of frustration and anger. He finally could not keep his silence any longer. He looked at Ed and then said, "You guys are missing the point. Only Ed can truly understand how I feel. This is not just about money, settlements, and legal costs. This case is about my reputation and future as a practicing cardiologist. There is no such thing as a jury of my peers. I will be judged in response to the sympathy that the plaintiff's attorney can manufacture in the minds of the jury. It will end up being more related to his skill as a plaintiff's attorney than the actual scientific facts of the case. He will produce expert witnesses that have the experience and skill to react in a courtroom and yet have no skill to function as practicing physicians. They will use hindsight as their weapon, and you will not be able to defend against that tactic. I have gone over this case in my mind a hundred times, and I can assure you that there was no malpractice on my part. As you are aware, I have no malpractice insurance. Only my home and retirement plan are protected.

However, thanks to Ed and his son I got out of the stock market last October and placed my money in gold, bonds, and foreign currencies. Those assets will be at risk if I lose this case, and they can attach future earnings as well. With those thoughts in mind, gentlemen, I hope we can come up with a defense that will bring some justice to this case."

Will Kitch said, "Unfortunately, my job as attorney for the hospital and its insurance company is purely related to the financial aspects of the case. If I feel it would be more cost-effective to settle with the plaintiff, then that is what I will recommend to the hospital's insurance carrier. Please understand that I am sympathetic to your feelings, but those are the facts of life."

Louis said, "We understand your position, Will."

Kathy stood up and said, "I think we should pursue the possible connection of this lawsuit and the murder of the nurse who cared for Mr. Kahn the night before his discharge. If you gentlemen would excuse me for a second, I'm going to call the detective in charge of the case and see what progress has been made."

They all nodded their approval, and Kathy left the conference room. She located the detective's card on her desk and dialed the police station. She was immediately transferred to Harry's extension.

"Hello, Detective, this is Kathy Ellington. I'm calling to see if you have found any connection to link Tanya's murder to our lawsuit involving Samuel Kahn. I am in the middle of a meeting with the defense attorneys, and if there is a connection it would be of utmost importance to our case."

"As a matter of fact, Kathy, I was getting ready to call his attorney to set up a meeting with Mr. Kahn and his wife. I felt it would be appropriate to include his attorney in this interview. If I understand the medical situation correctly, you feel that Tanya may have injected him with a drug that would counterbalance the anticoagulant effect of his blood thinner."

"That's correct, Detective."

Harry went on to say, "I'll let you know how the interview goes, but why would Tanya Ramsey do such a thing? I can't believe she would be motivated to jeopardize her career over money. However, we did find out that she received fifty thousand dollars from a previous patient's family from Dubai."

"That's interesting, Detective. I'll let the attorneys know that you are investigating that angle of the case. What about Tanya's husband?"

"We have definitely ruled him out."

Kathy said, "Nice speaking to you again, Detective. I hope to hear from you soon."

Kathy rejoined the meeting and informed them of her conversation with Harry. They listened with interest to Kathy and hoped that something good would come of the investigation. They knew that they had to be practical, however, and build their defense as if the case was going to trial. Even if there was foul play, it might not keep the Kahn family from pursuing the lawsuit. They resumed the conversation and began to go over the expert witness list. There were the usual hired guns that typically testified for the plaintiff's side of a lawsuit. They had a retired cardiologist and emergency room physician from Denver. There was also a hematologist to testify on the coagulation aspects of the case. Fortunately, Michael Sutton could not get a cardiologist who specialized in electrophysiology and arrhythmias to testify against Jack. This left an opening for the defense to bring in an atrial fibrillation specialist to testify on Jack's behalf.

"I'll get the head of the department of electrophysiology in the cardiology department at the University of Colorado Medical School to review the case," said Louis. "I'm sure he has testified for the defense side for our firm on previous occasions."

"Do we need any other expert witnesses?" Jack asked.

Louis replied, "We should have a backup in case he does poorly on the stand or has a time conflict. I believe we can save the money on any other experts unless the plaintiff's experts state something in their deposition that is false or needs to be challenged on your behalf."

"I believe you should consider a hematologist as an expert," Ed said. "They may try to claim that Jack missed diagnosing one of the hyper-coagulation syndromes. I reviewed the chart and found that Jack did actually order the appropriate workup during his second admission. An expert in that field would definitely be of benefit."

They all agreed, and at that point Will Kitch looked at Kathy and said, "I believe we are not needed any longer, and I would like to get started on my drive back to Denver." As Will got up to leave, Kathy rose and walked him out to his car.

As they walked, she said, "Will, I believe we should stay in the suit. A settlement makes no sense to me when there was really no malpractice by either Jack or the hospital. Even if Tanya was responsible in some way, we did not deviate from standard of care in our hiring or overseeing her nursing care."

"I agree with you, Kathy, and for now I will decline their offer. However, if they make a lower offer we are obligated to consider it. Talk to you soon." Kathy waved good-bye as Will drove away. She went back into the meeting and found Jack and Louis Reiner going over the opposing side's depositions.

Ed got up and said, "Guys, I'm going to leave you with your depositions and take Kathy to dinner for Valentine's Day. Talk to you tomorrow, Jack." Kathy and Ed left the conference room and headed back to Kathy's office.

Ed said, "I've made reservations at Poppi's Restaurant for seven o'clock, if that's okay."

Kathy smiled coyly and said, "That sounds great."

Ed then said, "I want to stop by and bring something for Laura and your mom."

"Ed, you are so thoughtful, thank you."

"You can thank me later! Are you going to be able to spend the night?"

"Better than that, I took the day off tomorrow. We can sleep in and then go skiing. See you at six thirty."

While Ed was driving back to his town house, he thought of his last Valentine's Day with Lynn. It was a tough time for both of them. She was not responding to her last round of chemotherapy. She was weak and had lost her appetite, but she had never complained. She always saw the positive side of things. He always felt that if she did not have such a great attitude during the last several months of her life it would have been intolerable for him.

She would do anything to keep from interfering with the lives of their boys. This had its negative effect, however, since they never spent the time at home in the last months of her life that they would have if they had known how terminal she was. She was insistent on keeping everybody around her from being negative. He had some guilt about this but always let her make her own decisions about the way things would be handled when it came to her illness. He was grateful now that his life was returning to normal, and he felt fortunate to have met someone like Kathy who had a way about her that made him feel so comfortable. Although he missed Lynn terribly, he was nevertheless thankful for the joy he felt whenever he thought of the romantic relationship he and Kathy were experiencing.

As Kathy got ready for the evening, she was excited about Ed, Valentine's Day, and where their relationship was going. *Surely he's fond of me,* she thought, *but could he ever think of anything permanent? Is he truly ready for a new relationship, and has he really recovered from the trauma of his wife's death?* She thought that maybe tonight she would try to get answers to these questions.

Ed arrived with flowers for Ruby and a teddy bear with a heart for Laura. They were thrilled. Laura gave Ed one of the heart-shaped cookies she had made. "I put it in a baggie," she said. "You can have it later."

"Well, thank you. I always love a cookie late at night."

Kathy said, "Goodnight, see you tomorrow. Mom, I'll have my cell phone if you need to reach me."

Poppi's Restaurant had been a favorite of Aspen locals for many years. It had a very romantic atmosphere and was located on the ground floor of a charming Victorian home. They were greeted by the owner, Michael, and were seated at a table in the front room of the restaurant. After a sumptuous dinner, they went back to Ed's town house. Ed started a fire and put on a CD. They opened a bottle of champagne together and toasted their good fortune.

"We are very lucky, Ed. We are in good health, have great jobs, and best of all we are together. I want you to understand that I love you very much and could spend the rest of my life with you."

"I know things are happening pretty fast, Kathy. I never thought I could fall in love again. But I have, and I love you very much."

Chapter 20

February 2008

It was the Monday morning following Valentine's Day when Harry entered the Glenwood Springs Rehabilitation Center. It had snowed heavily all night, as it had been doing for the whole month of February. Harry entered through the front door and was immediately aware of the distinctive odor that was so typical of nursing homes and rehabilitation centers. It was almost impossible for the staff to keep up with the frequent needs of incontinent patients. Harry was directed to Samuel Kahn's room. He introduced himself to Sam and Evelyn Kahn.

"I hope I'm not interfering with your rehab, Mr. Kahn. This should not take long."

Mrs. Kahn said, "I think we should wait for Mr. Sutton, if you don't mind."

Harry nodded affirmatively and asked, "Would you like some coffee from the cafeteria while we wait?" They thanked him but declined his offer. Harry went down the hall to find the cafeteria and noticed a man walking toward him that he was confident was the attorney. As they approached each other, Harry reached his hand out and said, "Mr. Sutton?"

"Yes, and you must be Detective McNally." They shook hands and decided to get some coffee together. Harry and Michael Sutton sat down in the cafeteria with their coffees.

Harry said, "I want you to understand that I'm not here to interfere with your lawsuit. I am investigating the murder of the nurse who was caring for Mr. Kahn in the ICU for several days prior to his discharge during his first admission. As you recall, this was prior to his readmission for his stroke."

"I understand, Detective. However, I don't see how Mr. Kahn is involved."

"I'm not sure he has anything to do with the nurse's murder, but there is an unusual connection. She apparently also cared for a renal failure patient who was visiting from Dubai, and this same family recently sent her fifty thousand dollars in addition to the money that her agency received at the time of her services."

Michael Sutton thought for a moment and then said, "I'm still having trouble seeing how this could relate to the lawsuit, but let's see how the interview goes. I'm sure you will go easy on them. They have both had their worlds turned upside down."

Evelyn and Sam waited for Harry to return. Sam had improved quite a bit over the last two weeks. He was walking with a walker if he was assisted by the physical therapist. Most importantly, however, was the gradual return of his speaking ability. He could speak several words and had regained his ability to gesture appropriately.

Evelyn rose to look down the hall to see if either Harry or their attorney were on their way. She suddenly turned and reentered the room. Sam noticed a look of horror on her face, and before he could ask what was bothering her, he saw the face of Pete Jensen enter the room. He was dressed in a maintenance uniform, carried a toolbox, and walked with a slight limp.

He smiled and said, "You both know we are watching you all the time. My partner and I are staying in the area until you return to New York. We will continue to protect the interest of our employer as long as it is necessary. Do you both understand our position?" Sam and Evelyn nodded yes. They were clearly distressed and anxious. Pete went over to the bathroom in Sam's room and began working under the sink. He looked back over his shoulder and said, "Compose yourselves and answer the questions that are asked without showing any hint of emotional distress." They both looked at him and nodded in the affirmative.

Harry and Michael Sutton entered the room together. Harry asked the maintenance man to leave. Pete Jensen rose from his position on the floor under the sink.

"I can finish this later," he said. As he was leaving, Harry noticed that the workman's shoes were not those he would have expected from a Colorado maintenance man. He made a mental note of the shoes and of the man's face. He also noted the expressions of fear plastered on the faces of Sam and Evelyn Kahn. Was their fear related to him or to the maintenance man?

Michael Sutton said, "I just want you both to understand that the detective is investigating a murder. This does not directly affect your lawsuit. I am here only to protect your interests, but you must be aware that you are obligated to answer his questions truthfully."

Harry pulled a chair up to the bed. "I hope your stay here has been beneficial."

"He has made significant progress, Detective," Evelyn said.

Harry then said, "As you have been made aware by your attorney, I am investigating the murder of Tanya Ramsey. She was your nurse in the ICU during your first admission to the hospital." Harry pulled out a recent photo and showed it to Sam. "Do you remember her, Sam?"

"Yes," Sam said.

"Was she a good nurse, and was she pleasant to you?"

"Yes."

"Would there be any reason you can think of that would cause her to want to harm you?" Sam answered, "No."

Harry then asked, "How were you feeling the evening before your discharge during the first hospitalization?"

Evelyn answered, "He was fine that night. In fact, his heartbeat was regular and he had no symptoms."

Harry went on, "Do you remember if Tanya or any other nurse gave you any injections that night?" Sam and Evelyn looked at each other at that moment. Evelyn started to answer when she noticed Pete Jensen walk past the room. She tried to look away, but both Harry and Michael Sutton noticed the look of apprehension on her face. Harry didn't react, but he asked again if there had been any injections given that night.

"I don't recall, Detective," Evelyn said.

Harry then looked at Sam and asked, "Sam, do you remember any injections?"

Sam looked at Harry for a long time before answering. He also looked at Evelyn and Mr. Sutton. Then he said, "No."

Harry's instincts told him Sam was lying. At that moment Harry noticed that Evelyn was diverting her eyes toward the bathroom sink. He casually rose and silently signaled to the Kahns not to say anything by putting his finger to his lips. He then asked, "Where are you and Sam from?" As Evelyn was beginning to respond, Harry slowly walked over to the bathroom sink.

Evelyn answered, "Manhattan, Detective, and from your accent I would guess that's where you are from too. What are you doing so far from New York?" Harry had already evaluated the area under the sink. He saw a listening device hidden behind the bend in the pipe.

He walked away from the bathroom and answered, "I needed a change of pace, Mrs. Kahn. I lost quite a few friends in the 9/11 terrorist attack, and I just needed to get out of New York. Well, I don't have any other questions. Do you have any questions for me?"

They were all silent, and Harry wrote a note he showed to all of them that read: "LISTENING DEVICE." He then crumpled up the paper and placed it in his pocket.

Michael Sutton rose and said, "I hope we have been of some help. It seems you are far from solving the crime."

"I'm afraid you're right, Mr. Sutton. Each day that goes by makes the case colder and colder. Thanks again for your time, and I would appreciate a call if you think of anything that would be helpful." Evelyn and Sam were silent, but Harry could see that they had expressions more of relief than fear as he would have expected. Harry felt that these people had probably been under surveillance and terrorized for a while by this man. The question as to why still needed to be answered.

Harry walked out to the main desk and asked to speak to the administrator of the rehabilitation center. He was informed that she was away from the building this afternoon on a recruiting mission to acquire more physical therapists. Harry then asked to see the head nurse. He was directed to her office, where he was asked to wait a minute while she finished with a phone call. After a few minutes, the head nurse came out of her office. Harry rose to his feet as she approached and introduced himself.

He then asked, "How many maintenance men are on staff at the center?"

"We have three on staff, and they rotate in eight-hour shifts so there is always one available. Why do you ask?"

"I am investigating a murder that took place in Basalt. The victim was a nurse who cared for one of your patients, and while I was interviewing him I noticed a man dressed in a maintenance uniform that just seemed out of place. May I please see the files on the three men?" "Certainly, Detective, follow me into my office." Harry noticed her office was pretty Spartan. She had a few photographs of Mount Sopris on the wall behind her desk and a family picture on the credenza. She opened the file cabinet and pulled out the three files Harry had asked for. He noticed that none of the employee photographs looked anything like the man who was hanging around Sam Kahn's room. "Would someone have hired out to a private plumbing company today for any reason?"

"No. I would have known about it," she said.

"Well, thank you for your time, and I'm sure I don't have to remind you to keep our conversation confidential." Harry hurried out of her office and made a quick search through the halls of the facility. He then went out to the parking lot to see if there were any utility trucks present or if the man dressed in the maintenance uniform was still around. He was somewhat frustrated to find nothing, but he now was convinced that there was a relationship between Tanya's murder and Sam Kahn's medical illness.

As Harry drove back to the station, he called ahead to ask the chief if he could meet with a sketch artist to attempt to come up with a visual picture of the man he had just identified. He felt that possibly they could reinterview the neighbors who had noticed the utility truck and workers at Tanya's house on the day of the murder. He felt that a sketch of this man might jog somebody's memory.

Chief Owens said, "Sounds like a good idea. I'll call around to see if any of the surrounding police departments have a sketch cop who can help us out."

"Thanks, Chief. I feel like I'm finally getting a break on this case."

Harry pulled up to the station at 11 AM and went directly into the chief's office.

"Harry," the chief said, "I've got good news. There happens to be a sketch cop working for the Aspen Police Department. He said he will meet with you this afternoon while the image is fresh in your mind."

"Thanks, I'll grab a quick lunch and head over to Aspen."

Chapter 21

February 2008

It was snowing heavily when Harry arrived at the Aspen police station. He introduced himself and asked the desk sergeant to direct him to the sketch cop. "That's Adam Archer, sir. He has been waiting for you. His desk is in the back to your right."

"Thanks, Sergeant." Harry walked over to Adam, who stood when he saw Harry approach. Adam was in his early thirties, tall, thin, and had dirty blonde hair. They shook hands, and Adam got out his sketch pad.

"How did you get into this aspect of police work, Adam?"

"I've liked drawing since I was a child. My parents always encouraged my artistic abilities, and when I completed the police academy in Denver, I attended the Forensic Facial Imagining Program at the FBI academy. While I was there I learned the psychological aspects and techniques to get the needed visual information from a witness. Very often they may not even be aware of how much their mind recalls. It takes active listening and then rendering what is heard to get the sketch done. My salary comes from the Aspen Police Department since my main job is detective work for the department, however now and then I get to assist in an investigation throughout Colorado."

"Sounds very interesting, Adam. I hope you can help me. I believe the man I am going to describe to you is involved in a murder case in Basalt."

"Okay, let's get started."

"He is a Caucasian about forty years old, six feet tall, and had a blonde crew cut. He has high cheek bones and very little facial fat. His nose was a little large for his face, and he has a scar about an inch long at the angle of his jaw just below his left earlobe."

"Great start, sir. Rather than take the time to use a computer, I'd like to sketch your description by hand."

It took only twenty minutes for the first draft, and Harry was amazed how close Adam's sketch resembled the man he saw posing as a maintenance man. After a few adjustments, the composite drawing was completed. Adam made several copies for Harry.

"I owe you one, Adam. You did a great job, and I don't know how I can thank you."

"Just solve the crime, Detective. That's enough for me."

Harry stopped by Aspen Valley Hospital on his way back to Basalt. He went to Kathy's office and asked Prudence, Kathy's secretary, if Kathy was in her office.

She smiled and said, "Kathy is not in today."

"Would you please take this sketch of a possible suspect and see if Kathy can show it around?"

"Certainly, Detective, no problem. Give me two so I can give one to Joyce Evans, the director of nursing." Harry thanked her and headed back to Basalt. It was still snowing heavily as he turned onto Highway 82.

Harry arranged for Officer Gully to meet him at Tanya's house so they could canvas the neighborhood with the sketch. They spent the rest of the afternoon asking the neighbors if they remembered seeing the potential murderer, but they got no positive responses.

Harry returned to the station and decided to call the phone number in Dubai that he had cross-referenced with the list he got from Tanya's home phone and the list from the home health agency. It was 5 PM when Harry dialed the Dubai number. It was 9 AM in Dubai when the call was answered by the secretary for Ahmed and Al-Shamir. Harry asked to speak to Al-Shamir in reference to his relationship with Tanya

Ramsey. The secretary placed him on hold for several minutes and then the call was finally taken by Ahmed, who stated that he was the personal assistant to Al-Shamir.

"I'm Detective McNally, in charge of the investigation of the murder of a nurse named Tanya Ramsey in Basalt, Colorado. I'm sorry to bother you so early in the morning, but your name and number came up when we cross-referenced her prior patient lists and personal phone calls. Do you or your employer remember her?"

"Yes, she was one of the nurses caring for Al-Shamir's father while he was visiting in Colorado. In fact, we were planning to bring him back to the United States for a renal transplant in the near future, and we were hoping to facilitate his recovery by bringing him back to your area. He seemed to thrive in those beautiful surroundings."

"Can you explain the extra fifty thousand dollars she received from Al-Shamir in the summer of last year?"

There was a long pause and then Ahmed answered, "Yes, that was given to her as an added bonus for the extraordinary care she gave to Al-Shamir's father and also to serve as a sort of retainer to make sure she was available in case we returned to the area."

"That was certainly generous of your employer." Ahmed did not respond, so Harry asked, "Do you know why anybody would harm Tanya Ramsey?"

This time Ahmed answered, "No."

"One last question, sir. Are any of your present employees in the Aspen area?"

Ahmed answered, "No."

Harry then said, "Well, thanks for taking my call, and if you think of anything that might help, please call." Harry left his number with Ahmed and hung up.

Just prior to leaving the office, Harry placed a call to one of his buddies at the antiterrorist section of the FBI in Manhattan. James Phelps had worked with Harry on several occasions in the past while Harry was working in Manhattan. They stayed in touch after Harry moved to Basalt, and Harry knew he could always depend on James if need be.

It was seven thirty in the evening New York time when Harry reached James on his cell phone and said, "How are you doing, old buddy?"

"Not bad, and you?"

"I'm doing fine, James, and don't miss you guys in the city one bit. I have a favor to ask. Can I fax over a sketch of a man I need to track down? I have a suspicion that he may be involved in a murder in our area, but more importantly he has the appearance of a prior military guy and may be functioning as a mercenary."

"Sure, Harry, I'll show the picture around and even run it by some guys in Interpol." "Thanks, James. Take it easy and stay safe." Harry got the fax number and hung up.

The weather was finally clearing as Harry got home. Grace was preparing dinner and had a scotch ready for him as he walked in the door. He took off his coat and shoes and removed his revolver and shoulder holster. He came into the kitchen with his scotch, sat down at the small dining table, and said, "How was your day, honey?"

"Pretty good," she responded. "How about yours?"

"I think I've finally gotten a break on the Ramsey murder case."

"That's great, honey. It seems this case has taken so much of your time"

"Fortunately Chief Owens has let me take all the time I need. This area is so different from Manhattan. There, I would have had multiple cases stacked up on each other. I have to admit that you had the perfect idea to move here. Rather than retiring I can keep working at a slower pace. I'm able to keep my skills up, and at the same time I am not in a pressure cooker. Anything on the agenda after dinner?"

Grace said, "It looks like the weather has cleared. How about acting like a couple of tourists and go into Snowmass Village and listen to the country-western band at the Silvertree Hotel? The Heart of the Rockies band is there tonight, and I've heard they are a lot of fun. I believe one of the guys in the band worked with John Denver and in fact wrote several of John Denver's biggest hits."

Harry said, "Sounds good to me."

Gary Goldman arrived at the Midtown Diner in Manhattan at noon to meet his friend Ralph Ruderman. Ralph and Gary had worked together at the SEC for better than ten years, and they remained friends even when Gary went into the private sector.

"Long time no see," Gary said as he approached the booth where Ralph was seated.

"Gary, you look younger than ever. I guess life is easier in the private legal sector."

"I suppose so, although things get pretty hectic at times. Being away from government politics to maintain job security has relieved a lot of stress in my life. In the private sector, if you do your job and bring in those billable hours, all is well."

"Well, I still enjoy prosecuting those high-flying, stock-manipulating guys who really hurt the small investor. They cause more distrust in our capitalist system and hurt the stock market more than the public is aware. Since the beginning of the Securities and Exchange Commission in 1934, the commission has not only indicted a large number of offenders but also serves as a deterrent for future crimes."

Gary raised his arms in surrender and said, "Hey, you don't have to convince me."

"So what's this meeting all about, Gary?"

Gary said, "I have a friend who was working for a hedge fund here in Manhattan. There have been several developments that make me believe there have been insider trading infractions. They trade oil futures, options on oil futures, and oil-related exchange-traded funds. To get right to the point, Ralph, I need to know if either the SEC or the CFTC have been investigating this particular hedge fund."

Ralph answered, "As I'm sure you are aware, there are always ongoing investigations involving acts of insider trading at both commissions. Why are you suspicious of this particular hedge fund?"

Gary responded, "For one thing, they have profits that far exceed even the best of the commodity-based funds. Their profits are in the range of greater than 45 percent annualized. Secondly, I believe there have been criminal acts committed to protect their interests."

"These are pretty significant accusations, Gary. What kind of criminal activities are you talking about?"

"I really don't want to discuss these right now until I have more information. So, who should I go to with my concerns?"

"We would handle the insider trading infringements since they are stocks and relate to the ETFs. But, I feel you should go directly to the CFTC in Washington DC since they handle commodities like oil. As an independent federal agency, they provide oversight of the commodity futures and option markets in the United States. Record-high oil prices have prompted lawmakers to press for scrutiny of whether speculative trading is artificially pushing up oil prices. I have a friend, Jack Collins, who was transferred to the Washington bureau of the CFTC a year ago. He's a great guy. I'm sure he'd be glad to help you. I'll give him a call, and I'll be in touch. He will want to know specifics of the facts to back up your suspicions."

They finished their lunch after catching up on friends they had in common. Gary thanked Ralph for his help. As he stepped out into the bustling crowd of midtown Manhattan, he could not help feeling that the city had permanently changed since 9/11.

Chapter 22

February 2008

IT WAS A clear, cold day when the Emirates Airline Boeing 777 landed in Newark. Ahmed was the first to deplane, and after passage through customs he found his usual driver, Hussein, waiting in the international reception area. They drove directly to The Jumeirah Essex House in Manhattan. Ahmed was comfortable staying in The Essex House since it had recently been purchased and was managed by the Dubai government.

As he entered the lobby he was greeted by two Arab men who were employed by Al-Shamir. They served as assistants and bodyguards and were always available to assist him while he was staying in New York. Abbud was a thin, dark man with a Semitic nose, coarse facial features, and medium height. He was dressed in a dark, custom suit and silk tie, and he carried himself with an air of confidence. Bihir was stocky and had a thin mustache and goatee. He was also dressed in a dark, custom-made silk suit.

The penthouse suite had been reserved for Ahmed. He entered the suite after the assistants searched the room and tested it for listening devices. He was obviously pleased with the accommodations. The suite was decorated in an ultramodern décor, and the view of Central Park through the large picture windows was breathtaking. It had recently snowed, and the park was covered with a smooth blanket of white. The snow-covered trees were glistening in the late afternoon sun. There were very few people in the park, and the taxi cab traffic through the park was rather sparse, giving Ahmed the pleasurable feeling that he was on top of a deserted Manhattan.

"Abbud, I have arranged a meeting for tomorrow with all of our trading groups. Please arrange to have them picked up and brought here after the markets close at 4 PM. Here is a list of their names and cell phone numbers. As you can see, they have arrived here from many major U.S. cities and are staying at several hotels in the area."

"I will see to it," Abbud answered.

"Bihir, please arrange for a light meal to be brought up to the suite for our guests to enjoy during the meeting. Sandwiches will be fine along with chips, cold drinks, and of course Arabic coffee." Bihir nodded, and both of the assistants left the suite.

Ahmed had another responsibility to attend to while in Manhattan. Al-Shamir's father needed a kidney transplant. There were no family matches available, and the family wanted the surgery to be done in the United States. Even though Al-Shamir's father was in his early seventies, a new kidney from a live donor would add at least ten years to his life and free him from his dialysis machine and its associated complications of infections, vascular access problems, and rapidly progressive coronary artery disease. There was also the inconvenience of being attached to the dialysis machine for several hours three times per week.

Ahmed somehow had to overcome the ethics of renal transplantation and long waiting lists for ordinary people needing a kidney. He had plenty of financial reserves for this from the family, but there were so many ethical hurdles to jump, he knew he had his work cut out for him. He would need to utilize his contacts with Muslim sympathizers in the medical field who had relationships with transplant teams and would respond to financial incentives.

Gary Goldman was sitting in his office working on a client's stock-related tax problems when his secretary came into his office and notified him that a Mr. Jack Collins was on the phone.

"Mr. Collins, I appreciate you getting back to me so quickly," Gary said when he picked up the phone. "The reason I needed to speak to someone at the CFTC relates to the possibility of insider trading in oil futures and related options from a trading group that has employed a close friend of mine. The problem is very delicate because I believe he and his wife's lives might be in jeopardy."

"Well, Mr. Goldman, do you feel comfortable giving me the name of this trading group and the name of your friend?"

"That depends on your ability to keep this confidential, and I need to be assured that you are the right person to handle this problem. First let me ask you: has your department has been investigating hedge funds and trading groups with extraordinary profits?"

"Our main focus has been foreign, oil-producing countries and their manipulation of oil prices," Collins responded. "We have also been concerned with the effect of speculators on the jump in oil prices. Do you remember when the Hunt brothers tried to corner the silver futures market?"

"Yes, I remember that incident. This seems very different, however, since the oil markets are so large and traded globally."

"That's true, but we are still obligated to track speculators. As far as your problem is concerned, I think the best approach for now is for me to speak to my boss and let us look into trading groups with large reported profits, and then maybe we can get together along with our head of the criminal activity division."

Gary said, "I appreciate the effort, and again I must reiterate the importance of confidentiality. Please move on this as soon as possible since I really fear for my friend's life."

Jack Collins said, "I'll get back to you within forty-eight hours."

Harry was awakened at 6 AM by the phone. "Sorry to call so early in the morning, Harry," said James Phelps, "but I think I have identified the man from your sketch."

"That was fast, James. Who is he?"

"This guy is ex-military with a dishonorable discharge related to drug smuggling while serving in Afghanistan. He has not been seen or heard from recently, but your sketch artist's rendition is almost as good as a photograph. Anyway, he has turned up on several investigative radar screens and was last employed by some anti-American terrorist organization. He apparently works strictly for financial compensation, having no real ties to any political belief system or political philosophy. How does this tie in with your local crime in Colorado?"

Harry answered, "I'm not sure how his background relates to my present case, except that the murder victim was previously employed by a wealthy Arab family. The victim also received an excessive amount of payment from this family for care given to the father with end-stage kidney disease. Do you have a name for this character?"

"His name when in the military was Peter Jensen. I'm not sure what name he is using now."

Harry said, "If I can locate this guy and pick him up for questioning, do you have any arrest warrants out for him?"

"We are always interested in speaking to this guy, but presently no arrest warrants are outstanding from our government agencies. I hope this has been helpful, Harry, and please keep in touch."

"Thanks for being so prompt, James. I may need some help in apprehending this guy. He sounds particularly dangerous, and I would certainly appreciate some government help."

"I'll see what I can do. Possibly the FBI can be of assistance in that area."

Penny noticed that Jack had undergone a mild but definite personality change. He seemed to get agitated by minor adverse occurrences and had difficulty sleeping at night. He was intolerant of any error made by his staff or those employed by the hospital. Penny decided to discuss this with Jack at dinner and ask him to seek help. At first Jack denied any problem, but with gentle coaxing he finally admitted that he was beginning to worry about the lawsuit more and more every day.

He said, "This is the first time my medical judgment has been challenged, and to be honest I don't feel in control of the situation. I don't feel comfortable in the legal arena, where the real medical facts may not prevail in the face of legal maneuvering. So far the cost of this lawsuit has been minimal since we have insurance for legal representation, but if I lose this lawsuit we have no malpractice insurance to cover the cost of a judgment against me and we could lose all our accumulated assets."

Penny said, "You and I know that you managed that case perfectly, and even if you do lose we will start all over again and rebuild our assets. They cannot take our home, your IRA, or your practice."

"I know, Penny, but I can't help my negative feelings. My attorney keeps telling me not to take this personally, but actually that's impossible. Physician and nursing training is the same, so you can understand that we come out of training with a set of personality features that make us vulnerable to the adversarial system of litigation. We are self-critical and therefore have a tendency to feelings of guilt and an exaggerated sense of responsibility."

Penny responded, "I think you should make an appointment with Arnold Zucker. He is a good friend and excellent psychiatrist. You need to ventilate your feelings about the case to someone who is not involved, and with his skills he can help you work through this."

Jack didn't answer right away, but finally said, "I know you are right, Penny."

Penny then said, "Are you comfortable with your attorney?"

Jack said, "He is young but very intelligent, and I feel he is competent and energetic. I also know his firm has a lot of depth and resources."

"You should also try to gain some control by helping select your expert witnesses and knowing exactly what your attorney is thinking."

Jack looked at Penny and after a long pause said, "You are the best. I feel better already. I'll call Arnold first thing tomorrow."

Chapter 23

February 2008

THERE WERE TEN hedge fund trading groups assembled in the suite of the penthouse occupied by Ahmed. Each of the teams were clearly surprised to find out that they were not the sole hedge fund investment strategist that Ahmed had chosen to invest and share information with. They were pairs of strangers assembled together for the very first time. Each of the teams were dissimilar in that they were from different major U.S. cities but were similar in that each had one partner of Arab descent. All of these traders had worked for large brokerage firms prior to starting their own hedge funds. They all had investors other than Al-Shamir, but he was their main source of investment funds, and more importantly he was their main source of information on the directional movement of oil prices. The average age of the traders was thirty-eight, and they were dressed in a manner that demonstrated their success. None of the traders had ever met Al-Shamir and had dealt only with Ahmed.

While they waited for the meeting to get started, they ate the sandwiches and had the soft drinks that were provided by their host. There was an absence of alcoholic beverages, and the sweet smell of coffee was present. The coffee was brewed in the Arabic tradition; therefore it was boiled three times before being served. The young traders utilized this time to get familiar with each other and exchange trading strategies.

Ahmed began the meeting at five thirty PM. The room got quiet as soon as he approached the large, circular table that was erected in the conference room just off of the suite's living room. Ahmed was dressed in a dark, pinstriped Armani suit, and although he was of relatively short stature, he had a commanding presence that was obvious to those present.

"I want to thank all of you for attending this meeting on such short notice," Ahmed said in English with a slight British accent. "I also want to extend our thanks for all of your past successes, and I hope we can continue to show these profits in the future. I would like to briefly give you our interpretation on the direction of oil prices over the next several months and into summer's end. Please hold your questions until I have finished."

"First, we are confident that the price of oil will exceed $150 a barrel by the end of the summer. I know this may seem impossible to some of you since by nature you use technical analysis and presently oil is already at overbought price levels. However impossible it may seem, the price will even become more parabolic in its rise for several reasons. There will be a large brokerage firm that will predict $150 per barrel by the end of the summer. This will in itself cause a rise in speculation. The Saudis will say that they do not want to see the price of oil rise so fast, but trust me when I say that they, along with all the other oil-producing countries, do want the prices to rise so they can do what the oil-addicted consumer countries have not done. This, of course, is to invest in nuclear power plants and wind and solar energy research and development." Ahmed looked around the room to be sure everybody was clear then went on, "There will be a push to blame speculators for the rising prices. This will in turn cause government agencies and the U.S. Congress to place rules limiting speculation. This will only delay the real action that is needed, which is to begin a program of mandatory research and development of alternative energy sources and begin drilling for oil in their own oil-rich areas. This will take time to get started because of the upcoming election and the stronghold that the environmentalists have on the Congress and the Liberal voters. The oil-producing companies and their shareholders also suffer from a lack of profit patience. They presently have no financial incentive to invest in future drilling sites and the construction of new oil refineries. As I'm sure you are aware, President Nixon established Project

Independence in 1974 with the goal of achieving energy independence by 1980. In fact, the U.S. dependence on foreign oil rose from 42 percent in 1980 to 52 percent in the year 2000, and it is now at 70 percent. Another mechanism that would help the United States would be an oil consumption tax or voucher system to reduce consumption. This will never happen in an election year. There will be a lot of talk but very little action."

"So the bottom line is continued higher demand on foreign oil and rising prices which will eventually cause a recession in the United States and then globally. This does not even speak to the effect that China, India, and other emerging markets have on oil consumption. There is one last point I want to be sure you understand. The present presidential election will do nothing to help drive the price of oil down. These candidates are spending so much time and energy trying to discredit each other and blame the present administration for the ills of the country that a constructive plan is far from becoming improvised. Are there any questions?"

The room was silent. Not one of these young and aggressive traders could even come up with a question. Ahmed allowed the traders to contemplate what he said. After several minutes of pure silence, he continued. "Secondly, we feel confident that the beginning of a bear market began in U.S. equities with last October's topping-out process. This gives you an opportunity to short the U.S. equity markets, especially those industry groups that are dependent on oil prices. Airline stocks that do not hedge their oil costs will be particularly vulnerable. In fact, all the transportation stocks will certainly have a tremendous loss of value. The discretionary consumer stocks will also drop as consumers try to balance their incomes against rising fuel costs. As the economic details of the recession become evident, the stock market indexes and associated ETFs will all be vulnerable. The Fed will be relatively helpless to stop the overall trend, and any rally in stock prices that may occur because of Fed or administrative suggestions of assistance will only produce further shorting opportunities. Are there any questions or opposing views?"

It was clear from the silence that Ahmed had their undivided attention and that each of the traders respected everything he had to say.

After a few seconds of silence, a young man from Chicago stood and asked, "How long are you projecting this bear market to last, and how deep do you think it will take the S&P 500?"

"I'm sure that question is on every market participant's mind, but I can only say at this time that this bear market has much further to go and will only come to a climactic end by some unpredictable event in the foreseeable future."

These young traders had not been involved in the markets long enough to really appreciate a truly prolonged bear market. They were only in their mid to late thirties and had only experienced rising or trading-range stock markets during their careers. Their reaction to this type of predictive scenario was somewhat disbelieving at first, but Ahmed's nature of delivery reflected his Oxford education, and he was very convincing even to the most skeptical of those present.

"I will continue to communicate with you at the usual oil-market turning points and prior to release of fundamental data for the purpose of short-term trading as this information becomes available to me." He thanked them again for coming and then looked at Mitch Carsdale and Jonathan Salem and said, "Please remain here so we can discuss your individual problem."

Mitch and Jonathan were visibly anxious after they were singled out from the group. They assumed it in some way must be related to Sam Kahn and his probing into their profits, but they assumed Ahmed had solved that problem. Ahmed spent some time with the other traders in the foyer prior to them departing to answer some individual concerns and questions. He was always calm and had a very commanding presence that served to reassure those in his company.

He finally returned to the conference table with Abbud and Bihir at his side. He sat down at the table across from the two traders as Abbud and Bihir positioned themselves at the entrance to the room.

Ahmed said, "Things have gotten out of hand in Aspen. I have the feeling that the time has come for us to begin to pull out of your hedge fund before more attention is focused on you from the authorities. We have taken steps in our other trading groups to have the accounting services done by those who are familiar to us in Dubai. Unfortunately Mr. Kahn has brought a lot of attention to your trading firm." Mitch was silent for a few moments. He looked around the room and noticed Abbud and Bihir guarding the doors.

Mitch nervously responded, "I appreciate your concerns, Ahmed, and agree with your plan to eliminate your investments with us. I only hope that if things cool off in the future you will consider us again for investment purposes."

Ahmed said, "Then it is agreed." They arose from their seats at the table, shook hands, and the two traders departed.

Ahmed spoke to Abbud and Bihir in Arabic. He instructed them to place Mitch and Jonathan under surveillance and notify him immediately if they were contacted by any of the authorities. He told them to arrange for listening devices to be placed in their offices and homes. The two bodyguards acknowledged that they understood his instructions and left him alone in his suite.

Ahmed walked over to the large picture window and watched the lights of the city begin to illuminate the streets around Central Park. He was deep in thought because his next concern was to arrange to get Al-Shamir's father on the top of the list of the United Network for Organ Sharing.

Harry had distributed the sketch of Pete Jensen to the employees of the rehabilitation center and most of the bars and restaurants in the down-valley area.

He contacted the FBI branch office in Denver to ask for assistance. The branch officer in charge was Erin Coffey.

She said, "Harry, I remember you. I was working with the FBI when we were working side-by-side with the NYPD in the investigations surrounding 9/11. What are you doing working in Basalt?"

Harry said, "I just felt the need to leave the City but wanted to keep working, so here I am. What are you doing in Denver?"

"I had an opportunity to get a better pay grade and become a branch manager. So how can we help you, Harry?"

"I'm investigating a murder here in Basalt. The case is getting complicated since my main suspect is an ex-military guy who has worked as a mercenary for foreign countries since his dishonorable discharge from the army. He has been harassing and spying on an accountant here who unfortunately suffered from a stroke. This accountant worked for a hedge fund that trades oil futures."

"I'm sorry, Harry, but I don't see the connection."

"Well, the person who was murdered was a nurse caring for this accountant, and she may have been involved in causing his stroke. I also have evidence that she worked for a wealthy Dubai family with ties to the oil business. It is possible that this mercenary, who by the way received his dishonorable army discharge for drug dealing in Afghanistan, could be linked to terrorism."

"Bingo, Harry, you just said the magic words."

Harry said, "I thought the implication of terrorism would catch your attention."

"You bet, Harry. I'll send two agents to Basalt tomorrow. I'll give them instructions to help apprehend this character."

Harry said, "I wouldn't be surprised to find out he has an accomplice. We have a witness who saw two workmen enter the murder victim's home around the time of the murder."

"The agents will meet you at your police station probably in the late afternoon since the drive from Denver takes about four hours. What's this suspect's name? We can see if we have anything on him in our files and cross-reference him with other federal agencies."

"Pete Jensen. Thanks in advance for your help."

Erin said, "It was great talking to you, Harry."

Chapter 24

February 2008

JACK COLLINS CALLED Gary Goldman within twenty-four hours. Gary picked up the phone after the first ring and said, "Hello, Goldman here."

"Gary, I think you may have hit upon something. My office staff used the technique of cross-referencing hedge fund trading groups that show profits in excess of 25 percent on an annualized basis with funds that specialize in oil-related products. We came up with a list of nearly fifty funds that fall into that category."

"That's interesting, Jack. Do you have the ability to know who the investors are in each of these groups?"

"Yes, we can get that information if the hedge funds are registered."

"Please cross-reference the clients of Capital Investors of America with the other groups, and let's see if any investor is present in more than one group."

Jack asked, "Is that the hedge fund that your friend works for?"

"Yes."

"Give me another twenty-four hours, and I'll get back to you with a meeting time and representatives from our criminal activity division."

Gary then said, "I really appreciate your time and effort."

"I hope it pays off," Jack said.

Gary Goldman decided to call Evelyn Kahn to see how things were going with Sam and to let her know the progress he was making with the SEC and the CFTC. It was 10 AM eastern time, so he decided to call Evelyn on her cell phone rather than in Sam's room. Evelyn picked up the call after the first ring. She was still in her hotel room, getting ready to go to the rehabilitation center.

Gary said, "How's it going, Evelyn?"

"Pretty good. Sam is speaking in short sentences now and can definitely walk with the support of the therapist. I would love to go home, but on the other hand these people here are so nice, caring, and skilled I'm hesitant to leave."

Gary then asked, "What about the lawsuit? Any activity or offers from the defense side?"

"Not yet, but Mr. Sutton feels the hospital may take our offer to settle for one million dollars. Personally I'm not so sure about that."

"Can you safely talk now?"

"I'm not sure," Evelyn said.

"Does that mean you are still being watched?"

"Yes."

"I just wanted you to know that I can arrange a private jet with nursing services for your return to New York."

"That's great, Gary. It will certainly take a lot of pressure off me."

"The air ambulance service utilizes the Aspen Airport private terminal. I was thinking of flying in to help and then flying back with you two on the air ambulance."

"You have been great, Gary. Thanks so much. You can't imagine how much we appreciate all you have done for us. I'd better get to the rehabilitation center before Sam worries about me being late. Thanks again."

Pete Jensen and Abdul Rahman met for breakfast at the Village Inn in Glenwood Springs. They had been taking shifts, alternating between the rehabilitation center and Evelyn's hotel.

"I'm really getting tired of this assignment," Pete said.

Abdul responded with a heavy northern London accent, "I can't argue with you there, my friend. I think we have the Kahns scared out of their minds. They have been very quiet, and we are hearing almost nothing of importance over the listening device. All they discuss is the lawsuit and his physical therapy." Jensen and Rahman ordered skillets and talked in hushed tones. They always had their eyes on the front door. They were dressed in work clothes and blended in with the locals who frequented the place.

"I can't tell you how upset I am over the accidental death of Tanya Ramsey," Abdul said.

Pete responded, "Yeah, that nurse shouldn't have freaked out like that. If she had not panicked and hit her head, our lives would be a lot easier. My main concern is that detective that spotted me in Mr. Kahn's room at the rehabilitation center. I'm not sure he would ever recognize me again or if he even knew what I was doing in the room, but it is a loose end. You know how I dislike loose ends. They always come back to bite you in the ass."

Abdul said, "I'm more concerned with the wrath of Ahmed than I am afraid of some local Colorado detective."

Their skillets came and they ate in silence for a while until Pete said, "Abdul, we have been working together now since July, and I have never asked you about your religion. I fought against the Taliban while I served in Afghanistan, and honestly I never really had an understanding of the beliefs of Islam."

Abdul thought for a while and then said, "I must start with some simple definitions, and then maybe it will become clear to you what the religion is all about. Islam is about submission to the will of God as well as observance of Islamic law. Islam is a diverse, worldwide community of believers striving to implement the Islamic ideal. Allah is the Arabic word for God. A Muslim is one who has submitted to the will of Allah. God's will is set forth in the Qur'an, which means recital. God intervened in history between 610 and 623 CE in western Arabia by dictating the divine text to the Prophet Muhammad.

"All Muslims believe in uncompromising monotheism and that God is all powerful, having created the entire universe. We also believe there will be a final judgment at which time all men and women will be judged according to whether or not they lived in accordance with God's will. Shari'a is a term translated as Islamic law. The Sunna is a written account of the lifestyle of the Prophet Muhammad and the first Islamic community. Muslim scholars have utilized the Qur'an and the Sunna to establish the Shari'a to assist Muslims in their quest to live according to the will of Allah."

Jensen then said, "It seems to me that there are many different interpretations of this law."

"I agree, and that's because the community of Islam implements and understands the Shari'a in different ways. There are, however, the Five Pillars of Islam that all Muslims follow to the best of their ability. These five are: the bearing of witness that Allah is the only God and Muhammad is the messenger of God; prayer five times a day preceded by washing; the giving of alms to those in need; the fast from dawn to sunset for the month of Ramadan; and lastly the pilgrimage to Medina and Mecca at least once in one's lifetime.

"Islamic scholars are called Ulama. They are recognized for their expert knowledge of the Qur'an and the Sunna. They are responsible for explaining and interpreting the laws and directing the behavior of their followers. They use several methods to interpret the Qur'an and the Sunna. An example of this is Hadith, which are the utterances of the prophet as an important source of understanding the Sunna."

Jensen said, "That's all well and good, but what's a jihad, and isn't that the cause of all the conflict?"

"Not exactly. The term jihad is literally translated as struggle. Jihad typically refers to the individual's struggle to meet God's challenge and do what God expects."

Pete then said, "I suppose the most important two questions that I would like answered as a Westerner are: what are the reasons behind Islamic terrorism, and why are the two major branches of Islam, the Sunnis and the Shiites, at war with each other?"

"Tough questions, but let me ask you a question first. Why would you give up all your beliefs and allegiances to your country and work for an Arab when you know we are in a struggle for world dominance?"

Jensen answered, "That's an easy question. First, I have been trained as a military person with no other skills, and as you are aware I have been dishonorably discharged from the army. I have no deep feelings for my country or the Christian religion. I am purely a mercenary, and if I wasn't employed by Ahmed it would be by somebody else, possibly African or South American militants."

"What about your family?"

"They disowned me when I got involved with drug smuggling in Afghanistan. So, you see, I'm in this for the money and whatever satisfaction I can get from doing my job well."

They were interrupted by the waitress bringing the check. They realized that it was already almost nine thirty in the morning and they had better get back to observing Sam and Evelyn Kahn.

They were getting up to leave when Abdul noticed the manager had been looking at them for a long time. The manager immediately looked away when Abdul looked back at him. "I can't believe these people. They act like they have never seen an Arab before."

"I'm not sure that's why he was staring. Let's get out of here," Pete said. He then added, "You take the first shift at the rehabilitation center. I'd like to snoop around a bit to see if there was any follow-up from that detective. I'll meet you at the Red Rocks Diner on Route 133 at 1:00 PM for lunch. Call my cell if you can't make it."

Harry was notified that the FBI agents were en route and would be at his office at about 2:00 PM with some information on Pete Jensen. It was 1:20 when his cell phone rang.

"Harry?"

"Yes, who's this?"

"This is Al Stark at the Red Rocks Diner. I think I have a fellow here eating lunch that matches the sketch you handed out the other day. He is here with some Arab guy. They seem pretty harmless to me."

Harry said, "I'll be right over. Do not engage them, and please don't spook them. I'm less than fifteen minutes away in Basalt." Harry let the chief know what was going on and took Drew Trestle with him. It was snowing lightly, but the visibility was good as they headed west on Highway 82 toward the diner on Route 133. Harry was driving his unmarked Bronco and was wearing jeans, a checkered shirt, and a leather jacket. Drew was wearing his police uniform and overcoat. He was also wearing a cowboy hat. Drew tried to reach the FBI agents on their cell phones, but they didn't answer, so he left a message that they were heading over to the Red Rocks Diner at the juncture of Routes 82 and 133 to follow up on the possible identification of Pete Jensen. Drew was obviously anxious about the confrontation and was somewhat concerned about how they would approach the suspects.

Harry could sense Drew's level of tension and said, "When we arrive at the diner, I think I should go in myself to be sure this is the man we are looking for. He probably will not recognize me, and if this is the right guy we can wait for him and his presumed partner to exit the diner before we approach them."

"What if they are armed and resist coming to the station for questioning?"

"If we approach them after they leave the diner, we can minimize the risk to innocent bystanders," Harry said.

The snow was falling heavier as Harry pulled up to the diner. He parked away from the front entrance along the south side. He checked his semiautomatic, 9 mm Beretta M9 pistol and left the safety on.

"That's a fucking cannon," Drew said.

"Yeah, I got used to carrying a big pistol in New York," Harry said. He placed the revolver back into his shoulder holster, zipped up his jacket, and headed into the diner. He was wearing a baseball cap that advertised fly fishing in Basalt.

As he entered the diner, he noticed Al Stark at his usual place behind the cash register. He looked calm and said, "How's it going, Harry?"

"Pretty good, Al. How's business?"

"Not bad."

The diner was in the old tradition of a railway car. The floor had a black-and-white checkered pattern, and the booths were made of blue and white vinyl. Harry took a seat at the counter, ordered coffee, and then got up to go to the restroom. He looked around and noticed the place was pretty empty. As he approached the restroom, he saw a Caucasian and an Arab sitting in a booth across from the men's restroom. He could see they were both wearing ankle holsters and was sure that the Caucasian was Pete Jensen. They were wearing construction-type work clothes except that instead of steel-toed construction boots, they were wearing combat boots. Harry noticed that Jensen gave him a curious look as if he might have recognized him. Harry casually nodded and went into the men's room.

"I know that guy," Pete said.

Abdul said, "Who is he?"

"That's the cop I was concerned about. I'm not sure he recognized me, but we'd better get out of here." Abdul waved to the waitress to bring the check. Pete got up just as Harry was coming out of the men's room. Harry brushed by him and took his seat at the counter. He finished his coffee just as Pete and Abdul were paying their bill at the cash register. Harry placed three dollars down on the counter and left just prior to their departure. He quickly got into his Bronco as the snowfall became very heavy, making the visibility poor. Harry and Drew waited in the Bronco for the two to come out of the diner. Drew was holding his Smith and Wesson 9mm pistol. They were planning to approach Jensen and his partner as they exited but were surprised because they came out of the back door and quickly jumped into a black SUV. It became obvious to Harry that the two men were going to make a run for it.

"He must have recognized me," Harry said.

"What should we do now," Drew said, somewhat excited.

"Stay calm. We'll follow them and pick the best place to pull them over. This will also give us a chance to call for backup."

The black SUV pulled out of the back parking lot and turned south, heading toward Main Street in Carbondale. Harry followed them closely. They were traveling at the speed limit. The road was covered heavily with snow as they passed Main Street and continued south. The peak of Mount Sopris, at nearly 13,000 feet, was barely visible on Harry's left because of the heavy snowfall. They began to pick up speed as they passed the sign reading, "Redstone—9 miles." There were very few vehicles on the road now. Drew again tried to reach the FBI agents and this time got through to agent Robert Farthing. Drew gave them their location and informed them that they were in pursuit of Jensen and his partner.

Agent Farthing said, "I am with Agent Maria Falconi. We are just passing through Glenwood Springs and should be in your area in twenty minutes."

Harry said, "Tell them to hurry and if possible arrange for a police helicopter out of the Eagle-Vail airport for backup. I believe these guys are going to make a stand somewhere between Redstone and McClure Pass when they realize the pass is closed for the winter. Drew, call Chief Owens and see if he can arrange a roadblock in Redstone or Marble with the Pitkin County sheriff."

While Drew was making the calls, Harry stayed in close pursuit of the suspects. Harry turned on his dash lights, which were fitted with shields to prevent reflection back to himself and Drew. He also turned on his siren. Jensen's SUV kicked up a lot of snow, obscuring the rear tail lights. It was getting more and more difficult to maneuver on the snow-laden road the farther out of Carbondale they traveled.

Pete and Abdul were driving at relatively high speeds now as they traveled parallel to Crystal River. The road was lined with occasional campsites used in the summer for fly fishing and hiking. Most of the residences were closed up for the winter.

Pete, who was driving the SUV, said, "We must get as far from Carbondale as possible before making a stand. I have been exploring this area over the last couple of days in case a situation like this arose." He added, "Reconnaissance is critical. I believe our best place to make a stand would be Redstone, before they can get backup in place. It is only a few more miles from here."

They were very calm and confident. Abdul reached for a case lying on the backseat. He snapped it open and pulled out a Kalashnikov AK-47 assault rifle and a Browning M1918 automatic rifle. There was loads of ammunition in the case along with two Glock 17 semiautomatic pistols.

"I think we can defend ourselves against these two local policemen," Pete said with an overconfident attitude.

"Allah will be with us," Abdul said.

"Yeah, Allah and my Kalashnikov," Pete said.

They passed a sign that read, "Redstone—2 miles." The road gradually curved eastward as it followed the frozen Crystal River. The SUV skidded on the curve, but Pete controlled the vehicle without a problem.

"Reminds me of driving in Afghanistan in the winter," he said jokingly.

Abdul tightened his seat belt. "I can never get used to these winters," he said.

"Relax, Abdul, I am in control."

Harry and Drew continued their pursuit at a safe distance. They had heard from Chief Owens and were notified that there were no Pitkin County sheriff personnel in the area, but they were sending two teams to serve as backup from the Aspen office. The FBI agents also confirmed that a helicopter would be on its way as soon as the weather cleared.

The SUV passed the sign that read, "Redstone—1 mile. Ruby of the Rockies." Pete noticed that the Bronco was still following but at a safe distance. He began to slow down a little so he could safely make the turn into Redstone. The snow was still falling, but it was a little lighter now. Pete saw the turnoff on his left. It was a narrow bridge that crossed Crystal River. On his right he noticed the historic coke ovens that lined the highway for about a hundred yards. He made a quick turn onto the bridge, causing the SUV to slide significantly. It banged against the guardrail but stayed on the bridge. Abdul was clearly shaken, but he remained silent.

"We need hostages," Pete said as he pulled the SUV up to the front entrance of the Redstone Inn. The snow had stopped falling, and the sky was beginning to clear.

A horse-drawn carriage was just leaving with two couples wrapped in blankets for a romantic ride through Redstone and the surrounding area, including Redstone Castle. The Castle was the original mansion owned by Cleveland Osgood, whose coal mining techniques and coke ovens were responsible for the area's development. The clock on the inn tower was clearly visible and showed that it was 3:10. Pete and Abdul grabbed their weapons, put on flak jackets, and stepped out onto the snow-covered driveway.

Chapter 25

February 2008

IT WAS WINDY and cold in New York City as Gary Goldman walked from the parking garage to his office. He was hoping that he would hear from Jack Collins this morning to shed some light on whether or not there was some connection between Sam's job, his illness, and insider trading violations. He picked up his messages at the reception desk, grabbed a cup of coffee from the kitchen, and settled down at his desk to go over his mail. In his stack of messages was a note to call Jack Collins at the CFTC as soon as possible. The rest of his messages and mail could wait, so he dialed Jack's number and was grateful to catch him at his desk.

"It appears that your guess was right, Gary."

"What did you come up with?"

"Well, of the fifty hedge funds that made extraordinary profits over the last two years, there were ten that had a common investor. This investor was from Dubai, and he was the major investor in all ten of the funds."

Gary then asked, "Is there enough of a coincidence for you to initiate an investigation?" "You bet your ass there is, and we would like to meet with you and your friend as soon as possible."

"I think that may put him in danger at this point in time, but when the time comes if you need a witness or testimony I'm sure he will be as helpful as possible. I just think that now is not a safe time for him to come forward. I will, however, consult with him and their attorney to let them know about your investigation."

"Okay, Gary, I think we have enough to get started at this time. I'll keep you informed."

Gary sat there for awhile, thinking that maybe he had gotten into a situation that common sense would tell him to avoid, but he knew that sometimes one must take a risk to do the right thing. He finished returning the rest of his calls and began working on the stack of files on his desk. He next had to decide whether he should call Louis Reiner and inform him of what was going on, even if he was the opposing attorney in Sam's lawsuit. He decided to sleep on his thoughts overnight.

It was Jack's day off, and his only responsibilities that day were to make hospital rounds, which he finished by 10 AM. His appointment with Arnold Zucker was at 11 AM, so he decided to stop by Kathy's office to say hello and catch up on the hospital gossip. Kathy was just leaving her office and was heading to the physicians' lounge to get a cup of coffee when Jack caught up to her.

"Good morning, Kathy, what's going on?"

"The usual crap," she said.

"Have you and the hospital made a decision on whether or not you will settle your part of the lawsuit?"

"They haven't made a definite offer as yet. Personally, I think it would be a mistake to settle this case. I feel that there was foul play and that there is a definite relationship between the plaintiff's illness and the death of Tanya Ramsey. I am also confident that your culpability in this case is minimal, and we should fight this case together all the way through the legal system."

"Well, I hope you are right. I wish I had your confidence about the outcome."

"Come on, Jack, you know you managed the case perfectly. You are just dwelling on the negative aspects too much." Jack didn't respond.

They reached the lounge, said good-bye, and Jack headed out of the hospital to his Jeep.

It was snowing lightly when Jack pulled out of the hospital parking lot and headed toward Main Street. Dr. Zucker practiced psychiatry out of his home, which was located in the eastern section of Aspen in a secluded area alongside of a creek just south of Cooper Avenue. He originally came from a wealthy, Northeastern family, got his bachelor of science degree from Harvard, and went on to graduate from Harvard Medical School. He did his psychiatric training at Massachusetts General and began practicing in the Aspen area after several years of teaching and an academic life in Boston. He married Susan while in medical school, and they had two children. Both of his children were now in college in the Northeast, so he and his wife were free to enjoy the cultural life and sports that the Aspen area had to offer. He had been able to maintain a steady but small practice of local patients, some of which were famous financial and theatrical figures.

Jack was relieved to find that there were no cars in the driveway as he pulled up. Arnold was standing at the front door to greet him as he made his way through the snow to the front door. Arnold was a tall, slender man, athletically built with a full head of wavy hair just touching his collar at the back of his neck. He was clean shaven and ruggedly good looking, and he was dressed casually in jeans and a turtleneck shirt. They shook hands and went inside.

The house was decorated with a Ralph Lauren motif. The ceilings were at least twenty feet high and featured knotty pine beams. There were large picture windows showing the creek and aspen trees mixed with evergreens in the yard. They went into Arnold's office, which was just off the living room. It also was decorated in the same fashion as the living room area but had a more male appearance with dark walnut floor-to-ceiling bookshelves and a dark mahogany desk. There was a leather couch and two large leather chairs that were on either side of a coffee table. Arnold offered Jack a soft drink. Jack gladly accepted the drink and sat across from Arnold in one of the leather chairs.

Arnold said, "I hope you are comfortable here, Jack. I will try to make this as easy as I can for you. First, I want you to know that I have the deepest respect for you as a physician and would choose no one else to care for me or my family if we needed medical care. I have also come to respect you for the moral person you are."

Jack smiled somewhat uncomfortably and didn't respond verbally.

Dr. Zucker continued, "I just have a couple of preliminary comments to go over with you before we start. First, everything we discuss here will be held in the strictest confidence, so I want you to say whatever comes to mind. I know it's natural to be somewhat guarded, but we will accomplish more if you can overcome this tendency. Secondly, I will not charge you for our time together. I never charge physicians, so don't even try to pay me. Lastly, I will let you decide what approach suits you best. We can utilize conventional psychiatric therapy or reality and behavioral therapy to attack your symptoms directly rather than delving into a presumed underlying cause. Drug therapy is also possible, and we can discuss that as well."

Jack thought for a moment, leaned forward, and said in a calm voice, "I must tell you that I have always been in good psychiatric health. I have no family history of psychiatric disease, and I have never used any psychotropic drugs. I drink a minimum amount of alcohol and exercise regularly.

"In September I was sued for malpractice. I had been going through the long, drawn-out process of pretrial preparation without much symptomatology until recently, when I began getting easily agitated and not sleeping well. I have tried exercising more vigorously, but I just can't seem to get a handle on my feelings. Penny has been great and supportive, and she urged me to see you before things escalated."

Arnold asked, "Are you having any other symptoms at this time?"

"Like what?" Jack said.

"Like feeling depressed, crying easily, sexual dysfunction, fatigue, or somatic symptoms?"

"Not really, except maybe a little depressed. More like angry, I would say."

"How about guilty?" Arnold said.

"I have reviewed this case a thousand times in my mind, and I would have handled it the same way now as I did then. I just don't think I did anything wrong in the management of the patient, but that doesn't seem to matter to the plaintiff."

"You didn't answer the question. Do you feel guilty?" Arnold asked again.

"I guess I do have that feeling, but I don't think I should."

Arnold looked at Jack for a long time and finally said, "I would have to say that in my experience unfounded guilt is the cause of most stress-related psychiatric problems, especially in physicians. I have a feeling that this comes from the techniques used in our training, and in addition to that you can throw in the teaching of guilt from our Western religions and parents. It is a miracle that any of us function at all. You also must have a feeling of not being in control of the situation. So, guilt and loss of control leads to uncontrolled anger, which you nicely suppressed from July to the present. I think your problem is not more complicated than that, Jack. What do you think?"

"I agree, but what can we do to make me feel better?"

"Well, there are several techniques at our disposal, but I think we can discard the long and drawn-out conventional approach of delving into your past and go right into reality and behavioral therapy to get you back on your feet again. There are certain reconditioning procedures to modify your response to the situation. We can also use crises therapy to undo your negative response to the lawsuit. Do you think a sleeping pill or antidepressant would help you?"

"I really feel that with your help I should be able to regain my psychiatric composure without the need for drug therapy. If things don't go well, I would be open to using medicines as needed."

"Fair enough." Arnold then reached into a drawer in his desk, pulled out a booklet, and handed it to Jack.

"These are some of the behavioral techniques I developed while teaching in Boston. They have worked well for my patients in similar situations of stress-induced depression. Look them over, and we can discuss them during your next visit, which can be whenever is most convenient for you, but the sooner the better."

They both stood and shook hands. As they were walking out of the office, Jack turned and said, "I can't thank you enough. I feel that I'm in good hands."

Arnold looked directly into Jack's eyes and said, "Don't worry, Jack; things will work out just fine."

Chapter 26

February 2008

PETE AND ABDUL entered the Redstone Inn wearing flak jackets under their work clothes. They had their automatic rifles slung over their shoulders and had their handguns pointing in front of them. The desk clerk was obviously startled as they burst through the front doors, breaking the quiet peacefulness that was the hallmark of the inn. Ann Colman had been the desk clerk at the inn for almost ten years. The lobby was empty except for her. She immediately reached for the phone to dial 9–1–1, but Abdul gave her a menacing look, and she replaced the receiver on its hook.

"What's the meaning of this intrusion?" she shouted.

"Just stay calm and quiet and you won't get hurt," Pete said in a hushed voice. He motioned for her to come out from behind the reception desk as Abdul searched the remaining parts of the first floor. The elevator door opened at that moment, and one of the guests stepped out to find Abdul standing there pointing his handgun at her. She was a woman in her early fifties, and she was very attractive with blonde hair and wearing cross-country ski clothes. She was obviously frightened by the scene in front of her and yelled out unconsciously. Abdul motioned for her to join Ann at the reception desk. She complied and seemed to calm down rather quickly. Pete tied their hands behind their backs and had them lie face down on the lobby floor.

February 2008

Harry and Drew pulled the Bronco up to the fork in the road in front of the Redstone Inn. They stayed back about thirty yards from the front entrance and took positions behind the Bronco, using it for protection. Drew contacted the FBI agents and the Pitkin County sheriff on his cell phone to notify them of their position and find out their estimated time of arrival on the scene. They held their handguns firmly in their gloved hands.

"I wish we had more firepower," Harry said.

Drew responded, "Hopefully the backup will be here soon. At least the sky is clearing now and that helicopter should have no trouble coming over the mountains from the Eagle-Vail Airport."

Abdul pulled out his international cell phone and dialed Ahmed's number.

Pete said, "Who are you calling?"

"Ahmed. He needs to know what's going on, and maybe there is some help in the area." He walked down the hall toward the dining room and bar as the connection was made. Ahmed answered and let Abdul know he was in Manhattan.

"Ahmed, Pete and I are on the run from local police. Pete was recognized by this local detective who was visiting Sam Kahn at the rehabilitation center when Pete was there adjusting the listening device. We are in a small town and have two hostages and weapons, but we could use help if there are any cell members in the area."

"There is no way I can help. You know what you have to do. Pete has no true loyalty to our cause, so you must eliminate him if escape is impossible. We cannot afford to give them any information. You must take Pete out before he is captured. We will take care of your family as promised. May Allah be with you." Abdul walked back to the lobby and shook his head negatively, letting Pete know that there was no help forthcoming.

Harry noticed that the inn tower clock showed 4:10 when two Pitkin County sheriff cars pulled off Route 133 and stopped next to them. The officers jumped out of their cars wearing bulletproof vests. One of the officers was carrying an M24 sniper weapon system. He was known in the area for his sharpshooting abilities. He was once an Olympic hopeful and had learned to shoot and hunt in the Colorado Rockies.

141

"Drew, get the phone number for the Redstone Inn," Harry said. Drew called the Basalt Police Station to inform Chief Owens of their location and got the number of the Redstone Inn. Harry asked the sheriff deputies to spread out and cover the exits. He suggested that the sharpshooter take a position on the roof of the general store across from the front entrance of the inn to hopefully get a clean shot at the perpetrators.

Abdul searched the rear exit of the inn and discovered that it backed up to a wooded area with deep snow on the ground and clearly offered no avenue for escape. He pulled two fragmentation-type hand grenades from his inside jacket pocket. He came back into the lobby and informed Pete that their only way to escape was to use the hostages as human shields and try to make it back out to Route 133.

Pete was still very calm and noticed the two hand grenades Abdul now had strapped to his belt. Just then the phone rang at the front desk. Pete answered, "Hello."

Harry said, "This is Detective Harry McNally. We have the inn covered, and it would be wise for you to cooperate and come out peacefully before anybody gets hurt. We only wanted to talk to you and are making no formal charges at this time."

"We have no intention of cooperating. We have two hostages and an inn full of other potentially innocent bystanders that you could put in jeopardy if you don't let us walk out of here. We are armed, and I assure you we are dangerous."

Harry could hear the helicopter approaching from the north. He also assumed that the FBI agents would be arriving any minute now. "There are FBI agents on the way, and they are expected at any moment," Harry said.

"I don't give a rat's ass. We will leave here with the hostages and take Highway 133 out of this area. You will stay back and not interfere, or we will kill these hostages. You can bet on it." Harry could not understand why they would take this attitude when they hadn't been charged with any crime. Even if they were involved in the death of Tanya Ramsey, the evidence against them was only circumstantial. Their involvement with Samuel Kahn must be the key to their fear of being apprehended. This led him to the conclusion that they must be desperate enough to follow through with their threats. He also wondered why this ex-military man was teamed up with an Arab.

Harry knew from his training in New York that his main role as a negotiator at this moment was to contain them as long as possible since the longer they were with the hostages, the less likely they would be to take their lives. Once they went from the containment phase into the mobile phase of the hostage situation, there were more things that could go wrong that would increase the chance of death to the hostages. He also knew that in this situation the hostages were being used solely as bargaining chips for escape. Therefore, the best approach was to make the containment visible and hope that their desire to survive was greater than their need to have their demands met. The hope was that the offer for safe surrender with dignity would work as a strategy.

"Is there anything I can get for you at this time?" Harry asked.

"We need you to arrange for a helicopter to meet us in Marble. We will decide on our destination after we are in the air with the hostages. We want you to be sure that Highway 133 is cleared all the way to Marble."

"I can arrange for your demands, but I need to be sure that the hostages are unharmed," Harry replied.

Pete put Ann Colman on the phone. "We are okay, sir. There are two of us who are hostages at this time. One is a female guest. The staff in the kitchen and guest services have been informed to stay in the kitchen and not interfere. The few guests in the inn probably saw the police lights and have stayed safely in their rooms."

Pete grabbed the phone and said, "Enough talk. Get started on our demands."

The clock on the inn tower now showed 4:35. The snow had stopped falling. The sky was clear as the FBI's black GMC turned off Route 133 and skidded to a stop beside Harry's Bronco. They approached Harry and introduced themselves. Their names were Maria Falconi and Robert Farthing. Harry filled them in on the details of the hostage situation.

"Any new information on this Jensen character?" Harry asked.

"He seemed to drop off the face of the earth after his dishonorable discharge from the Rangers," Maria Falconi answered.

Robert Farthing was looking around to see where Harry had placed the sheriff's men. He noticed the sniper set up on the roof of the small general store across from the inn entrance. "Is that guy any good?" he said as he pointed to the officer with the sniper rifle.

"Supposed to be," Harry said. They all looked up as they heard the familiar sound of a helicopter approaching. They were looking for a place to set down and finally chose Route 133 near the old coke ovens.

Harry called the inn again, and Pete picked up the phone. "The helicopter is ready for you. We are just waiting for the road to be cleared to Marble."

"Fine. One more thing. Be sure you understand that I will not hesitate to kill these women if you try anything that even looks out of the ordinary."

"I understand," Harry said.

Abdul was watching the hostages closely, and when Pete got off the phone he wandered over to the front entrance. He was surprised to see the amount of police cars that were present with their red and blue lights flashing. He had the sudden realization that the situation was far worse than Pete realized. He knew Pete was a well-trained soldier, but they were definitely in a severely compromised position. One mishap with the hostages and they would be easy targets. He knew they could not be captured alive. Ahmed had made that fact very clear.

The tower clock now read 5:05. The sun would be setting soon. Harry got word that the snowplow truck was nearly there. He felt things would go smoother if the transfer took place while it was still light, so he called Pete.

"Plan to leave in a few minutes. You can follow the snowplow truck to Marble, and the helicopter can follow you there. One more thing. The helicopter is not large enough for you and the hostages. You can leave the hostages in Marble, and the pilot can then serve as your hostage. Sorry, that's the best we can do."

Pete thought for a moment, informed Abdul of the change in plan, and then said, "No problem, McNally." Pete noticed Abdul was sweating profusely and looked very nervous. "Be cool, Abdul. It's going to be all right." Abdul just stared at Pete and was silent.

They went over to the hostages and pulled them up by their hair. Both women screamed in pain as well as surprise since up to this point they had been left alone.

Pete said, "Let's rock and roll, girls. If things go well, you will be safe in Marble in less than thirty minutes." Abdul took Ann Colman to the front entrance first. He had his right arm around her neck and was standing directly behind her. She was about his height, so she was a perfect shield for him. His revolver was holstered in his shoulder holster. He was still obviously nervous, especially as he approached the door. Pete didn't like the way Abdul looked. He was also concerned with the way Abdul was continuously checking the fragmentation hand grenades on his belt. Pete situated himself behind the other hostage, with his left arm around her neck and his revolver in his right hand pointing at her head. She didn't struggle at all and remained quiet.

Abdul and Ann Colman exited first and began slowly inching their way toward the SUV still located just to the right of the front entrance. There was about two inches of fresh snow on the ground, which caused them to make fresh tracks leading from the front entrance. The sheriff's sniper, who was lying prone on the roof of the general store, had a perfect view of the front entrance. He had been instructed not to take a shot unless the perpetrators fired first. Abdul was still holding Ann Colman closely as he got within ten feet of the SUV. He looked back at Pete and his hostage as they exited the front entrance. Suddenly he threw Ann to the ground, pulled both hand grenades from his belt, and began screaming in Arabic, "Allah Akbar, Allah Akbar, Allah Akbar!"

Pete realized immediately that Abdul was intent on killing him, the hostages, and himself with the hand grenades. Suddenly he heard the crack of the sniper rifle. Abdul's head snapped back, blood shot out from the right side of his head in a pumping fashion, and he fell to the ground before he could detonate the hand grenades. Pete couldn't believe his eyes. He loosened his grip on his hostage, dropped his gun, and raised his hands in the air. He knew that Abdul had been instructed to kill him and blow himself up. Pete was an opportunist mercenary, not an Islamic terrorist, so he knew he would be better off being held by the FBI than he would be back in circulation as a mercenary with the terrorists searching for him.

Both of the hostages ran over toward Harry's Bronco. Harry and the other officers came out from behind their vehicles, wrestled Pete to the snow-covered ground, and handcuffed him, and Harry read him his rights.

Chapter 27

February 2008

GARY GOLDMAN AWOKE from a restless night's sleep. He knew that he had to inform the Kahns, Michael Sutton, and Louis Reiner of the information that he and Jack Collins from the CFTC had discovered during their investigation. It might negatively affect the lawsuit, but since the Kahns safety might be at stake, he knew they all needed to be informed of the findings. He decided to call Evelyn by the end of the day, and if she was agreeable the attorneys could be informed.

Harry drove into work early in the morning. He wasn't confident that he had made the right decision to allow the FBI to hold Jensen. He knew that he had made a deal with the FBI, but he would have felt more comfortable if he could have interrogated Jensen himself since his job was to solve the Tanya Ramsey case, and he knew that this was probably low on the priority list of the FBI. Abdul's body was also taken by the FBI for identification and cross-referencing to see if he was in some way connected to any known terrorist organizations. Abdul's body first went to the FBI medical examiner for an autopsy and identification utilizing his fingerprints and dental records. Harry decided to ask the chief if he could drive into Denver to be present at the interrogation. He also wanted to inform Todd Ramsey of the developments in the case, but he decided to wait until after the interrogation of Pete Jensen. Lastly, he needed to inform the Kahns

146

that they had apprehended the man who had them under surveillance at the rehabilitation center.

Evelyn arrived at the rehabilitation center early in the morning. She was excited to see Sam because over the last few days he had made significant progress with his physical therapy. He had progressed to walking without the assistance of a walker and now only needed a cane to support his previously paralyzed lower extremity. Most importantly, however, Sam was speaking in longer sentences and no longer showed signs of depression. He was anxious to be discharged and return to New York to be with the rest of his family and close friends.

They were beginning to get the records ready for their transfer to a home health agency in Manhattan for rehabilitation at home rather than being admitted to an inpatient facility. Evelyn had decided to take Gary Goldman up on his offer to hire a private jet for their transportation back to New York, but she was confident that they no longer needed an air ambulance for his transfer. Gary, however, insisted that a private jet would make Sam's transfer go a lot smoother.

Kathy had been thinking about attending a meeting of hospital administrators that took place each year in Fort Lauderdale. This would give her an opportunity to see Ed again and to get out of the cold weather for a few days. She realized how much she missed being with him even though it had been less than two weeks since Valentine's Day. She thought about surprising him and just showing up in Fort Lauderdale, but she decided that wasn't a good idea because she just had a certain amount of insecurity about his life outside of Aspen. She couldn't wait to call him in the evening to let him know that she was planning to come to Fort Lauderdale.

Jack was on call for the emergency room this week for cardiology. He was very busy with multiple hospital admissions since this was peak winter tourist season in Aspen, and it was very common for visitors to the area to drink alcohol heavily, and at this altitude it was not uncommon to get cardiac arrhythmias and acute myocardial infarctions after the extreme exertion of skiing. In spite of the increased workload, Jack's spirits had been much better since his visit with Dr. Arnold Zucker. He was looking forward to enjoying the challenges of the art of practicing medicine again, and he was not allowing the malpractice case to interfere with his life as much. He and Penny had spent a couple days last week skiing together, and their lives seemed to be returning to normal. He knew he had other issues to work out with Arnold, but he was hopeful that his depression would be self-limiting.

Ahmed tried on several occasions to reach Abdul on his cell phone. He was concerned because Abdul was always responsive to his calls. Ahmed considered sending Bihir to Colorado to find out what was going on, but he did not think it wise to increase their exposure in the area, especially since Jensen had already been spotted by the police. He decided to wait for Abdul to call him and hope that Pete Jensen's evasive skills were as good as his military resume indicated.

He was also having difficulty with his contacts in New York in arranging a match for Al-Shamir's father's kidney transplant. The ethical issues involved in transplants were difficult to overcome, even with all their financial strength. It seemed that money could not buy everything so easily in America.

Ed was especially busy in his practice because during the month of February, there was a large influx of tourists to the Fort Lauderdale area. Many wealthy Canadians came to the area during the winter months and were not hesitant to utilize the medical care in the United States to get things done that they would have to wait months for in the Canadian system. Colonoscopy screening for colon cancer prevention, for instance, was especially difficult to get scheduled in the more remote parts of Canada. So, many Canadians had the procedure done while they were in Fort Lauderdale for the winter.

Ed's practice had begun to utilize electronic medical records, which were initially difficult and time-consuming, but with time and patience the system was working well. As busy as he was, there was always time to think of Kathy, and in fact they had managed to touch base on a daily basis since Valentine's Day. Ed found himself looking forward to their daily conversations and wondered if she felt the same way. He was having difficulty sorting out his own feelings as well as trying to understand how such an attractive, athletic, and independent woman could have an interest in him.

Chapter 28

February 28, 2008

HARRY HAD ARRANGED to be present for the first interrogation of Pete Jensen and decided to bring Grace along for the ride. They were planning to spend the night in Denver, and this would give Grace a chance to do some shopping while he was busy at the FBI office. It was snowing heavily all along I-70, causing traffic to move very slowly. There was a standstill at the Eisenhower Tunnel for over an hour as the usual array of truckers and tourists returning from skiing in Summit County, Aspen, and Loveland all converged at the tunnel. Harry and Grace eventually arrived in Denver around 2 PM, and Grace dropped Harry off at the Denver FBI field office. He went directly to the Domestic Terrorism Division and was greeted by Latoya, the receptionist who was expecting him. She escorted him down a long corridor and then handed him off to an armed guard who escorted him to the interrogation area. After they passed through several locked doors, he saw agent Maria Falconi standing outside a room with one-way glass on one wall. She was wearing a tailored black pantsuit with a pinstriped shirt. Harry approached her, and as she recognized him she turned and extended her hand for a handshake.

"How are you, Harry?" she said.

"It was a tough drive from Basalt. What's going on?"

"My partner has been interviewing that Jensen character. So far he hasn't gotten much out of him except a lot of hostility toward our government, hatred of the army for his dishonorable discharge, and a downright nasty attitude in general. He apparently was raised by his grandmother in upstate New York. He was a good athlete in high school, never went to college, and joined the army after several odd jobs in his hometown. His military records show that he excelled as an infantryman and became a gunnery sergeant prior to being transferred to Afghanistan. His trouble began when he was caught selling arms to terrorists there. I don't get the feeling from his interview today that he did it out of love for their cause—it was purely for the money. That about brings you up to the point we're at now."

"Anything about the murder in Basalt?" Harry asked.

"We were waiting for you," she responded.

Harry then asked, "Have you gotten any information on Jensen's Arab partner?"

"Not yet, but we are working on it."

"Have you gained any insight into this guy's personality or weaknesses that we can explore?"

"Only that he is not that well educated and is apparently a loner, but he does not appear to be a heavy drinker or drug abuser."

Harry said, "I would guess that he lacks street smarts,"

"Why do you say that?"

"Well, he's been caught twice already. Once by the military in Afghanistan and once by us."

Maria smiled in agreement and said, "Let's give my partner a break and see what information we can get from this guy. Why don't you take the lead, Harry?"

Harry and Maria entered the room to relieve Robert Farthing. Harry noticed that Jensen was dressed in the same clothes he was wearing when he got arrested. He was unshaven and clearly had not had a shower since he was arrested. He was handcuffed to the chair with his hands behind him. Maria and Harry left their weapons outside, as was customary in the interrogation area.

Harry said, "If it's all right with you, Agent Farthing, can we remove his handcuffs?" Farthing glanced at Maria to get her approval. She nodded yes, and then Harry asked Jensen if he wanted some coffee. Harry and Maria were trying to gain some rapport with Jensen and take a different approach than Robert Farthing had taken prior to their entering the room.

Jensen said, "Coffee would be just fine; black, please." He stood as Farthing removed his handcuffs, flexed his wrists, and rubbed them as if to regain his circulation.

As he sat down again, Harry sat across from him, stared into his eyes, and said, "I want to be upfront with you, Mr. Jensen. I do not work for the FBI. I am investigating the murder of Tanya Ramsey in Basalt. I have evidence that puts you and your deceased associate at the crime scene at the time of the murder. I also know that her husband did not commit this crime, and nor does he have the financial capability of hiring someone to do it for him. If you come clean with me on the circumstances of that crime, it is possible that we may be able to help out with some of your other charges."

"Are you guys joking? This is the worst good-guy-bad-guy routine I have ever seen. I have been interrogated by the army, and they could not break me. Why do you think I didn't spend any time in the brig in Afghanistan? All they could do was dishonorably discharge me. You have nothing on me except resisting arrest."

Harry looked at him coolly and was silent for several minutes. Maria and Robert stood there and also said nothing. All of a sudden, Harry jumped up, grabbed Jensen by his shirt, pushed him against the wall, and said, "Listen to me, you sorry bastard. You held two women hostage, resisted arrest, and endangered a multitude of police officers. You have been harassing a poor stroke victim in a rehabilitation center in Glenwood Springs, and I'm sure you and your fucking Arab partner are involved in terrorism. This leaves you to deal with the FBI. We will have enough evidence to nail you on the Ramsey murder, and these guys will be able to link you to some terrorist cell. So play it cool and see how far you get." Harry then pulled Jensen back to his chair and said, "Handcuff this son of a bitch. He wants to play it the hard way."

Harry stepped back and walked out of the interrogation room. Farthing handcuffed Jensen to the chair and then also left the room. Maria sat across from Jensen but said nothing. Jensen was obviously shaken and for the first time asked for a lawyer.

Maria said, "I'm sure you are aware of the U.S. Patriot Act that was passed after 9/11. We can hold you indefinitely without allowing you legal representation because of your association with a suspected Islamic terrorist. We can interrogate you in any manner we choose, and we can bring in the CIA if we see fit. We already have your partner's cell phone, and we are tracking all his calls as we speak. We will be checking your financial records, and we will freeze your assets. We intend to interrogate your grandmother, and we can do this without allowing her to have an attorney present either. You should have cooperated with Detective McNally. You are in deep shit, Mr. Jensen."

Jensen said, "How about that coffee?"

Maria got up to leave, turned, and said, "Don't hold your breath."

Harry was watching through the one-way glass. His mind went back to the days just after 9/11. He remembered the confusion and chaos of the local and federal agencies as they tried to decipher the reasons for the attack, who was responsible, and how many people were dead or wounded. It became clear that the September 11, 2001, attacks were a coordinated suicide mission engineered by Al-Qaeda, utilizing four hijacked commercial airliners to crash into the Twin Towers, the Pentagon, and the White House.

There were no airplane survivors, and the death toll of innocent civilians from over ninety countries was in the thousands. The post-crash medical and psychological problems continued to take their toll on the survivors and the relatives of those killed. The most devastating statistic for Harry was the loss of 411 emergency workers who responded to the scene and died as they attempted to implement rescue and firefighting efforts.

The aftermath brought about many changes in homeland security with its subsequent enhanced airport surveillance. Possibly the worst outcome of the aftermath was the negative effect of the term "war on terrorism." This led to hate crimes against Muslims and feelings of insecurity in U.S. citizens. The expression "war on terrorism" had also glorified the terrorists and gave the misleading impression that they were warriors in the true sense of the word, when in fact they were nothing but cowards killing innocent civilians, including women and children.

Harry's thoughts were interrupted by Maria as she exited the interrogation room. "This guy needs more time in isolation without food, a shower, or fresh clothes," she said.

Harry said, "I think you're right. I know the type. He is not in this for a cause, and he certainly would not give his life or freedom for an Islamic jihad."

Robert Farthing then asked, "Will you be staying in Denver for a while, or are you heading back to Basalt?"

Harry answered, "My wife and I are staying here for another night, so I'll be back tomorrow. Maybe by then he will be ready to talk."

Harry left the building and walked to the hotel a few blocks away. He decided to call Mrs. Kahn to let her know that he had apprehended the man responsible for placing the listening device in her husband's room. He also informed her that the perpetrator's partner was killed during the arrest, so they could feel safe for the present. He remembered that he had promised to call Kathy Ellington at Aspen Valley Hospital since Jensen's apprehension would have important implications in the medical malpractice case if indeed he was the murderer of Tanya Ramsey. Harry decided to call her tomorrow after he reinterrogated Jensen and hopefully had more information to give her.

Harry arrived at the Hotel Teatro in twenty minutes, just as the sun was setting and the downtown city lights were beginning to glow. The Hotel Teatro was located across from the Denver Center for the Performing Arts. The hotel lobby walls were decorated with costumes and photographs from the Denver Center Theater Company. Harry went over to the concierge to make reservations for dinner. He decided to try Kevin Taylor, the restaurant located in the hotel that was well-known for its romantic atmosphere and quality cuisine. He knew the cost for this one-night stay would reach far beyond their budget, but he also realized that he had been so engrossed in this case that he had spent very little time with Grace and certainly owed it to her to splurge a little.

Chapter 29

February 2008

GARY GOLDMAN ARRIVED at his Manhattan apartment in the early evening, after a long day at the office where he was involved with defending two clients against the IRS. Both clients had liens placed on their homes, and their bank accounts were garnished by the IRS. These cases were so difficult to defend because of the bureaucratic entanglement present in dealing with the IRS. He was exhausted but knew he had to call Evelyn this evening. He reached her at 7 PM Colorado time.

"Gary, I'm so glad you called. I have great news for you. Sam has made so much progress since you last saw him, and I believe we can get him home whenever you can arrange that private jet you mentioned. He will not need an air ambulance."

"That sounds great, Evelyn. I also have some news for you, but you may find it disturbing. My investigations with the CFTC have uncovered some disturbing connections between the hedge fund that Sam worked for as well as many other hedge funds that trade oil and oil-related products."

"Gary, I got a call a few minutes ago from Detective McNally, from the Basalt Police Department, explaining that they apprehended and are questioning the men who had been keeping Sam and me under surveillance. He also believes that these men may have been responsible for killing the nurse that cared for Sam prior to his discharge from the hospital during his first admission."

Gary then said, "If that is the case, it may affect your lawsuit."

"Yes, we understand that, but our safety is far more important than any medical malpractice lawsuit."

Gary said, "I agree. Are you planning to call Michael Sutton and inform him of these recent developments?"

She answered, "Yes."

"Evelyn, now may be the best time to get out of Glenwood Springs. I will arrange for the jet to leave Aspen in two days if that's okay with you."

"I'm sure we can be ready to leave by then. I have already arranged for home care with physical therapy back in Manhattan, and Sam can see his internist when he gets home and consult a neurologist if necessary. I can't wait to get out of here."

Gary said, "One more thing. Sam will need to be available to answer some questions that the CFTC may need answered."

Evelyn responded, "Let's see how he feels when we get home."

"That's fine, Evelyn. I'll call you with the flight information tomorrow."

Gary turned on his computer and navigated to privatejets.com. He arranged for a Learjet 31 to leave at ten in the morning. They would also handle the limo service to transport Sam and Evelyn from Glenwood Springs to the Aspen Airport for a small extra charge.

With that complete, Gary decided to call Louis Reiner to inform him of the events now taking place. He had placed his number in his cell phone after their last meeting. He had doubted he would ever use it, but now it seemed like the right thing to do.

Louis answered his cell phone, saying, "This is Louis Reiner."

"Louis, this is Gary Goldman, a close friend of Sam Kahn. We met in Manhattan, and I'm sure you thought that we would never speak again. However, I have some information that I'm sure you will find interesting."

"I remember you, Mr. Goldman. What's on your mind?"

"First, the CFTC and I have been investigating the activity of the hedge fund that Sam worked for, and we have found a relationship with other funds that have been making extraordinary profits similar to those profits of Mitch Carsdale and Jonathan Salem. These funds all have a common investor from Dubai. Secondly, Evelyn Kahn just told me that the detective working on the murder of the nurse who cared for Sam in the ICU has apprehended the men that have been keeping Sam under surveillance since he has been in the rehabilitation center."

"That is very interesting information, Mr. Goldman, since my client has been insisting all along that his care was by the book. He said that the evening before discharge Mr. Kahn was perfectly anticoagulated, and it would be very unusual to come back so quickly with embolic phenomenon."

"That leaves the hospital responsible for the malpractice because they hired the nurse that may have tampered with Mr. Kahn's medication," Gary said.

Louis said, "That's not necessarily true if the hospital did their usual and customary investigation into her qualifications."

"I'm sure the attorneys will work that out, but somebody needs to be held responsible," Gary said.

Louis thought that he would call Jack Simpson and Will Kitch first thing in the morning. He would also prepare a summary judgment to present to the judge to get Jack dismissed from the case and would run this by Abe Kaufman to get his approval.

Kathy was completing her end-of-month financial summary for the board of directors as the last bit of sunlight was disappearing from the evening sky. She had decided to go to the administrators meeting in Fort Lauderdale, and Prudence made her travel arrangements prior to leaving for the day. Kathy was anxious to call Ed to see what he thought about her visit.

She dialed his number and he answered. She said, "So, Dr. Harris, how would you like to see me in your neck of the woods? After all, you have never seen me in a bikini at the pool."

"Are you kidding me, Kathy? When are you coming and for how long will you be here?" Kathy answered, "I have a chance to attend an administrators meeting being held at the Harbor Beach Marriot. Is that far from you?"

Ed said, "It's so close you can stay at my place, and I can drop you off at the hotel for your meetings on my way to work and pick you up when you are finished. I have to tell you that each day without you gets harder and harder."

"So, Ed, I take it you miss me?"

"You bet. So when will you be here?"

"The meeting starts Thursday morning, and I will be finished at noon on Saturday, but I thought I would stay until Sunday. I'll e-mail you my flight information."

Ed then asked, "What topics are they covering in the meeting?"

"There are several hospital issues. First they will be covering electronic medical records and the concept of going entirely paperless. I see a lot of problems in the present available systems, but apparently there are newer forms of technology that use voice recognition for the physicians who will be reluctant to type all their orders and progress notes. The main problem is the cost, especially for a small hospital like Aspen Valley. They will also be discussing the use of hospitalists to cover admissions from the emergency room and also how best to utilize hospitalists for the care of ICU patients. Then there are the usual administrative issues that would bore you silly."

"You're right about that! I was supposed to be on call this weekend, but I will trade with one of my partners so we can spend more time together Saturday and Sunday. What time on Sunday are you leaving?"

"I'm taking the afternoon flight back to Aspen with a connection in Denver."

Ed said, "Bring casual clothes and a couple of bathing suits. I'll teach you to windsurf, and we'll go snorkeling. Talk to you tomorrow."

Ahmed waited until 2 AM to call Dubai so he would not awaken Al-Shamir. The hotel operator made the connection without difficulty.

Ahmed said, "Assalmu alaykm, I have some bad news. I have not been able to locate Abdul and Pete Jensen in Colorado. I am also having difficulty in arranging for a donor for your father's kidney transplant. The rules are very strict here, and one cannot purchase a donor as easily as we thought."

"This is very disturbing information, Ahmed. Did I send the wrong person to handle these matters? I have always relied on you and your family to serve me. Have I not taken care of you and your family over all these years?"

"Of course you have. With your permission I will try to locate our operatives in Colorado utilizing the available cell members functioning there. I will also put the word out to our many cell members in New York that we need a donor for your father."

Chapter 30

February 2008

HARRY AWOKE WITH a start after another restless night with the same nightmare that had periodically plagued him since 9/11. The dream always awoke him at the same point in a breathless panic. He was diving in murky water, attempting to find his missing friends. He could hardly hold his breath another second but knew that if he didn't keep going he would never find them. The dream usually occurred in the early AM, leaving him drained of energy and yet unable to fall back asleep. He had many counseling sessions with the NYPD psychologist assigned to him, but nothing seemed to change his recurrent dream. They diagnosed his problem as posttraumatic stress disorder. Fortunately the dream had occurred less frequently since he moved to Colorado.

He got out of bed carefully so as not to awaken Grace. He made some coffee that was supplied by the hotel and sat in the dark in a large chaise lounge and contemplated how he would approach Jensen during the second interrogation. Hopefully Jensen would be softened up a bit more after another night without a shower, significant food, and sleeplessness since the lights in his cell were kept on constantly. He had not been allowed legal representation or contact with his family or friends. He had basically dropped out of sight. Harry finally decided that the best approach would be to appeal to Jensen's sense of survival and offer him a deal if he would admit to Tanya's murder and give them information regarding his employer. The sun was beginning to rise when Harry awakened Grace so they could have breakfast together before he went back to the FBI building.

The dining room at the Teatro was as elegant for breakfast as it had been for dinner. Harry could see from the look on Grace's face that she was thrilled. The tables were set with the finest linen, crystal, and china. The waiters were solicitous and ever present, reminding them of the service at the Plaza Hotel prior to its condo conversion. They had a leisurely breakfast and spent time talking about their daughter, who had just gone through a divorce in Baltimore, Maryland. They had been ignoring the subject up to this time since it was so painful to discuss the sequence of events that led to the separation and now the divorce proceedings.

Their daughter Hope worked as a paralegal in a large law firm in Baltimore. She fell in love with and married one of the young associates working on the litigation team. He had hidden from her and his employers at the law firm the fact that there were many relatives on his mother's side with a severe form of bipolar disorder. He apparently became symptomatic shortly after their marriage and refused to take medications or seek psychiatric help. He began using an array of illicit drugs and subsequently had many extramarital sexual encounters, especially when he was in a manic phase of his illness. He was uncontrollable, and Hope had to leave Baltimore and return to Manhattan, where she was fortunate to get a job and begin a new life. Grace had spent many hours in Baltimore and then in Manhattan, both consoling and assisting Hope in reestablishing her life. The stress of watching their only child go through this tragic marriage only added to Harry's already fragile post-9/11 stress. They both felt a little better after taking the time to discuss Hope this morning and decided that it would do them both some good to continue an open dialogue about her. After a few moments of sitting in silence, Harry motioned to the waiter to bring the check. They walked out of the restaurant, hugged each other for a long time, and went their separate ways.

Ahmed awoke early and had a quick breakfast in his suite. He dressed and called for Bihir to arrange for a flight for the two of them to fly to Denver first class. He had the address of the mosque in Denver that had, as one of its members, a leader of an active terrorist cell. He thought he could enlist their help in locating Abdul Rahman and

Pete Jensen. He also planned to have the cell members tested to see if any of them were a match for the much-needed kidney transplant. Al-Shamir had been donating heavily to several of the mosques that were associated with terrorist cells in Denver, so Ahmed felt comfortable in this effort.

Harry walked into the bureau building, went through the metal detector, and showed his credentials to the guards. He then took the elevator to the third floor and went directly to the offices of Falconi and Farthing. They were on the speaker phone with the bureau chief in Washington. He was considering calling in the CIA to complete the interrogation. They waved Harry into their office and motioned to him to take a seat. The chief was trying to explain that they were trying to show cooperation between the two agencies, and this was a perfect case to give them since it was probably related more to international terrorism than a local FBI matter.

Maria tried to explain that Jensen was wanted for murder of an American citizen in Colorado and the link to terrorism was only because of his relationship to Abdul Rahman. The chief gave them twenty-four hours to get some significant information from Jensen or they would have to relinquish him to the CIA. The chief hung up, and it seemed that the matter was closed.

Harry said, "I would like one more crack at this guy this morning before you turn him over to the CIA. We don't really have much on him at this point, and without a confession I would hate for you guys to look back on this form of treatment of a prisoner."

"We do have some information that you are not aware of, Harry," Robert Farthing said. Maria added, "We have information on Jensen's partner. Even with his head partially blown off by your sharpshooter, we were able to utilize his fingerprints and identify him." Harry said, "You have to admit that was quite a shot, and if he did not take the initiative to take that shot we would have had two innocent civilians dead, and we would not have Jensen to interrogate."

Maria continued, "This guy Abdul was on every antiterrorist organization's watch list. He has apparently worked for multiple terrorist cells. He has been involved with terrorist activity in Europe and the Middle East. This is the first time he has shown up in the United States, and the CIA is taking his presence very seriously. As I'm sure you are aware, since we have been in Afghanistan and Iraq there have been no major attacks on our soil."

Harry listened to what they had to say and then said, "I understand how important this guy Jensen is to you guys, but I would like to remind you that I have a personal interest in him since I believe he was responsible for the murder of a nurse in my jurisdiction, and the family would like to bring closure to this matter. In addition, he had a stroke victim and his wife under surveillance and has been terrorizing them for over a month. I really would appreciate one more crack at this guy."

Farthing and Falconi looked at each other. Maria said, "Harry, I know you have been around and you probably have more experience than both of us put together."

"Are you trying to say I'm old?" Harry said jokingly. They all smiled, and the decision was made without another word being said.

Pete Jensen was brought up from his cell in shackles and placed in the interrogation room. He appeared quite different than the day before. He looked weaker and almost needed to be dragged through the halls to the interrogation room. He was unshaven and still had not had a shower. He had dark circles under his eyes, and it was obvious that he had not even brushed his teeth. His hair was matted. His fingernails were dirty, as were his clothes. Harry observed him through the one-way glass. He could see that Jensen was fidgety, and possibly this would be the best time to get a confession from him. However, a confession for the murder of Tanya Ramsey was not a federal offense, and he knew he had to offer him an attorney.

Harry stepped into the interrogation room carrying two cups of coffee. Agents Falconi and Farthing waited outside and were content to observe Harry and Jensen through the glass. Harry sat across from Jensen and offered him a cup of coffee. Jensen drank it down as if he hadn't had anything to drink in years. Harry was concerned about Jensen's state of mind, so he started by asking Jensen his name, his date of birth, the present date, his location, and his prior army serial number. When those questions were answered appropriately, Harry leaned forward and quietly said, "Do you know what the term 'extraordinary rendition' refers to?"

"Not exactly," Jensen answered.

Harry noticed that his voice was very hoarse. He thought this was possibly from screaming in his cell or just from generalized weakness.

"The term refers to the extrajudicial transfer of a terrorist suspect to a location where that suspect can be harshly interrogated to the point of torture. The key terms here are extrajudicial and harshly interrogated. If you think you have been treated badly here, you cannot imagine what forms of torture the CIA will put you through to get information as it relates to terrorism. You see, Pete, things have changed dramatically since 9/11 and the declaration of war on terrorism by President Bush. I can tell you this—today is your last day here because the FBI is about to turn you over to the CIA. They have identified your partner, Abdul, as a high-ranking Islamic terrorist. I'm sure you will be transferred to Guantanamo or some other 'black site' detention center for a more severe form of interrogation."

"Are you done with your speech, Detective?"

Harry stared at Jenson for several seconds and then said, "This is no time for you to cling to some macho form of arrogance. I am telling you the way it is, and you should understand that these believers in radical Islam don't give a rat's ass about you or any Judeo-Christian person. They are training their children to hate while we teach our children to love and to be tolerant of others. They have a long-term plan of taking over the planet and will not be satisfied until they kill or convert everyone, including moderate Muslims. They will not get you out of this situation. You are worthless to them now."

Pete sat there without saying a word for several minutes. It was obvious that he was having difficulty making a decision. He finally said, "What can you do for me?"

"If you tell me what I need to know in regards to the murder of Tanya Ramsey and help us locate the person who employed you, then I believe I can keep you in our justice system, where you will have an attorney and be incarcerated in the U.S. penal system."

"I need to see that in writing, Detective McNally."

"I'll see what I can do." Harry got up from his chair and walked out of the room. He wanted to get some feedback from Falconi and Farthing.

Harry asked, "What do you guys think?"

"I believe we can arrange for his release to you if he gives us what we want," Falconi said. Agent Farthing nodded his approval. They left to speak to their superiors.

Harry called Chief Owens to bring him up to date on the latest developments and get a letter faxed authorizing the transfer to the Basalt jail. If Falconi and Farthing could get a similar letter from their superiors, Harry felt he could get Jensen to fully cooperate.

It took about an hour to get all the necessary paperwork together. Harry reentered the interrogation room carrying coffee and some fresh doughnuts. He placed them on the table in front of Jensen. He also showed him the signed affidavits needed for his release to the Basalt Police Department. Jensen had a resigned look on his face.

Harry said, "I don't know if you remember that at the time of your arrest there was a lot of confusion. Everybody thought that because of Abdul's suicide attempt with the hand grenades that we were arresting Islamic terrorists. In all the confusion I'm not sure that you heard me read you your Miranda Rights. So, to be sure, before I hear your confession and take custody of you I will read them to you. When I am finished I want you to record your statement by writing out your description of your involvement in the murder of Tanya Ramsey."

Agents Falconi and Farthing entered the room and stood against the wall while Harry read Jensen his Miranda Rights. Jensen declined the presence of an attorney and began writing down his confession. He stated that her death was secondary to head trauma after she panicked and fell, striking her head on the coffee table. He explained that they were there only to frighten her so she would not talk about her role in the medication switch of Sam Kahn. He also stated that they had both Evelyn and Sam Kahn under surveillance because Sam had information as it related to a kind of trading scheme. He didn't know much about that aspect of things.

It took Jensen a long time to finish his written statement. He was clearly very weak and had episodes of psychological breakdown with fits of crying mixed with anger manifested by striking his fists on the table. He was still shackled to the table, so he could not get up and walk around to ease his tension. When he finally finished, they all felt that before answering any questions they should return him to his cell and allow him to shower, shave, and put on some clean clothes.

Harry called Chief Owens again to keep him informed and have him arrange for transportation back to Basalt, utilizing some of the Pitkin County sheriff's men and vehicles. The chief agreed and congratulated Harry for his diligence and attention to every detail. Harry informed him that he would be returning tomorrow unless something went wrong with the questioning this afternoon. He then called Grace to let her know how things were going and to ask her to make dinner arrangements at another elegant restaurant to celebrate him solving the case.

Chapter 31

February 2008

AHMED AND BIHIR landed in Denver at noon on Wednesday. They were greeted at baggage claim by their private driver, Akif. Bihir and Akif gathered the baggage, and they promptly left the airport complex via Pena Boulevard. They went directly to the northeast area of Denver where the mosque was located. Ahmed had arranged to meet with the imam of the mosque that Al-Shamir had been heavily funding. Ahmed needed information, and apparently there was a terrorist cell actively functioning from this particular mosque. He needed to know the whereabouts of Abdul Rahman and Pete Jensen. He had information that there were cell members who had access to employees working in the Denver division of the FBI.

While they were waiting for the imam to meet with them, they took a tour of the school located in the basement of the mosque. Ahmed was pleased to hear the familiar chanting from the children of "hate to America" and "death to the infidel." The children were dressed in uniforms and had headbands all bearing the same Arabic letters. The mosque was laid out in accordance with Muslim prayer and was organized around a courtyard. There was a prayer hall for men and a separate hall for women. There was a library for study of the Qur'an and an office for the imam. This mosque was obviously well funded. The imam completed the afternoon prayer session and then met with Ahmed privately in his office.

166

The private jet arrived at the executive airport adjacent to La Guardia at 1 PM carrying Sam and Evelyn Kahn. Their children and Gary Goldman were waiting for them with a wheelchair and a special van built for the handicapped. As they maneuvered Sam out of the plane, the family surrounded him and began hugging and kissing him. After they were settled in the van, Gary spoke to Evelyn and Sam to inform them that he had arranged for special agents from the government to protect Sam so he would be available to testify against Mitch Carsdale and Jonathan Salem.

Kathy's plane arrived right on time at the Fort Lauderdale International Airport at 2 PM from her connection in Dallas. Ed arranged his schedule so he was off that afternoon. He was excited and nervous at the same time. He knew that this would be a test of their companionship and love toward each other since it would represent a more real-life situation with him working every day and her at meetings all day. He had arranged for dinner reservations at several of the nice restaurants in the area and had actually arranged for her to have dinner with his kids on one of the evenings during her visit.

Ed met Kathy as she approached from the gate. She was wearing jeans, a white T-shirt, and a black blazer. Her hair was a little longer than the last time he saw her. When she saw him, she smiled. As she reached him she put her arms around him and kissed him. He kissed her back.

"I missed you so much," she said. Ed was sure that the feelings he had were also shared by Kathy. He grabbed her carry-on and computer bag, and they headed down to get the rest of her baggage. The baggage claim area was crowded as usual with locals and those using Fort Lauderdale to begin a cruise to ports in the Caribbean and Panama Canal.

"Well, Mrs. Ellington, you are in my neck of the woods now, and I hope you're ready for a few days in paradise!"

"Actually, Ed, anywhere with you would be paradise." They laughed like teenagers escaping from the real world. The drive from the airport took only twenty minutes, even though this was peak season for tourists on the beaches of Fort Lauderdale. Ed took the scenic route from the airport over the Seventeenth Street Bridge so Kathy could see Port Everglades with all its many cruise ships awaiting the arrival of their passengers. They then followed A1A along the beach to his condominium located on the east side of A1A.

The private elevator arrived at his penthouse apartment, and as he opened the door Kathy let out a gasp as she took in the view of the Atlantic Ocean. Ed showed her around the apartment. She could see that the feminine touches of his deceased wife were still present, and the apartment was beautifully decorated. They stepped out on the balcony and walked around to see the views of the Intracoastal Waterway, downtown Fort Lauderdale, and the surrounding areas.

"Ed, this place is beautiful! This is more like a vacation home than a permanent residence. I could hang out on this balcony enjoying the view all afternoon."

"Wait till you see the sunset over the Everglades and the sparkle of the city lights. Let's change and take a walk on the beach."

They walked for about a mile on the sand along the beach toward Las Ollas Boulevard. It was cool with the ocean breeze coming in from the east. They could smell the salty air blowing in off the ocean as they walked in silence for several minutes, holding hands and enjoying the calmness of listening to the waves approach the shore. They passed the many condominiums and large, oceanfront residences across the street from the beach and along A1A.

Kathy finally broke the silence and asked, "Where do you think this relationship is going?"

Ed did not answer right away. Finally he said, "I have been thinking about you day and night. You are in my thoughts when I awake in the morning and when I go to sleep at night. I am confident that I love you. I also feel better about myself now that I am finally going out and living for more than my work and my kids. I do have a problem, however, that I need to work out. I also would like to know how you feel about our future together."

"Ed, I know I am in love with you. I certainly didn't plan for this to happen, but it feels right to me. You are the most special, wonderful man I have ever known. I know I don't want to lose you. I hope to grow old with you and devote my life to loving you. It took me a long time after my divorce to adjust to being independent and caring just for myself and Laura. I didn't think I would ever have another loving relationship again. I have searched my own feelings, and I am confident that we are right for each other."

Ed stopped walking and turned her toward him. They faced each other, and Ed placed his hands gently on her face. They kissed each other gently but passionately. They were somewhat overwhelmed by the moment of closeness. They stood motionless on the beach for a few minutes and then turned and headed back toward Ed's building.

Ed said, "I would like to try to explain my problem to you. I am certain that I am not the only man to have lost his wife that he loved in the prime of their relationship, but when it happened it felt like I was all alone in the world. I was fortunate to have great kids and friends who all tried to be comforting, but they had their own grieving to go through, and honestly I always had the feeling that my presence in their lives made it more difficult for them to work through their loss. I have this need to overcome a feeling of guilt. I know that I don't have a reason to feel guilty, but nevertheless it is present."

Kathy then asked, "Did you get professional help after your wife passed away?"

"No. I thought that by keeping busy I would eventually overcome my grief. There is also the problem that relates to the cycle of trying to forget and at the same time trying to remember."

Kathy thought for awhile and then said, "I don't follow you."

"I know it sounds weird, but let me try to explain. I would go through periods of wanting to bring back memories of Lynn when she was in good health. She had a vibrant personality and always seemed calm even though there was chaos all around her. However, my mind seems to focus on the last few months when we were going through hell together. This made me want to forget, which brought up feelings of guilt for not trying to remember. This thought cycle has occurred over and over again. It seems to be occurring less now as time has passed. I probably should have seen a therapist, but you know how we doctors are. We always think we can heal ourselves."

"I'm no expert on grief counseling, Ed, but when I was an ICU nurse we attended a symposium on this subject. They stressed the variability of the grieving process. One of the most important factors determining a person's ability to handle loss relates to the time one has to prepare for the loss. You were probably well prepared and therefore you did not go through any of the pathological signs such as depression, insomnia, isolation, and anorexia."

"I suppose you are right, but I still have these feelings of guilt occasionally, and I feel it is because I avoid trying to remember."

Kathy then said, "I have always felt that guilt is an important part of our human conscience and helps us distinguish right from wrong. Problems occur when guilt is not based on any wrongdoing. Your guilt must come from the feeling that you in some way should have been the one to get sick rather than your wife, or more likely you have the feeling that her illness somehow could have been avoided. There is no logic behind either of those feelings. I am so confident that you will eventually work through all this. I want you to understand that I have no intention of replacing your deceased wife. I will never be jealous of her, and I will not attempt to displace any of your innermost thoughts and feelings that you may continue to harbor for her. I can exist along with her in your mind if that is what you need." Ed looked into her eyes and smiled gratefully. They began holding hands again and resumed walking along the beach.

They approached Ed's condominium as the sun was setting, which caused his building to cast a long shadow on the beach. They decided to sit on the beach for a while and allow the surf to wash over their feet. Ed had a total sense of relaxation and a feeling of respect and love for Kathy. He was looking forward to the next few days.

Chapter 32

February 2008

IT WAS LATE in the afternoon when Pete Jensen was brought back to the interrogation room. He was shaved, showered, and had a completely different demeanor. He was relaxed and seemed resigned to his fate. He was dressed in an orange jumpsuit and was handcuffed with his hands behind his back. He had ankle shackles in place which impaired his ambulation and balance. The two guards assigned to him seemed more cordial than prior to his confession. Harry, Maria Falconi, and Robert Farthing entered the room together.

Harry said, "We have reviewed your confession and need to fill in some of the details. I must ask you again if you desire to have an attorney present." Jensen again declined. Harry thought this was unusual, but he went on to ask, "Who has been paying you and Abdul for this assignment in Colorado?"

Jensen responded, "I never had contact with the man. He always communicated with Abdul by cell phone. He paid me by depositing money in an offshore account in Aruba."

Maria then said, "We will need the account numbers in Aruba."

Pete said, "No problem."

Harry said, "Go on, Pete."

Pete continued, "I overheard Abdul speak to this man on several occasions, and I believe his name is Ahmed. I don't know anything else about him except that he flies into New York on occasion to check on his investments."

"Where does he fly in from?" Maria asked.

"I believe it is from Dubai. Abdul mentioned it one time when he had to call him. He had to wait for the appropriate hour to reach him because of the time difference."

"What was the relationship between Tanya Ramsey and Sam Kahn?" Harry asked.

"All I know is that she was his nurse while he was in the ICU in Aspen."

Robert Farthing then asked, "What was the relationship between Kahn and this fellow Ahmed?"

"I don't know."

Harry then said, "So let me get this straight. You're claiming that your job was to keep both Tanya Ramsey and Sam Kahn from talking, but you never knew what it was that they knew? You are also claiming that the death of Mrs. Ramsey was accidental and occurred because you were there to scare her?"

"That's right."

Harry then asked, "Why did you have a listening device in her house and in Mr. Kahn's rehabilitation room?"

Jensen smiled and said, "So you found those devices. I guess we underestimated you, Detective. We used them so we could know what was going on at all times. They were hooked up to recording devices, so we were never more than an hour away from what they were saying since we frequently reviewed these recordings."

Farthing then said, "Abdul was clearly an Islamic radical. He was going to detonate those grenades and kill you as well as those innocent bystanders. What was so important about Tanya Ramsey and Sam Kahn that he would have been instructed to commit suicide?"

"I have no idea. It was as shocking to me as it was to you."

Harry looked at Jensen for a long time and then asked, "What happened to you, Pete? You were a decorated army sergeant and served in multiple dangerous and strategically important missions. I can't believe you got into this situation just for the money."

Jensen sat quietly for several minutes and then said, "I became disillusioned by our government's actions and poor decision making on the part of the politicians in Washington. I lost close friends fighting in countries that didn't appreciate our help, and there was no logical reason for our presence there. We fought against genocide, corrupt governments, and fear of dictators who encroached on the lives of their own citizens. Our soldiers returned home broken both physically and mentally, and for what? Now we are in Iraq for the wrong reasons, and you tell me—what the fuck are we doing there? We are hated by most of the planet, and the terrorists have us making judgments out of fear rather than common sense. We are manipulated by the press as well as the government."

Harry quickly answered, "What makes you think things are any different in other countries? These poor people are brainwashed as well. They volunteer themselves and their children to blow themselves up. Tell me that makes any sense."

Pete had no answer. He sat there with a dejected look on his face and then said, "Do you have any other questions?" Harry looked at Maria and Robert to see if they had any questions. They nodded no and left the room.

Harry then said, "I will make arrangements for your transfer to the county jail in Basalt. I would recommend that you reconsider getting an attorney to represent you. Do you know the difference between first- and second-degree murder as opposed to the charge of manslaughter?"

"I do know that our intent was not to kill Tanya. The death was accidental."

"Yes, but it occurred while you were committing a crime. Your case is further complicated because there is a connection to terrorism. All I am trying to do is inform you that it would be wise for you to seek the advice of an attorney."

Pete said, "Thanks, Detective, I'll consider your advice." Harry then left the room, and the guards entered to take Pete back to his cell.

Harry called Chief Owens to inform him that the confession and interrogation went well and Jensen was ready for the transfer back to Basalt whenever it could be arranged. Chief Owens said he would send some of the sheriff's men to assist with the transfer that would take place tomorrow in the early morning.

Harry then called Michael Sutton at his office in Denver. The phone was answered, "Sutton and Associates, can I help you?"

"This is Harry McNally from the Basalt Police Department. Is Mr. Sutton available to speak to me?"

"May I ask what this is in reference to?"

"Yes, tell him it is about the Sam Kahn case."

"Please hold, Detective."

Sutton came to the phone promptly and said, "Hello, Detective, how can I help you?"

"I am calling to inform you that we have apprehended and have a signed confession from Pete Jensen for the murder of the nurse that was caring for Mr. Kahn at Aspen Valley Hospital. If you remember, he was the gentleman posing as a maintenance man at Mr. Kahn's rehabilitation center."

"Yes, I remember that incident."

"It seems that there is some link between the nurse's death and a terrorist organization, and she very well may have been responsible for Mr. Kahn's hospital complications. I trust you will inform the opposing attorneys of these recent developments?"

"Certainly, Detective. Do you think my client is still in jeopardy?"

"I can only tell you that these people are highly organized and will stop at nothing in pursuit of their goals. During the apprehension of Pete Jensen, his partner attempted to detonate grenades that would have killed himself, Jensen, and several innocent bystanders."

"That seems unbelievable, Detective. If my recollection is correct, that man was not of Arabic descent. How did he get involved in this kind of situation?"

Harry answered, "He was functioning as a mercenary."

"I see. Well, thanks for the call, Detective. I will notify Mr. Reiner and Mr. Kitch as soon as we hang up. This does place a different light on the civil medical malpractice case. It seems that the hospital will take the brunt of the negligence, now doesn't it?"

Harry answered, "I certainly don't want to comment on that, Mr. Sutton. If I were you, I would try to assure that Mr. Kahn is kept safe. That would be my first priority."

Sutton said, "He and his wife are arranging to fly back to New York, but I will call them this morning. Thanks again."

Michael Sutton hesitated to call the other attorneys, sitting in his office and carefully considering the consequences of his malpractice case. He finally decided that he would inform Louis Reiner of the recent development in the case. He asked his secretary to get him on the phone. She soon buzzed his office and notified him that she had Mr. Reiner on the line. Sutton informed Louis of the recent facts. Louis then informed him of the connection between Mr. Kahn's employers and their possible CFTC infringements and that he was going to file a summary judgment on behalf of his client.

"How does Abe feel about your chances of getting a summary judgment?" asked Sutton.

"He is all for the idea, Mr. Sutton."

"Well, good luck. You know I will try to block such a filing since it is unclear who is really responsible for the injury to my client."

"Be serious, Sutton. You know Dr. Simpson was not negligent in this case, and it seems obvious that the nurse was responsible for altering Mr. Kahn's anticoagulation."

"That may be so, but it is not so obvious to me, and I doubt a judge will go along with a summary judgment."

Louis said, "We'll see."

"I trust you will call Mr. Kitch," Sutton said.

"Sure, I'll notify him this morning."

Jack Simpson was in the middle of office hours when the call came from Louis Reiner. His medical assistant lightly knocked on the door of the examining room. Jack opened the door, and his assistant said, "Mr. Reiner is on the phone, and he said he has some good news." Jack excused himself from his patient and went into his consultation room to take the call.

"Hello, Louis, what's going on?"

"There have been some interesting developments in your case. To make a long story short, we are planning to submit a motion to the judge for a summary judgment. It appears that the nurse caring for Mr. Kahn in the ICU was involved with some terrorist organization and presumably did alter his anticoagulation."

Jack asked, "What is a summary judgment?"

"It is a legal term for a motion that claims that there was no medical malpractice on your part. In your case we are claiming that the events that led up to his stroke and splenic infarct were out of your control. We will claim that there is no 'question of fact' which requires a trial of your peers, but rather all that is needed is a decision on the law which a judge can decide." Jack said, "I'm not sure I understand the difference, but it sounds good to me."

Louis then said, "We will get some papers over for you to sign in the next few days. Don't worry, Jack, I'm confident that everything will be all right."

"Thanks, Louis, I feel better already. By the way, how is Mr. Kahn doing?"

"I understand from his attorney that he is finally returning to New York and is progressing nicely."

"That's great. Thanks for calling. Bye." Jack felt like the entire weight of the world had been lifted from his shoulders. He knew that this was not over yet, but at least things were going in the right direction. He called Penny to let her know and asked if she had time to call Ed and Kathy. She informed him that they were together in Fort Lauderdale and she would call right away.

Chapter 33

March 2008

IT WAS SNOWING lightly in Denver when two of the Pitkin County sheriff cars pulled up to the government building to pick up Pete Jensen for his transportation back to Basalt, Colorado. Pitkin County government vehicles were all converted to either hybrids or to use natural gas. These two vehicles were black Ford Explorers which had been converted to use natural gas for cost savings, less negative greenhouse effects, and a statement toward making the United States independent of foreign oil.

Jensen was brought into the underground parking area. He was still handcuffed, shackled, and accompanied by two FBI agents. He was transferred into the backseat without difficulty, and the Explorer left the parking garage with Tim Conway driving and Carey Underhill riding shotgun. They were armed with holstered pistols and a shotgun. The other Explorer followed closely with two of the sheriff's men in the front seat. Harry and his wife were waiting in the front of the building in their own car and began following a short distance behind. The caravan made its way through the city traffic without difficulty and then onto I-70 West. As they approached the foothills, the snow began falling a little heavier, which caused them to slow down a bit as they passed the town of Genesee Park.

At the cutoff to Blackhawk and Central City, Carey Underhill said jokingly to Jensen, "How about a quick gambling stop at Central

City?" Jensen didn't answer and seemed preoccupied. Tim Conklin and Carey Underhill looked at each other but didn't say anything. The visibility was good until they reached the area of Idaho Springs, where it became obvious that this amount of snowfall was going to become a problem. There was snow piled up on both sides of the road from the snowfall the night before. The flakes were getting larger and began to decrease the visibility. The drivers were in contact with each other by cell phone and were considering stopping awhile to see if the snowstorm would let up, but they decided to push on at a slow pace.

They had been driving for almost three hours, passing many large trucks that were pulled over on the side of the road. As they neared the town of Georgetown, Harry noticed that they had fallen back from the caravan by several car lengths.

He said, "Grace, I really am concerned about this storm. I know these sheriff's men are good mountain drivers with a lot of experience since most of them grew up in Colorado, but I think it would be wise to stop in Georgetown and wait it out."

"I agree with you, darling, but it seems that they are intent on getting home before nightfall."

"Well, I'm going to take it slow. This Ford Bronco isn't quite as steady as the big Explorers they are driving."

The area between Georgetown and Silver Plume was particularly slow because of the steep grade and slow-moving tractor trailers. However, once they passed Silver Plume the snow had let up a little, and they began making better time.

"We will be approaching Loveland Pass and the Eisenhower Tunnel soon," Tim Conklin said to Jensen. He again did not respond and was studying the terrain carefully. He had a concerned look on his face but remained silent. The second sheriff's Ford Explorer was directly behind the one containing Jensen. The officers seemed relaxed at this time and were all looking forward to getting home. Jensen sat up on the edge of the backseat, and it was obvious to the officers that something was disturbing him.

Tim Conklin said, "Jensen, are you okay?" He did not answer and had a faraway look in his eyes.

Jensen was having a flashback to an event when he was in Afghanistan. He was riding shotgun in a newly arrived mine-resistant, ambush-protected vehicle. These new vehicles were designed by Navistar to provide better mobility and safety for the troops patrolling the hilly and rocky terrain laden with roadside bombs. Jensen's vehicle was suddenly attacked by a roving band of Taliban warriors with Russian-made RPG-29 and RPG-27 weapons. The vehicle withstood the hits, but when Jensen's squadmates attempted to exit the attacked vehicle they were killed by assault rifle fire. Jensen played dead and somehow survived the assault, but he began having recurrent flashbacks of the account at unexpected times.

The caravan began the steady climb toward the Eisenhower Tunnel. It was barely snowing as they passed the first of the ski lifts that were still carrying skiers up from the base of the Loveland ski area. They were within fifty yards of the tunnel entrance when it became obvious to Carey Underhill riding shotgun that Jensen was in a trance of some kind.

All of a sudden, a single rifle shot was fired from the mountainside somewhere above the Eisenhower Tunnel. The high-powered bullet struck the front windshield, causing the glass to fragment around the bullet hole. The bullet struck the right shoulder of the officer who was driving, causing him to suddenly swerve the Explorer into the guardrail dividing I-70 just east of the Eisenhower Tunnel.

Conklin managed to get the car safely stopped. He put the emergency lights on.

Carey Underhill yelled out, "Tim, are you okay?"

Tim answered, "I've been hit in the shoulder. This hurts like a son of a bitch. Call for backup from the Silverthorne sheriff's office and get an ambulance out here right away." Carey noticed that there was blood coming from Tim's shattered shoulder. He reached into the glove compartment for the first aid kit and applied a pressure bandage under the driver's shirt. He then checked to be sure Jensen was safe in the backseat. He noticed Jensen was still in a daze and was sweating profusely. His eyes were staring straight forward and had a glazed look.

The second sheriff's Explorer was right behind the lead vehicle. The driver pulled over to a position ten yards behind the first vehicle. The westbound traffic had come to a complete stop at this time, with cars and trucks in disarray at the entrance to the tunnel.

Harry and Grace were back about one hundred yards at the time of the shot. They were not aware at first that anything had happened and figured that the traffic was coming to a standstill because of the road conditions. After a few minutes Harry called the lead sheriff's vehicle on his cell phone. When there was no answer, he became anxious that something was wrong. He then dialed the backup vehicle. Officer Hayes answered the phone and said, "Harry, we're under attack. The lead car received gunfire and swerved out of control. We don't know what the fuck is going on. Get here as quick as you can."

Harry told Grace to stay in the car with the doors locked, and to move to the driver's side in case the traffic began moving so she would be able to make her way to the soft shoulder off the road and wait for him. Harry drew his revolver and began running toward the mouth of the tunnel.

There were several cars parked in the parking area just east of the Eisenhower Tunnel. They were obviously there waiting for the weather to clear prior to heading toward Vail Pass, which could be very difficult in a heavy snowfall. Vail Pass Peak had an elevation of 10,662 feet. It was significantly steep on either side of the peak, with grades of 7 to 8 percent.

Among these vehicles was a black Honda. There were two men inside waiting for the signal to attack. As soon as they heard the gunshot, they pulled black hoods over their heads and exited their vehicle.

Dressed in black jumpsuits, the two hooded men came out of the parking area carrying French-made FAMAS assault rifles. They were running straight at the demobilized lead Explorer containing Jensen. The two officers in the backup vehicle began running toward the lead vehicle. Just as they were a few feet away, another rifle shot was fired from the mountain above the mouth of the tunnel. The bullet struck Officer Hayes in the thigh, causing him to yell out in pain and drop to the ground. The second officer dove for cover beside a Jeep Wrangler that had pulled over near the guardrail. He could not see exactly where the shot had originated from. He yelled forward to the officers in the lead vehicle to get down on the floor and wait for backup. He then saw the two hooded men approaching the lead Explorer. He pulled out his holstered revolver and fired at the lead approaching man. His bullet hit the attacker in the chest. The man fell quickly onto the snow-laden road just in front of the Explorer. The second hooded man turned and fired his assault rifle at Hayes, killing him. He then opened fire on the lead Explorer.

The bullets produced multiple holes in the doors and rolled-up windows. Carey Underhill was crouched on the floor in the lead explorer, and he was hit in the abdomen. Blood oozed through his fingertips, and he became pale and clammy. The hooded attacker came up to the Explorer and fired inside, killing Jensen immediately. He then turned and started to run back toward the area where his car was parked.

Harry had been approaching rapidly by this time and witnessed the entire event. It was obvious to him that the entire attack was meant solely to eradicate Jensen. He got to the scene as the killer was turning to leave. Harry already had his pistol out of his shoulder holster. He aimed and fired while running straight at the hooded killer. He made a decision to just wound the man so he could be interrogated later to establish what this killing was all about. His shot hit the assailant in the right shoulder, causing him to drop his assault rifle. Harry fired a second shot, this time striking the man in his left knee. This completely immobilized him, and he dropped onto the road. The snow was falling very lightly as Harry stood over him and removed his hood. The assailant was a young Arab in his early twenties. He was writhing in pain as blood oozed from the gunshot wounds. The snow-covered road was turning a crimson red around him. By this time the eastbound traffic on the other side of I-70 had slowed to a standstill. The cars and trucks heading west around the crime scene were scattered around and were facing in multiple directions as people fearfully tried to get out of the way of the gunfire.

Harry realized that although two of the assailants had been immobilized, there was still at least one more attacker at a higher elevation that could still be dangerous to those in the immediate area. He pulled the captured Arab behind the Explorer so he would not be visible from the area above the mouth of Eisenhower Tunnel. He was crouched down with the Arab assailant when the remaining sheriff's officer crawled up to him.

"What in the hell is going on?" he said.

Harry responded, "I have no idea why these people felt obligated to kill Jensen, but more importantly, how did they know we were traveling today and what the timing would be? There must be a terrorist infiltrator in the FBI or your sheriff's office, though that is less likely. Maybe we will get lucky and get some information from this young man."

Harry could hear sirens coming through the tunnel and hoped these were the Silverthorne sheriff's men and the paramedics to take care of Officer Conklin and the assailant he had wounded. Harry scanned the area above the tunnel entrance, trying to find the sharpshooter's location. He wondered how he got there and if he would try to escape or sacrifice himself for the sake of their movement. He was concerned for all of the innocent bystanders that were stranded in their cars and filled with fear that they may become a target as well.

Two EMS vehicles pulled across the break in the median from their position on the eastbound side of I-70 to where Harry, the wounded officer, and the Arab assailant were positioned. They were followed by two Summit County sheriff's cars. They were all wearing ballistic vests and helmets. The paramedics quickly loaded the wounded men into their ambulances and headed west to the Saint Anthony Summit County Medical Center.

This new level-three facility located in Breckenridge was set up for trauma as well as the usual general medical needs. Fortunately, there was no further gunfire from the remaining assailant above the mouth of the tunnel. Harry quickly briefed the officers on the situation and the need to capture or kill the remaining assailant. They decided to ask for help from the Colorado National Guard since they had the equipment and manpower to perform a search in the deep snow. The Colorado Army National Guard field unit in Boulder was known for their quick mobilization and training in mountainous snow conditions, and they had a helicopter division that could bring the necessary soldiers in a short time. The sheriff's men made the call.

The eastbound traffic had begun to clear out by this time from the area adjacent to where Harry was located. The highway patrol had stopped all of the eastbound traffic entering the tunnel from the west, so that side of the highway was now free of innocent bystanders. The westbound traffic was backed up for several miles now. Loveland Pass was closed due to the recent snowstorm, so there was no other way to travel west from Denver and the adjoining towns on the eastern slope.

The sheriff's men set up barricades one hundred yards back from the mouth of the tunnel and directed the remaining cars to advance through the tunnel heading west. There was still no more gunfire, and they were able to work more confidently. Harry and the remaining sheriff's men were scanning the area above the tunnel with high-powered binoculars. The snow had stopped falling by now. It was after four in the afternoon and getting dusky, especially since the sky still contained dark, snow-laden clouds. It was obvious to Harry and the officers that they would need to track through the snow from the parking lot area and go above the tunnel to find the shooter, assuming he was still there. The absence of further sniper fire suggested that he was already gone and was not the foolish zealot that would give his life for the cause, whatever that was.

Harry made his way back to their car, where Grace was waiting patiently. She had the engine turned off and was bundled up in her overcoat.

"What's going on, Harry?" she asked when he opened the door.

"The lead cars were attacked, and Jensen was killed along with three of the sheriff's men. We wounded and captured one of the assailants. One of the other sheriff's men was wounded, but I think he will be all right."

"What's the delay about now?"

"There is still one remaining gunman somewhere above the tunnel, but I believe he has already escaped, probably over the mouth of the tunnel to the Loveland ski area and lost himself among the late-afternoon ski crowd. We have called for the National Guard to carry out a search for this assailant. I think the traffic will be getting underway as soon as the National Guard helicopters have landed and they begin their search."

Chapter 34

March 2008

HARRY AND GRACE didn't get home until after midnight. They were both exhausted and went directly to bed. Harry's sleep was interrupted by fragments of the recent events that needed to be put together. He spent the night tossing and turning as he wrestled with the pieces of the case. He had difficulty separating his dreams from the real facts and sequence of events. When he finally awoke, he realized that he again needed to reach out to James Phelps in New York at the antiterrorism division of the FBI.

The sky was filled with dark clouds as another low-pressure system moved in from the west, forewarning another heavy snowfall in store for the Aspen area. Harry pulled into the station parking area at 7 AM and went directly to his desk to try to organize his thoughts. Harry pulled out his notepad and began trying to link the recent events to the murder of Tanya Ramsey.

He knew she was probably in some way responsible for the medical problems of Sam Kahn. He also knew that Pete Jensen and his Arab accomplice had a definite interest in both Sam Kahn and Tanya Ramsey. It was apparent that even though Pete Jensen was just a mercenary, he was working for a network of very sophisticated Arab terrorists that would not hesitate to give their lives for their cause, except for the single shooter who escaped from his position at the Eisenhower Tunnel. This sharpshooter was somebody high up in the command and not foolish enough to give up his or her life so easily. They would possibly be able to get some answers from the captured Arab being cared for at the Saint Anthony Summit County Medical Center in Breckenridge. What was unclear to Harry was the link between Islamic terrorists, Sam Kahn, and Tanya Ramsey. Harry searched through his list of recent contacts as they related to the case and found the phone number for Michael Sutton. He called the attorney's office, and his secretary immediately transferred his call to Mr. Sutton.

"How are you, Detective?"

"Just fine, Mr. Sutton. I'm sorry to bother you again, but I'm having trouble trying to understand the relationship between your client and Islamic terrorism. Can you help me out in any way?"

"Mr. Kahn worked for a hedge fund that traded oil and oil-related products. A very close friend of Mr. Kahn's investigated such a relationship. He found that his employers could have been involved in insider trading."

"What is this friend's name?"

"Gary Goldman. He lives in New York and is a very close friend of Sam Kahn." "Thanks for the input, Mr. Sutton. I'll keep in touch."

Harry next placed a call to James Phelps but got his voice mail. He left a message to call him back and then decided to visit Todd Ramsey to see how he was doing and to inform him of the recent events. It was seven thirty in the morning, so he decided to call first.

Susie answered the phone, saying, "Hello, Ramsey residence."

"Hi, Susie, this is Detective McNally. Is your daddy at home?"

"Hold on, please."

Todd answered, "Hello."

"Todd, this is Detective McNally. I wanted to drop by this morning since I have some information for you that would be better delivered in person."

"I'm getting Susie ready for school, but come on over if you don't mind a little chaos." "No problem, I will be there in a few minutes."

As Harry pulled up to the Ramsey home, he realized he had not been in that area of Basalt since the murder investigation. He noticed that the entrance walkway was already shoveled free of snow, and the front yard was well kept.

Harry rang the bell and heard Ramsey yell out from inside, "Come in, the door is open!" Harry was greeted by Susie and Todd as he approached the kitchen. Harry was impressed with the condition of the home, but more so with the appearance of Todd Ramsey. He was clean-shaven, already dressed in his instructor's uniform, and had already prepared breakfast for Susie.

"Don't look so surprised, Detective. I don't drink and I have been able to turn my life around. Susie and I are doing just fine together. So, what's on your mind?" He then motioned for Susie to return to the kitchen. She quietly returned to the kitchen, and Harry could hear the sounds of the Disney channel on the television. They sat across from each other in the living room.

"Todd, I just wanted you to know that we apprehended the men responsible for Tanya's death. It turned out that they were only here to frighten her, and as she struggled with them she fell and struck her head."

"Why were they trying to frighten her?"

"She had apparently been paid by an Arab family to administer a drug to a patient at the hospital where she was employed. I believe she was probably forced to do this since by all accounts she would never have committed a crime like this."

"I'm sure of that, Detective. Is there anything else I should know?"

"No, I believe you and Susie are safe, and I can't see any reason for them to bother either of you. I hope this information helps you bring some closure to the loss of your wife."

As Harry rose to leave, Todd said, "Let me tell you, Detective, closure is overrated as a concept to stop grieving. A day does not go by that I don't think of Tanya, and the knowledge of the cause of her death does not in any way relieve me of my feelings of sadness. If I had been a better husband, she probably would not have gotten involved with these people. Closure does not help resolve my guilt or my sadness. I know you meant well by coming over this morning, and I appreciate your efforts."

"Todd, I believe it is the act of approaching closure that helps the ones left behind since in realty closure is never fully attained." They shook hands, and Harry let himself out the front door after yelling good-bye to Susie.

Harry's cell phone rang as he was pulling into the station. Harry recognized James Phelps' number and said, "James, how are you doing?"

"Freezing my ass off here in New York. What's on your mind, Harry?"

"Do you remember the guy you were able to identify for me from the sketch artist?" "Yes, I believe his name was Jensen."

Harry filled him in on all the details of his arrest, interrogation, and obvious involvement with terrorists. He then said, "James, I believe this case should be handled by your department with coordination between the other involved agencies. It seems apparent that the CFTC should also be involved since these terrorists are somehow involved in the oil markets. There is an attorney out of Denver named Michael Sutton who has been involved in this case as counsel to Sam Kahn, who was an accountant working for one of these hedge funds. Sutton has information that will help you find out who from the CFTC is working on this case. We also were able to wound and apprehend one of these terrorists. He is presently in a hospital in Breckenridge, Colorado, and I am concerned that his life also may be in danger. If he is handled appropriately, possibly he can lead you to the leaders of this group, their purpose, and method of funding. My gut feeling is that this group of terrorists has ties with a much larger Islamic terrorist organization."

"Harry, I have learned from our past working relationships to trust your instincts. I will take this to the top of our agency and work on coordinating and sharing information with whatever agencies should be involved. Would you want to be involved?"

"I'm afraid I've already taken too much time with this case, but I'll talk to my boss and see if I can at least be there for the interrogation in Breckenridge. Let me know when you and your guys will be arriving. There is one more thing of importance. I believe these terrorists have someone inside the FBI in Denver. Good luck, James."

Kathy's flight back from Fort Lauderdale to Denver went smoothly, however as was usual this time of year, her flight from Denver to Aspen was delayed because of poor visibility. She spent several hours in the Denver Airport waiting for the snowfall to decrease enough for the United Express to resume flights into Aspen. She decided to have dinner at Wolfgang Puck's restaurant in the airport and work on applying some of the new management concepts she learned at the meeting in Fort Lauderdale. She was deep in thought when she heard the announcement that her flight was ready to board. She closed her computer and headed to her departure gate.

The flight was boarding quickly because the unpredictable weather in the mountains often gave a small window of opportunity for these forty-minute flights. She took her seat by the window. Her thoughts drifted to Ed and her recent visit to Fort Lauderdale. They spent time together walking barefoot on the beach and watching the sun set over the Everglades from his condominium, and the nights they spent together were both romantic and relaxing. She closed her eyes for a moment, recalling the sheer joy and desire of being with him. She had never known such passion and desire for a man. He was a gentle lover. She started to feel a longing for him and smiled at herself. They were so good together, and the comfort level between them was obvious from the beginning. She was lucky that his kids were happy for them. Laura loved him and was thrilled at the prospect of having older brothers. The main problem in their relationship was obviously that they were both dedicated to their work in different communities too far apart for her to think about. She was confident that they could maintain their relationship from a distance, but for how long? She looked out the window as the plane was crossing over the foothills and approaching the snowcapped Rockies. The sun was just beginning to make its way down in the west and appeared to burn a hole in the mountain peaks.

Sam Kahn continued his physical therapy, speech therapy, and occupational therapy in New York. His progress was remarkable. He and Evelyn had been under continued surveillance from the FBI and the CFTC. He would presumably be their lead witness in the insider-trading violations perpetrated by his bosses and probably many other trading groups. There had been no threats on Sam's life and no contacts to warn him to keep his mouth shut. Sam could now walk with a walker, complete simple tasks of daily living, and converse in simple sentences. Evelyn was thrilled with his progress, but she lived in continued fear for their lives. She understood how ruthless their adversaries were and knew their financial position was such that they considered themselves above the law.

Gary Goldman spent a lot of time with Sam and Evelyn trying to assure them that they were being protected. They considered some program of protective custody but knew that he would be easy to find with all the therapy that was required. The agencies involved were also hoping to apprehend anyone who made an attempt on Sam's life.

Jack and Penny were waiting for the summary judgment to be ruled on by the judge. As confident as they were that the outcome would be in their favor, it was still difficult to put the lawsuit behind them until the final verdict was in place. Jack stopped seeing the therapist and placed his entire energy into his work and skiing on the weekends he and Penny were not on call at the hospital. Their financial situation was in great shape thanks to Ed's advice last October to sell their stocks and buy corporate and government bonds. Their life was also romantically back on track, helped by their common interests and the strong bond they felt for each other. As soon as Jack began feeling better emotionally, they took advantage of all the local romantic restaurants and bars that made the area so popular.

Chapter 35

March 2008

JAMES PHELPS AND his assistant Gina were the first to arrive at the entrance to the Hyatt Main Street Station Hotel and Conference Center in Breckenridge. It was close to the hospital that was caring for and closely guarding the Arab gunman captured at the Eisenhower Tunnel. There had been many changes in the antiterrorism organizations during the Clinton and Bush administrations. After 9/11 there was an acceleration of changes that would better organize the fight against terrorism. Phelps now worked out of Washington DC at the National Counterterrorism Center, better known as the NCTC. This was the lead organization and had a cooperative relationship and interdependence with the FBI's National Security Board, Homeland Security, the CIA, and the Department of Justice. Phelps pulled a team together that would utilize the skills of the CIA and the National Clandestine Service.

Gina had arranged for the necessary guest rooms and for use of the small conference room at the hotel. The first agent to arrive was Amran Pinto, a Sephardic Jew born in Morocco but raised in the United States from the age of twelve. He went to college at NYU, where he studied foreign languages and political science. He spoke most of the Arabic languages and could speak in dialects from multiple Arab countries. He was lean, tall, and dark skinned, and he had a deep scar running above his left eyebrow. He had short, black hair and appeared much younger than his stated age of thirty-five. He was known for his interrogation skills. He shook hands with Phelps and Gina and took a seat. He began reading the file that outlined the facts of their mission and the possible worldwide financial impact that would result if they failed.

The next agent to arrive was Loretta Smyth. She was from the Financial Crimes Enforcement Network, which was also now part of the NCTC. She was a short, attractive blonde in her mid-thirties and had an athletic appearance. She turned the heads of every man in any room she entered. Her assignment would be to investigate the financial aspects of the case, including making contact with Sam Kahn, his attorney Michael Sutton, and Gary Goldman and his SEC friend who had worked on the connection between the hedge funds and the insider-trading information. She was also to take over the assignments of the FBI's field agents to guard Sam Kahn and try to apprehend any suspicious person that came close to him or any of the Kahn family. Loretta had her Masters degree in accounting, but her on-the-job training in the agency afforded her the ability to become an expert with firearms. She was a tough field agent who was dedicated to her work, and because of her continued movement from one assignment location to another she never had any long-lasting relationships. She came from a wealthy New England family that had originally made their money prior to the October 24, 1929 panic which resulted in the ever-infamous Black Tuesday crash of the stock market five days later. It seemed that her grandfather had advanced notice or was just lucky and had sold all his stocks on September 3, 1929 and went short on many of the high-flying stocks. He later reversed his position and began buying stocks again in the summer of 1932, catching a long bull-market run all the way up to the period prior to World War Two. He bought a seat on the New York Stock Exchange, and from that time on the family continued to gather wealth. It was always difficult for the family to understand Loretta's career choice.

The last three agents to arrive were from the CIA's National Clandestine Service. They were all previously trained and had experience in the Army Rangers with special ops assignments. They were all selected to join the CIA after demonstrating the skills necessary to work under extreme conditions in and out of the United States. The leader of the group was Andy Regalto. He was in his early forties and of Italian descent. His black hair was cut short and was beginning to gray at the temples. He had high cheekbones, a thin face, and a muscular body. He displayed the confidence necessary to be the leader of this elite group.

Jeff Ronson was black, tall, and athletic, carrying the appearance of a basketball player. His expertise was explosives. He was quiet and had a no-nonsense aura. The third member of the group was Leslie Rosario. She grew up in a tough neighborhood in Queens, New York, and had served in the infantry, where she became a sharpshooter. She was at the top of every training program that she signed up for, and because of her performance ended up in special ops with the National Clandestine Service. She was a striking Latina with long, black hair, which she wore pulled back in a ponytail. Her eyes were dark and piercing and already showed the expression of a woman who had experienced too much of life's dark side.

James Phelps started the meeting with a brief review of the material in their folders. Phelps assigned Loretta Smyth to depart to New York for the purpose of putting the financial details together after interviewing Sam Kahn, his attorney, and his friend Gary Goldman with his SEC contact. She would start in Denver with Kahn's attorney and then go directly to Manhattan. He assigned Amran Pinto to interrogate the captured Arab presently guarded by local authorities from the sheriff's office and assigned his agents to take over the protection of the prisoner. Prior to everyone leaving the conference room, James apologized for the fact that there was no time for skiing. They all laughed and were obviously anxious to get on with their assignments and get to know each other since their lives would depend on the abilities and characters of the other members of the team.

Phelps then called Harry on his cell phone. Harry picked up the phone immediately and said, "Hello, James, are you in the area yet?"

"Arrived today, and I must tell you we have a top-of-the-line team working on this project. The NCTC has placed a high priority based on your thoughts and conviction about the importance of this project."

"I hope you are not having second thoughts, James."

"I trust your judgment, Harry, but you'd better be right or they will have my ass."

Chapter 36

March 2008

AHMED WAITED NERVOUSLY in the office of the imam for the arrival of Al-Shamir. The mosque was quiet today. The afternoon prayer session was almost completed, and the last of the school children had been sent home. Bihir waited outside the mosque on the sidewalk so he could greet Al-Shamir and escort him into the mosque to meet with Ahmed. The traffic was slow moving since there had been a heavy snowfall the night before, leaving the streets slushy and icy in places.

It was almost five o'clock when the limousine pulled up to the curb. Al-Shamir exited the limo accompanied by two of his personal bodyguards. The bodyguards wore typical Western wool suits, but Al-Shamir was wearing traditional Arabic clothing. His head was covered with a black, knit kufi in the Saudi style, and he wore a black, Arabian Jubba-style jacket over a deluxe Saudi-style dishdasha. He moved quickly into the mosque. Bihir escorted him to the office where Ahmed was waiting.

Ahmed stood and greeted Al-Shamir with a kiss on both cheeks. Neither of the men smiled as they greeted each other. Al-Shamir motioned for the bodyguards to leave them alone. He sat calmly while Ahmed explained that Abdul and Jensen were both dead. He did the best he could to keep the details to a minimum, but he had to explain the events and consequences of the Eisenhower Tunnel debacle, including the capture of one of the mosque's cell members.

193

Al-Shamir sat quietly listening and then calmly asked, "What is being done to eradicate the captured cell member?"

"We have been looking for an opportunity to make contact with him," Ahmed said. "We have another man in the hospital working as a transporter for the radiology department. He is waiting for a chance to eradicate him, but unfortunately the police are watching him closely."

"Why didn't you kill him when you had the chance at the tunnel?" Al-Shamir asked.

"I couldn't get a clean shot without jeopardizing my position and line of escape."

"So you thought your life was more important than the mission?"

Ahmed sat quietly without responding.

Al-Shamir hesitated as he waited for a response, and then he went on to say, "I am sure you understand that our entire funding organization of the Islamic jihad is presently in danger of being unraveled. The money we donate to support these radical mosques throughout the country is derived from our trading profits and utilizing insider information. What you don't know is that we are only a small part of a larger organization of funding from multiple Islamic countries that have as their only goal to assure the entire planet is under Islamic domination." Al-Shamir did not raise his voice, show anger, or threaten Ahmed, but Ahmed could feel the tension in the air. He began to sweat nervously, which was unusual for him.

Ahmed finally asked, "What is your plan?"

"It seems obvious that we must eradicate any witnesses who can link us to these mosques. So to start, we must infiltrate the hospital in Breckenridge and eliminate the single surviving cell member from the Eisenhower Tunnel attack. This must be accomplished, even if it takes the action of a suicide bomber. Next, we must eradicate that accountant in New York. I will leave the details up to you."

Ahmed nodded and said, "I understand, sir."

Al-Shamir rose and finally said, "This must be taken care of by you personally, Ahmed."

Ahmed bowed in respect and said, "I will not let you or the movement down."

Al-Shamir left the office, and after a quick tour of the mosque he was escorted back to his waiting limo. Ahmed sat and contemplated his next series of steps to assure success, but he could not escape the fear that failure would surely mean that his family in Saudi Arabia would be targets of Al-Shamir's wrath.

Loretta Smyth left Michael Sutton's office and went directly to the Denver International Airport for her nonstop flight to New York City. She had made arrangements, with Sutton's help, to meet with and set up the surveillance of Sam Kahn and Gary Goldman, who they feared were in danger. They held the key to the financial dealings of this ring of terrorists. She had her laptop open and was setting up the schedule that she would need for protection of Mr. Kahn and his family. She would need the help of the FBI, through their national security branch, to man the needed schedule. If they were lucky, they could perhaps capture some of the cell members in the New York area which could lead to further arrests. She knew that she would be responsible for going over the financial records and information that Gary Goldman and his SEC friend had accumulated. The chain of financial evidence was always the most crucial in cases of this nature, and if not appropriately collected and organized it could lead to disaster in court. She closed her laptop and boarded with the other first-class passengers.

James Phelps, Amran Pinto, and Andy Regalto entered the Saint Anthony Summit County Medical Center through the service entrance at six in the morning while it was still dark. The sky was clear, and the forecast for the next few days showed a high-pressure area over the Rockies. They had their assignments, and Phelps had already met with the hospital administrator to inform him of their purpose and to get a list of all the employees so they could run them through the data bank of potential terrorists. After reviewing the list of employees, they found a man by the name of Fakih Hassani, who had recently gained employment in the department of radiology as a patient transporter. They cross-referenced him with a list of terrorists, and even though they found no reference that linked him to terrorism, it seemed logical to pursue this man since there were no other employees with Arab-sounding names. Phelps had no problem with racial profiling and understood all the ramifications concerning violation of the Fourteenth Amendment, but since the 9/11 attacks it made no sense to ignore the fact that almost all of the terrorist activity in the world had involved a classic profile of young, single males of Middle Eastern descent.

Phelps stationed the other two operatives, Leslie Rosario and Jeff Ronson, outside of Hassani's apartment building two blocks off Main Street on East Adams Avenue, across the street from the Breckenridge Elementary School. They were waiting for the word from Phelps that Hassani was at work so they could investigate his apartment. The sun was beginning to rise as Hassani left his apartment building, presumably headed for work. The two operatives waited fifteen minutes to be sure he was gone for the day and then entered the building without difficulty. They went to Hassani's third-floor apartment and carefully manipulated the lock open using a pick and tension wrench.

Hassani lived in a studio apartment, and it was clear that he lived alone. There were empty pizza boxes lying around, and the place looked like it had not been cleaned in a long time. They did, however, notice that there were several half-filled glasses of soda and several eating utensils on the small dining table, suggesting that Hassani recently had company. They figured at least two other people had been in the studio apartment. They carefully searched the apartment for any clues that would link him to a possible attempt at a rescue or more likely eradication of the prisoner held on the surgical ward at the hospital.

Leslie looked under his bed and said, "Jeff, come here."

Jeff asked, "What did you find?"

Leslie carefully pulled out from under the bed four vests with materials to make suicide bombs in a box. The explosive components were separated, and the shrapnel had already been arranged in the vests. Jeff snapped open his cell phone and called Andy Regalto.

"Andy, we found the materials needed to make suicide bombs."

"How many vests are there?"

"Four."

"Place everything back the way you found it for now. Did you find anything else of importance?"

"Leslie is turning on his computer now to see what communications and e-mails he has been receiving. Also, it appears that he has had some buddies here to help him."

"Finish investigating, and keep the place under surveillance. Maybe we can get all of them at once and break this cell wide open." Leslie downloaded his entire hard drive onto a zip drive so they could review it later. Jeff cut and crossed the wires that would be used to detonate the explosives within the vest. He did it in such a way that the person wearing the vest would not be able to tell the wires had been tampered with. He then placed the vests and all of the explosive materials back in their place under the bed. Leslie and Jeff quickly exited the apartment without being seen.

Amran Pinto got off the elevator on the third floor and walked toward room 322. One of the Summit County sheriff's men was standing guard at the door, and another was located across the hall at the nurse's station. Pinto identified himself to both officers and entered the room with the leader of the sheriff's team. A third officer was in the room, sitting in a chair at the prisoner's bedside. Pinto nodded to the officer and asked both of them to leave. He took a long time assessing the prisoner, who was an Arab male in his early twenties. The prisoner was resting comfortably, but his left leg was elevated off the bed in a traction setup with a stabilizing rod through his left knee, where he had received a gunshot wound. His right shoulder had a bulky dressing, and his right arm was in a sling. He was unshaven and wore a white skullcap on his head. Amran Pinto introduced himself in Arabic with a dialect that was common in Riyadh, Saudi Arabia. He informed the prisoner that his job was to get as much information from him as possible. He told the prisoner he would use any form of torture that was needed and assured the prisoner that he would keep him alive and not allow him to martyr himself for Allah. He informed him that he needed to know what group he worked for, the purpose of the attack on Jensen, the location of the cell that he worked with, and the identity of his immediate superior. Pinto assured the prisoner that as tough as he may be, he would succumb as all of his prior prisoners had done. The prisoner broke out in a cold sweat and tried without success to stare Pinto down. Pinto knew that it would not take much to break this young man.

Fakih Hassani reported to work on time at the radiology department. He had a quiet demeanor and carried out his job of transporting patients without much conversation. Most patients appreciated his attitude, as they were already preoccupied with their illness and their future. Small talk in most instances was not really appreciated.

Andy Regalto was dressed in scrubs and was posing as an operating room technician. He was able to keep an eye on Hassani for most of the day on an intermittent basis. During his lunch break he tried to befriend Hassani in the hospital cafeteria by telling him he was new on the job and in the area. Hassani was not too friendly, but he was pleasant and answered most of the questions Andy asked him. He declined Andy's offer to meet after work and have dinner together. Andy thanked him for the information he had given him and said he would see him tomorrow.

Leslie Rosario returned to the hotel and began downloading the information obtained from Hassani's computer. She hoped that the e-mails were not in code since it would take a long time to decode the information. She was soon pleasantly surprised to find the hard drive was so easily accessible and there was no need for decoding. She thought to herself that these people were either stupid or so brazen that fear of being caught had not entered their minds. There were the usual e-mails from advertising agencies, multiple hits on a particular pornographic Web site, and e-mails from several friends she presumed were his Islamic cell contacts. She also found a detailed floor plan of the hospital, and to her dismay there were maps and floor plans of several other hospitals in the Colorado Rockies. She traced these hospitals to popular ski resorts. Vail Valley Medical Center, Yampa Valley Medical Center in Steamboat Springs, and the Aspen Valley Hospital were on the list.

She called Jeff Ronson and said, "Jeff, is there any activity at Hassani's apartment?" "No," he answered.

Leslie said, "I finished working on Hassani's computer. These guys are planning a multiple hospital-site attack across the Western Slope ski resorts. I think we should round them up now and not wait for them to act."

Ronson responded, "Call Phelps and let him know what you found. I'll continue my surveillance here until I hear from you."

Leslie informed Phelps of her findings, and he suggested that they needed to wait and see if they could get them all at once. He also stressed that it would be optimal to take them alive since they could undoubtedly lead to bigger fish. He told Leslie to rejoin Jeff at Hassani's apartment complex.

Harry was just pulling up to his home when his cell phone rang.

"Harry, its Phelps. I wanted to let you know that we have made a lot of progress in a short time. We have uncovered a terrorist cell working out of Breckenridge, and we believe they will try to rescue or more likely eliminate the wounded hostage you captured at the Eisenhower Tunnel. We also found information that suggests these guys want to terrorize other hospitals at popular ski resorts. They have floor plans for the Aspen Valley Hospital, Vail Valley Medical Center, and Yampa Valley Hospital in Steamboat Springs. We also uncovered the materials needed to make four suicide bombs."

"Do you need help taking these guys down?"

"No, I think we can handle this without your help, but thanks for the offer. We will need to bring in additional operatives now anyway to help at the other three locations."

Harry got out of his car just as the snow began to fall. He entered his home through the mud room, took off his coat and shoes, and fixed himself a drink. Grace was not home yet from her errands, so Harry decided to light a fire in the fireplace and relax until she arrived. He thought about the reasoning behind suicide bombings at ski resort hospitals. This would certainly be devastating to the future economics of the area and clearly plausible since at present there was absolutely no precedent that would keep the local law enforcement on alert.

He had thought that moving to Colorado and settling in a small town would eventually allow him to heal from the events of 9/11. It was apparent to him now that this would not be the case until the Islamic extremists were defeated. Their funding needed to be cut off, and there needed to be a better understanding of the underlying psychological motivation of the suicide bombers. Suicide bombing in particular as a weapon was very difficult to understand from a Western perspective. Suicide is contrary to Islamic law, so suicide bombers must consider themselves as martyrs in a fight for freedom rather than committing an act of suicide. A better understanding of the loss of self-esteem, humiliation, and hate seemed to be the key to combating this form of terrorism.

Harry decided that it would be prudent to alert Kathy at the hospital. He found her office number in his cell phone and was lucky to catch Prudence before she left for the day.

Prudence remembered him and said, "Please hold for a moment? Kathy is in the process of finishing an interview with a recent graduate for the position of assistant administrator."

"Of course, Prudence, and how are things at the hospital?"

"It has been pretty hectic since we are in the peak of our season now, and almost all the beds are filled. She is coming out of her office now, Detective. I'll connect you in a second." Kathy said, "Hello, Harry, how can I help you?"

"I'm not sure how to tell you this without alarming you, but I have information that there may be an attempt at a suicide bombing at your hospital. They also have plans to hit the hospitals in Steamboat Springs and Vail."

"How do you know about this, Harry?"

"A team from the NCS working in Breckenridge discovered the plot while they were guarding a terrorist that we captured at the Eisenhower Tunnel."

"What can I do to protect my patients and staff?"

"My friend who is in charge of the operation is dispatching some agents to your facility as we speak. Go over your employee list and see if there is anybody that could be involved from the inside—possibly a recently hired employee or an employee that fits the terrorist profile. I'm sorry to ask you to profile, but at this time it makes the most sense. Call me if you turn up any suspects."

Chapter 37

March 2008

THE WEATHER WAS beginning to change in the Aspen area. It was already getting warmer, and although the depth of snow was higher than it had been for many years at the four ski resorts in the Aspen area, everybody had the sense that winter was over and spring skiing was about to commence. Ed decided to get one more ski trip in before the ski season ended. He was able to get a flight into Denver with a connection on United Express to Aspen.

The sky was clear, and the temperature was thirty degrees when he stepped off the plane at Aspen Airport at the foot of Buttermilk Mountain. He always had the same feeling of excitement combined with a sense of pending relaxation every time he felt the cool, crisp air of the Rockies. The mountains were covered with snow, and he knew it would be a great ski week. He rented a car and was at his town house by 2 pm, just as the stock market was closing in New York. He had anticipated an attempted rally this quarter that would fool everybody into thinking that the bear market that began last October would not continue to destroy wealth. Oil was on a rampage, and it was predicted that crude oil futures would hit one hundred dollars a barrel. Bonds had been trading in a tight range since the beginning of the year, but he knew that when the bear market in stocks resumed, the bond market would rally in earnest as a safe haven for conservative investors.

He called Kathy at work to let her know he had arrived. He then called Jack and Penny and left a message for them to call him back so they could make arrangements to ski together as well as have dinner this weekend.

Ed lit the fire in the fireplace, put on some classical music, and relaxed on the couch with a glass of wine. The phone rang and Ed answered, "Hello."

"Hi, Ed, it's Penny. How are you?"

"Great! What's going on?"

"Good news! Jack is meeting with his attorney today and signing the final papers for a summary judgment. He will be dropped from the case since it has become clear that Mr. Kahn's complications occurred because the nurse tampered with his medications, and that resulted in his failure to remain anticoagulated. However, the hospital is still involved in the case since the nurse was an employee."

Ed said, "So when are we going to celebrate?"

"Jack is off this weekend, so we thought we would ski together tomorrow and have dinner together tomorrow night if that's okay with you and Kathy."

Ed said, "I can't see why not. Let's meet at nine at the new base village in Snowmass." "Sounds good. See you at nine." Ed was concerned that the attorneys for the hospital would want to settle the case, and he knew this was not the view that Kathy held. He hoped she would be able to prevail in the decision-making process, but he also knew that at times the insurance companies would rather settle a case for a reasonable sum of money than take a chance on losing, especially when they were the only defendant.

Loretta Smyth arrived at Sam and Evelyn Kahn's apartment in Manhattan in the late afternoon. She had arranged to meet with the Kahns, Gary Goldman, and Ralph Ruderman from the SEC. She also had arranged for several shifts of operatives to guard the Kahns. The apartment was on the twelfth floor. It was small but well decorated with hardwood floors, stylish wallpaper, and large floor-to-ceiling windows which provided a beautiful view of the city.

Loretta introduced herself and showed her identification to Gary Goldman and Ralph Ruderman. She looked directly into Sam Kahn's eyes and said, "I appreciate your cooperation, and I want you to understand that we feel this whole ordeal will soon come to a close. However, at the present time we are concerned with your safety. We have you under constant surveillance. We will not discuss who they are or where they are located, but this a priority case for us." Sam and Evelyn nodded as if they understood, and then they both looked to Gary Goldman for reassurance. Loretta then turned to Goldman and Ruderman and added, "We are also willing and able to protect both of you if you so desire, but we feel that your risk level is low at this time."

Gary then said, "I agree, Miss Smyth, and we will defer to your judgment. I believe we may have only scratched at the surface of this ring of hedge funds that are probably linked to the Middle East and are utilizing insider information. We have identified a single investor that is involved with at least ten hedge funds reporting extraordinary profits for several years. All of these funds trade oil, oil-related options, and ETFs."

"How high were the profits, Mr. Ruderman?"

"Always in excess of 20 percent per year and on several occasions as high as 50 percent return to the investors."

"I will need to know the names of these funds and, more importantly, the name of the investor involved with all of these groups. I must tell you that these people are definitely involved in funding terrorism, and we are very close to closing down one of their cells in the Colorado area." Ruderman handed Loretta the file containing the names she needed. Loretta added, "Thank you for your cooperation. It's about time that all of our agencies cooperated in matters as important as this. Let's take a look at the data you guys have collected."

Loretta, Gary, and Ralph sat themselves around the dining room table and began pouring over the data. Sam and Evelyn went into the kitchen, where Evelyn began to prepare dinner. Loretta noticed the difficulty Sam had in getting up from a sitting position. After finally balancing himself with his walker, he slowly made his way into the kitchen with Evelyn's help.

Evelyn whispered to Sam, "I really feel good about her. I have a sense that she will protect us and keep us safe. How do you feel about her?"

Sam smiled and said in a soft and stuttering voice, "She is too beautiful to be that tough!"

They both laughed, and then Evelyn said, "I'm glad you're getting better, Sam."

After an hour of discussion, Loretta stood up and said, "This information is really helpful. I will set up a task force of agents to track down each of these hedge funds and begin questioning the managing partners. We will also try to locate Al-Shamir. He is probably the supplier of the inside information." They all shook hands, and after saying good-bye to Sam and Evelyn, they left the apartment.

Loretta began walking toward her hotel in midtown just as the sun was setting over the city. She flipped open her cell phone and called James Phelps to inform him of the information she had just received and to let him know what she planned to do next. The streets were relatively empty at this time, but she noticed that two young men across the street were walking in the same direction as her. At first she didn't think anything was unusual, but to play it safe she began to walk faster and noticed that they also quickened their pace. Fortunately, one of the operatives placed in the apartment across the street from the Kahn's apartment also noticed the two men and notified another of the operatives who was posing as a cab driver. He pulled his cab around the corner and slowly passed Loretta to let her know he was nearby if his assistance was needed. Loretta adjusted her earpiece of the two-way micro headset that her team was using for communication at close distances.

The voice on the other end came in clearly and said, "Should I pick these guys up or let them follow you for a while?"

"Follow," she said. She only had another two blocks to walk to the Grand Hyatt on 42nd Street. The two men continued to follow her but made no attempt to contact her or get any closer than a comfortable following distance. As she entered the hotel lobby and mixed in with the crowd, she said into her two-way device, "Just follow those guys and see where they lead you. I'll be okay here in the hotel."

The two men hung around in the lobby awhile and then left in separate directions. The operatives decided that their services were best served back at the Kahn's apartment, so they did not pursue either of the men and returned to their post across the street from the Kahn's apartment to complete their shift.

Loretta ordered dinner from room service and spent the rest of the evening organizing the teams to investigate the hedge fund managers and track down their clients and respective financial records. When she was finished, she double locked her door and went to sleep with her pistol at her side.

Chapter 38

March 2008

PINTO LEFT THE prisoner's room after less than an hour of interrogation. He had been able to obtain the information he needed without extreme measures of torture by just applying pressure to the prisoner's surgical sites and threatening to alter his traction setup. The terrorist's name was Ismail, and he was born in Denver soon after his parents moved here from Saudi Arabia. Ismail was only eighteen years old and had no plans to further his education as he was satisfied with his job as a clerk in a neighborhood grocery store. He was educated in the Denver school system and belonged to a mosque in the northeast area of Denver. Ismail's only friends were the young men associated with the mosque and, as was typical of his circle of friends, he had not dated or had any female relationships. He was a member of a terrorist cell that was associated with the mosque, and the cell's funding came directly from that mosque.

The only name other than those in his cell that he was familiar with in relation to the murder of Pete Jensen was a man named Ahmed. Ismail didn't have any information in regards to the mechanisms of funding of the mosque and sadly he didn't even know why they were assigned to kill Pete Jensen other than the fact that Jensen was a traitor to their cause. When asked about the nature of their cause, Ismail answered very bluntly that the goal of the Islamic jihad was to convert or eliminate all nonbelievers in pure Islamic beliefs. He was taught that everyone should practice pure Islam as it was practiced during the time of Muhammad the Prophet. Pinto thought to himself that this type of indoctrination was so typical of political and power-hungry extremists who used religion as their motivating tool to get young and inexperienced men and women to perform such ungodly acts on their behalf.

Pinto entered the administrator's office and went directly through the side door to the conference room where he met with James Phelps and Andy Regalto. He quickly went over the details of his interrogation and assured them that he had obtained all the information that this young man could offer to them. He was also convinced that the prisoner had no knowledge concerning Fakih Hassani or the other Arabs in the Breckenridge area.

Phelps decided that it would probably be better to detain Hassani and his buddies as soon as possible rather than continue with his original thought of tracking them for a while. They could transfer the entire cell directly to the Guantanamo Detention Center in Cuba. Phelps decided that they could transport them out of Colorado from the Eagle-Vail Airport, which was less than one hour away with the help of the Colorado National Guard. The airlift squadron was based at Buckley Field in Aurora, Colorado, and had the role of meeting both state and federal mission responsibilities. Phelps felt he could arrange a pickup at the Eagle-Vail Airport without much hassle or red tape. He would go to his superior to get this arranged.

It was late in the afternoon and the sky was still clear. Jeff Ronson and Leslie Rosario were keeping watch over Hassani's apartment building. Just as Hassani was rounding the corner to enter his building, he was joined by three other young Arab men. They quickly entered the building and disappeared from sight.

Ronson had planted a listening device in the apartment under the dining room table after he had replaced the materials the terrorists planned to use to make the suicide bombs. It was nearing sunset, and the agents knew it was time for the men to get ready to recite Maghrib, which was the fourth prayer of the day and took place immediately after sunset. Since there was no mosque in Breckenridge, Jeff and Leslie figured they were going to pray together at Hassani's apartment. They adjusted their earpieces so they could hear what Hassani and his accomplices were saying.

"Let's straighten the apartment before prayers," Hassani said. The others agreed, and they worked in silence. Hassani opened his computer and went directly to his e-mail page.

He said, "We have a message from Ahmed." The others were rolling out their prayer rugs, but they immediately came over to view the computer screen. Ahmed's message was brief but clear. Hassani read the message aloud for the others to hear. "I am on my way to Breckenridge and will take charge of the operation. I expect to arrive by car at 7 PM and will come directly to the apartment. I will call for directions as I approach Breckenridge on I-70."

They looked at each other with expressions of surprise as well as apprehension. It was time for prayers. They knelt on their prayer rugs, which were facing toward Mecca, touched their foreheads to the floor, and commenced praying.

Leslie immediately called Phelps to inform him of Ahmed's arrival time and to see if he had specific orders for them. He decided to leave Pinto in Ismail's room to protect him in case there was an attempt to silence him, and he decided that Andy and he would join Leslie and Jeff for the capture of the terrorists. He notified the local police chief of their plan to capture the terrorists and asked him for backup, but he told the chief to stay clear of the area until he notified them to move in. The chief was agreeable and seemed to know his limitations and the limitations of his men.

The sun had completely set and the temperature had dropped to twenty degrees when James Phelps and Andy Regalto arrived at the building across from Hassani's apartment complex. They opened the back of their Ford Explorer and pulled out a variety of weapons. Phelps handed Andy Regalto the M4 Carbine, Leslie Rosario the Precision Arms sniper rifle, and Jeff Ronson used his own Colt .45 pistol. Phelps positioned Leslie on the rooftop across from Hassani's apartment where she would have a clear shot into the apartment. Phelps took the Glock 22 pistol and positioned himself with Andy and Jeff in the shadows across the street from Hassani's apartment complex. All cell phones were off since they were communicating with earpieces and the speaking devices attached to their wrists. They also could hear what was being said in Hassani's apartment. They were concerned about collateral damage but felt that the element of surprise would afford them the opportunity to capture the terrorists without the use of force.

208

Ahmed was sitting in the backseat of the Lincoln Continental as it made its way along I-70 from Denver toward Breckenridge. Bihir was driving, and Abbud was in the front seat. They were riding in silence, and it was obvious that Ahmed was in deep thought. He had dispatched several men from a cell which operated out of a mosque located in Soho in the lower eastside of Manhattan. They had been keeping Sam Kahn and his wife under surveillance since the Kahns had returned to New York. They reported back to Ahmed as soon as Loretta Smyth, Gary Goldman, and Ralph Ruderman showed up at the Kahns' apartment. They had followed Loretta back to her hotel and were waiting for orders from Ahmed to move forward in regards to Sam and Evelyn Kahn as well as Loretta Smyth, Pete Goldman, and Ralph Ruderman.

This particular cell was very large and was indebted to Al-Shamir. The mosque that supported the cell had received huge funds from Al-Shamir over the last several years and anticipated a large endowment this year since oil prices had been very volatile, which translated into significant profits for Al-Shamir. Ahmed had also planned to terrorize three ski resorts in Colorado and had cell members from the Denver mosque ready to be routed to Steamboat Springs, Vail, and Aspen. He hoped Al-Shamir would be satisfied with his plans and allow Ahmed back into his good graces. Ahmed's main concern at this time was that he did not know what danger could be waiting for them in Breckenridge since he didn't know if the captured cell member had divulged any information to the authorities. He also had not gotten any information from his informant inside the Denver FBI.

His thoughts were interrupted when Abbud turned and said, "We are approaching the Eisenhower Tunnel and should be in Breckenridge in about half an hour. Should I call ahead to Hassani and get the final directions to the apartment?"

Ahmed answered, "No, we will call when we get closer to our destination."

Phelps, Regalto, and Ronson sat in the shadows across from Hassani's apartment with a good view of all the entrances. It was getting colder, but they knew it wouldn't be long before the action began. Phelps had instructed Pinto to move Ismail to another floor in the hospital and not leave his side. Phelps had concerns about the other people living in the apartment, but there was not enough time to move them out. He felt if they were spotted it would ruin their chance for a surprise attack.

The Lincoln carrying Ahmed, Bihir, and Abbud came to a stop at the Chevron station just off I-70 at the exit to Breckenridge. Abbud got out to fill the gas tank while Bihir made the call to Hassani's apartment. Bihir got directions, and soon they slowly made their way toward the apartment complex.

As they approached the neighborhood, Ahmed said, "Drive by slowly but don't stop. I want to be sure it's safe to enter the complex." The Lincoln passed the entrance slowly, went around the corner, turned back on Main Street, and then parked on South Ridge Street, one block away. The entrance to Hassani's apartment was easily visible from this position. There was very little traffic on the street at the time, and no pedestrians were present on the sidewalks. Bihir and Abbud exited the car and walked toward the apartment building.

Phelps and his team watched closely as the two men entered the building. They heard the knock on the door by way of their listening devices, and then heard Bihir and Abbud enter the small apartment. Bihir made a quick search of the studio apartment while Abbud motioned to Hassani and his accomplices to wait in silence. When they were satisfied that the area was secure, Abbud opened the window facing the street so Ahmed could see him. Abbud left the window open and then quietly asked Hassani to show him the suicide vests. Ahmed waited in the Lincoln for several more minutes.

Phelps motioned to the other operatives to enter the building and notified Leslie to keep a close eye on the apartment through her sniper rifle sight.

Ahmed was just about to leave the Lincoln Town Car when he saw the operatives approach the building with their weapons out. As they ran into the building, Ahmed quickly pulled out his phone to call Bihir and warn him.

Ronson and Regalto were up the stairs and on the second floor quickly. The agents were just about to kick the door down and enter when two doors away a young woman carrying a baby entered the hall from her apartment. Regalto motioned for her to quickly leave the building. When the hall was clear, they kicked down the door and entered Hassani's apartment.

To their surprise, Hassani and his Arab accomplices were wearing the suicide vests with their hands on the trigger devices. Bihir and Abbud were standing beside them and appeared to be unarmed.

Regalto spoke into the microphone mounted on his wrist, "Boss, come up here pronto. These guys are threatening to blow themselves up, and it appears that there are enough explosives to take out a city block."

Phelps left his position across the street. He glanced at the Lincoln, but he could not see if there was anybody left inside since it was dark and the windows were tinted. He entered the building and ran up the stairs, taking the steps two at a time. As he entered the room, both Ronson and Regalto turned to address him, at which point Bihir reached under his overcoat to remove his Colt .45 from his shoulder holster.

Suddenly there was the crack of rifle fire from across the street, and Bihir went down with a bullet right in the center mass of his chest. Abbud rushed to his side, but it was obvious that he had died instantly. The other Arabs appeared frightened and began sweating profusely.

Phelps didn't know if they had recognized and fixed the explosive mechanism after Jeff had cut and crossed the wires. He had to decide if it was worth the gamble since these guys looked serious about giving their lives for the cause of Allah.

Abbud stepped back from the dead body of Bihir and shouted to the others, "Do it now, Allah Akbar!" Phelps knew that there was nothing he or anybody could say that would stop these young men from performing the act of suicide that they had been programmed to perform since early childhood. The amount of built-up hate and desperation could not be overcome by any words at this time.

He looked at them and said, "Is there anything we can do to stop this insane act?"

They looked at Phelps as if he had no understanding and simultaneously chanted, "Allah Akbar!" They then held their trigger mechanisms in the air and pushed on the red buttons in unison. The silence in the room was profound. The suicide bombers kept hitting the firing mechanisms over and over again, but to no avail. It was clear that Ronson's manipulation of the wires had not been noticed. Ronson and Regalto instructed the young men to lay face down on the floor. They were handcuffed and gagged. Abbud was watching in disgust, but he did nothing. He was also cuffed but not gagged by Andy, who had a grip on his right elbow. Suddenly they heard the screeching of tires through the open window.

Phelps ran to the open window and saw the Lincoln Continental backing up South Ridge Street. He spoke into his mouthpiece to Leslie, "Can you get off a shot at that Lincoln? I think it contains the leader of this group."

Leslie pointed her sniper rifle in the direction of the moving Lincoln and said, "Sorry, Boss, I don't have a clean shot."

Phelps quickly pulled out his cell phone and called the Breckenridge police chief and asked him to attempt to locate and apprehend the Lincoln and its driver. Abbud was glaring at Phelps, and with a sudden twisting motion he freed himself from Andy Regalto's grasp and began running toward Phelps, who stood at the open window. Jeff Ronson was standing over the suicide bombers on the floor, but he saw what was happening and quickly fired two shots from his Colt .45, bringing Abbud down.

Phelps rushed to Abbud's side and saw that he was bleeding from his mouth and gasping for air. Phelps said, "Who is your leader?"

Abbud looked up at Phelps and muttered through gritted teeth, "Allah, Allah, Allah." He was dead in less than a minute.

Ahmed left the car two blocks from the apartment complex and disappeared on foot into the crowd that was gathering on Main Street. Phelps called Pinto at the hospital to be sure that the prisoner was in a safe location. Pinto informed him that he had moved the prisoner from the surgical floor to the medical ward one floor below and he would stay with him throughout the night.

Chapter 39

------◆◆◆◆◆------

March 2008

IT WAS SIX in the morning, and the temperature was eighty-two degrees when the Colorado National Guard Airlift Squadron plane landed at the Guantanamo Bay Naval Base located on the southeastern shore of Cuba. The plane was carrying the five prisoners from Breckenridge along with Amran Pinto. There were three National Guard soldiers present to aid Pinto during the flight. The prisoners were handcuffed and chained together in such a fashion that kept them from moving off their assigned seats along the inside of the plane across from Pinto and the guards.

These prisoners were to be held along with many other alleged enemy combatants who were not protected by the Geneva Conventions since they were not members of a known armed force of a country and did not wear a uniform that would identify them as members of an organized army. They would be interrogated to get information about the terrorist organizations they were associated with. An attempt would be made to secure information on the mechanisms of funding for those organizations. Everybody working at Gitmo knew that their days were numbered since there was such a growing world opinion against the persistence of the detention center and its role as an interrogation center. Interrogations had been carried out around the clock recently in hopes of getting critical information for the fight against terrorism. Amran Pinto was to begin his questioning as soon as the prisoners were processed. He knew the pressure was on, so he would use any of the techniques available to him to get the needed information.

Loretta Smyth had begun her day early, contacting the respective FBI agents assigned around the country to track down the other nine hedge funds involved with the investor named Al-Shamir. She was going to handle Mitch Carsdale and Jonathan Salem of Capital Investors of America herself.

She decided to call them to set up a meeting posing as a representative of a wealthy client that wanted to invest in their fund. She had obtained the fake identification and business cards that were needed. She made arrangements with the partners of the Washington firm she was pretending to represent to answer any questions that were asked to backup her story. She went by the name of Mindy Reynolds, and her title was Investment Advisor for the firm of Edgemont Investment Advisors. The secretary for Capital Investors of America scheduled the meeting for this afternoon at their offices in midtown Manhattan.

Loretta checked with the agents guarding Sam and Evelyn Kahn and was informed that it was quiet at that location. She advised them to stay on their toes and also told them she would need backup to deter the Arab men who had followed her last evening if they showed up again in the morning. She did not want them to know that she was meeting with Salem and Carsdale. She was assured that there would be an agent watching her back closely.

The weather had turned cold and windy, so she decided to take a cab from her hotel. As Loretta walked through the lobby, she again noticed the two Arab men from the evening before hanging out near the front entrance. They were well dressed and blended in with the rest of the hotel clientele. She walked through the lobby without paying any attention to them and was hopeful that her backup was in place. The two men began to follow her out the front door, but when she looked back out of the rear window of her cab, she noticed that they were not following her any longer and were instead handcuffed and being escorted into a black Ford Explorer by two of her backup operatives.

Loretta arrived at the meeting a little early and spent the time chatting with the secretary to find out what Mitch Carsdale and Jonathan Salem were like. The secretary's name was Adi, and she was a young woman in her twenties. She was more than willing to talk about her bosses.

Loretta asked, "What are your bosses like?"

Adi smiled and said, "Jonathan is all business, but Mitch is more sociable, single, and quite a womanizer. I'm sure he will like you, Mindy."

Loretta removed her coat and gloves and said, "Thanks for the info; I'm sure it will come in handy."

Adi said, "No problem."

Loretta then took a seat in the waiting area. After a few minutes, Jonathan came out to the reception area and introduced himself. He escorted her to a conference room located in the rear section of the office space. As they walked through the offices, she saw several young men and women in front of computer screens with real-time charts and quotes in front of them. They were busy and didn't even look up as she passed. Some were on the phone talking to floor brokers, and others were making trades on line. They arrived at the glass-enclosed conference room, which afforded a view of the entire bank of trading desks.

Mitch stood and introduced himself as Loretta entered the room. He was obviously awestruck by her beauty. He offered her a drink as she approached the conference table. She declined the drink and opened her computer bag. She handed each of them her card and then took a seat at the conference table.

Loretta opened the conversation by saying, "I can see you gentleman have quite an operation going on here. I took the liberty of reviewing your performance and comparisons to other hedge funds in the Morningstar Hedge Fund rating service, and I can tell you that I was amazed by your growth statistics as compared to the S&P 500, especially in the last fifteen months."

Jonathan smiled and said, "As you know we trade oil futures and oil-related products such as drillers and large oil companies, and as I'm sure you are aware we have been in an oil-related bull market since the beginning of 2007."

"Yes, I am aware of that, Jonathan, but you have returns in excess of 12 percent every month, even when the oil market was in a trading range for an entire quarter like we had at the end of 2007."

Mitch smiled and said, "That's why they call it a hedge fund."

215

Loretta looked into his eyes, held his gaze for a long time, and then said, "I also compared you to all the funds that trade oil and are large enough to be considered in Morningstar, and with the exception of a handful of other funds, your fund was always rated in the top 2 percent. I reviewed your risk-analysis profile to see if your fund was taking extraordinary risk and if it had standard deviations that exceeded other funds. Again I found no significant excess risk taking."

Jonathan seemed a little nervous and said with a slight stutter, "We are proud of our trading skills, Miss Reynolds, and I can assure you that our risk profile is low compared to other commodity-trading funds."

Loretta then inquired, "Can you go over your fee structure and bonus situation?" Jonathan rose and said, "I will get you our standard contract, which has our fee structure and performance fee. You will also see that our minimum initial purchase is one million dollars, and you can redeem semiannually." He left the room, and Loretta saw him stop at one of the trading desks and give an order on his way to his private office.

Mitch said, "If you don't have any plans for the rest of the afternoon, maybe you would like to go out for drinks when we are finished here?"

"Sounds good to me, Mitch. To tell you the truth, I was so impressed with your performance ratings that I haven't even made any other appointments today. Do you mind if I ask you a question about Jonathan?"

Mitch asked, "What kind of question?"

"He is obviously of Arab descent, and I was wondering if he is a Muslim."

"Yes, he is an active member of a midtown mosque."

Loretta then said in a somewhat sultry way, "So, since he doesn't drink, it will only be you and I having drinks?"

Mitch smiled and said, "If that's okay with you." She smiled.

Jonathan went to his computer in his office and looked up the firm that she claimed to represent. He found their Web site but did not find her name mentioned in their advertisement. He was somewhat suspicious, so he called the firm and inquired as to her credentials. He spoke to one of the partners and was pleased to find out that she was one of their newest and most promising young financial analysts and advisors. He still felt that something was wrong, but he could not put his finger on what it was. Maybe she was too good to be true?

Jonathan returned with the contract, offered it to her, and said, "Miss Reynolds, I think you will find this contract very straightforward."

She quickly reviewed the contract and then asked, "I see that we can add one million dollars to our investment on a yearly basis, but how long is the initial lockup period?"

Jonathan answered, "One year is standard for most funds, but we are so confident that we will have very few redemptions that we allow the first redemption in six months. We do, however, require thirty business days advance notice for redemptions."

Loretta stood, shut down her computer, and took off her jacket. She was wearing a black silk fitted blouse and tight-fitting pants that showed off her athletic body. Both Jonathan and Mitch could not keep their eyes off her. When she looked up at them Jonathan quickly averted his eyes, but Mitch held her glance as she knew he would. She said, "I hope you don't mind my asking, but do you use technical or fundamental analysis as your main trading tool?"

Jonathan said, "Supply and demand is what makes commodities move, so we use fundamental analysis as our main tool."

"What service do you use to get that information?"

Jonathan stood and said, "That is proprietary information, Mindy. None of our clients have that information."

Loretta then said, "I don't see why it should be a big secret, but if that is one of your stipulations, so be it. I can't think of any further questions, gentleman. Could you point me to the ladies room, please?" Mitch directed her to an additional set of offices and restrooms on the other side of the bank of computers.

When she left, Mitch thought to himself that they had acquired another client that would bring in a 1 percent fee and 20 percent of profit performance bonus. Mitch smiled and said, "I will close this deal over drinks, and I hope I will get a lot more tonight." Jonathan did not smile back and remained silent.

Loretta worked her way into the accountant's office. She was curious to see who had replaced Sam Kahn. She was not surprised to find a young Arab man sitting in front of his computer going over reams of trading printouts. She introduced herself as a new client.

The young man stood, shook her hand, and said with an accent that was clearly British, "It's a pleasure to meet you."

Loretta then said, "How did such a young man get such an important job?"

He smiled and said sheepishly that his uncle was a major investor in the fund and that the previous accountant had taken ill suddenly last summer.

She said, "Lucky for you." She turned and was about to leave, but then she turned back and asked in a casual manner, "Who is your uncle?"

He was about to answer when Mitch approached from around the corner and said, "I see you met our accountant."

She answered, "Yes, I have, Mr. Carsdale, and I believe it's time for that drink you promised." She took his arm, and they went back to the conference room where she packed up her computer. She looked at Jonathan and said, "How can I be sure that you guys are not running some form of Ponzi scheme?"

He responded in a somewhat condescending tone, "If you review our client enrollments and profit payments, you will see that there is no evidence of a pyramid system being formed, and you will also see that our clients take their quarterly profits out of the fund on a regular basis."

"I would like to go over those client enrollments and payment schedules, if you don't mind."

Mitch interrupted and said, "We will prepare that information for you, but we will have to keep our clients names confidential."

She said, "Of course." She said good-bye to Jonathan, put on her jacket and coat, grabbed her computer, and left the office with Mitch.

They walked for a while in silence, and then Loretta said, "Where are we going?"

"I thought you would like the Latitude Bar, which is just a few blocks walking distance. It's one of my favorites, and if we feel like staying for dinner they have pretty good food." "Sounds good, but I doubt I can stay for dinner. I have a lot on my plate for tomorrow." "We'll see about that," he said. It was still cloudy and cold as they entered the bar. They checked their coats and went directly to the third-floor VIP lounge. They sat in a booth by a fireplace.

The waitress who came over to take their order immediately recognized Mitch and said, "How can I help you, Mr. Carsdale?"

He looked at Loretta and said, "Is champagne okay with you?"

"Can we save it for another time, Mitch? I will just have a glass of chardonnay."

The waitress looked at Mitch for his order, and he said, "Make that two of your best chardonnays."

As the waitress walked away, she looked back over her shoulder at Mitch with an expression that said, "Not tonight, Mitch."

Mitch said, "So, do you think we have a deal?"

"I can't see any reason that my client would not take my advice and place his money with you."

"How much money do you have to place for your client?"

Loretta answered, "Ten million for oil and another ten million to place in gold funds. I believe the downtrend in gold is about to end and thought we could catch the bottom here."

"It is pretty risky for you to place so much money on a contra-trend move."

"The market rewards risk takers, Mitch, but enough market talk for now." She moved closer to him, and he could smell the fragrance of her perfume. He was overwhelmed by her beauty, and it seemed to him that the attraction was mutual.

The waitress came over to the table, placed the drinks in front of them, and said, "Enjoy."

As they clinked glasses, Loretta said, "To a long-lasting relationship." They both took a taste of the wine.

He put his glass down and said, "Where did you say your office was?"

"I'm from Washington DC."

"Are all the women there as beautiful as you?" She smiled and took another sip of her wine. "Will you be in the city much longer?" he asked.

"Depends on how things go tomorrow."

He then asked, "Are you married, engaged, or dating anybody?"

"Recently ended a relationship," she answered.

"Did you get burned badly?"

"Not at all. I just felt that I wasn't attracted to him any longer. He is a very kind and gentle soul, but to be honest I just wasn't attracted to him any longer and our relationship lacked excitement."

"Well, let's see if I can provide you with a little excitement while you're in the Big Apple!"

She laughed and said, "I think I might take you up on your offer. Perhaps tomorrow night, assuming I complete all the deals I've been working on. So please tell me there is no wife in the suburbs waiting for you to come home."

He didn't answer right away but then said, "If there was a wife somewhere, I believe I would get a divorce just so I could be with you."

They both laughed, and then she looked at her watch and said, "I really have to get going."

He picked up his glass of wine, took one last sip, and said, "Can I assume we will get together tomorrow for dinner?"

She stood and said, "I'm looking forward to it."

They left the Latitude Bar just as the afternoon rush-hour traffic was beginning to accumulate. It was still cold and windy.

Mitch said, "Shall I get you a cab?"

"No, thanks, I think I will walk since it's only two blocks to my hotel."

He responded, "Suit yourself." They began walking in opposite directions, but she could sense that he was watching her, so she turned, smiled, and waved good-bye.

She looked around carefully for anybody that might be following her and was satisfied that her encounter with Mitch and Jonathan had gone unnoticed. Her next move was to get inside that office with a couple of operatives and find the addresses of the investors, with special attention to Al-Shamir.

It was three in the afternoon when Ahmed reached the Denver mosque. He was frustrated with the recent events since he had lost Abbud and Bihir, along with several young cell members, to the authorities. He still had not assured the safety of the trading groups, which meant there was the possibility of losing the future profits and subsequent funding of the jihad. He also had failed Al-Shamir in obtaining a suitable kidney donor for his father. He needed to spend an hour or so with the imam at the mosque to try to come up with a plan that would allow him to recoup his standing with Al-Shamir and the leaders of the jihad.

Phelps, Ronson, Rosario, and Regalto were packing up their equipment when Pinto called from Gitmo with information he had obtained from the captured cell members.

He said, "Boss, I know this is early in the interrogation, but these guys were going to utilize one of the suicide bombs at the hospital in Breckenridge, and they intended to utilize the remaining three suicide bombs to attack other hospitals at ski resort locations in Colorado. This correlates with the information Leslie got off their computer yesterday. We have disrupted that plan, but as you know their leader escaped and we must assume he is going to carry out this mission. I'm not sure how much more information these guys have, but rest assured I will get it out of them."

Phelps smiled and said, "I know you will."

Ed finished a great day of skiing with Penny and Jack. He called Kathy when he got back to his condominium in Snowmass Village. "Kathy, I really missed you today."

"I would have loved to join you guys, but we have been searching through our list of employees for a possible terrorist or accomplice to a terrorist act. I have to tell you, it is so weird profiling your own employees. So far we have not come up with anybody who fits the profile of a terrorist."

Ed said, "Maybe the whole thing is just a hoax or scare tactic?"

Kathy answered, "I don't think Harry is the type of detective to overreact. In any event, it would be better to be as prepared as possible."

Ed said, "I guess you're right. This is getting so disturbing. I can't leave you at the hospital alone. What about Laura and your mother? Are they okay?"

"Yes, they are staying home and I will give them a call later. I'm also waiting for a call from Harry to see if we need to evacuate the patients and staff or if they will be sending agents here to help defend the hospital. Ed, this is really a mess."

Ed said, "I'll come over to the hospital to be with you, and maybe I can be of some help." "That would be great. I'll be in my office. Please come soon."

Chapter 40

March 2008

AHMED KNEW IT would not be long before the Denver mosque was raided. He assumed the captured cell members would not be able to resist the interrogation techniques of the operatives who had caught them, but he had acquired enough additional cell members to at least carry out the mission at one of the ski resorts. He had the name of a real estate company in Aspen that had previously arranged rentals for Al-Shamir and his family. The cell was now to occupy one of the Meadow Ranch condominiums in Snowmass Village. This location was quiet and only fifteen minutes from Aspen Valley Hospital. The imam picked his most reliable and dedicated cell members to assist Ahmed and in addition gave him one of his own cars to use for transportation to the mountains. He also informed Ahmed that he was having the other cell members tested to see if there was a match for the much-needed kidney for Al-Shamir's father's kidney transplant.

Ahmed and the three cell members left for Aspen following afternoon prayers. They had loaded the needed equipment to make explosives into suitcases, and for all intents and purposes they looked like a group of young men going on a ski vacation. Their ages ranged from nineteen to twenty-five. They all carried their prayer rugs and wore white skullcaps. They were all born in the United States and would probably have turned out to be average Muslim Americans except for the fact that they were all trained in the religious school of this particular mosque, which introduced them to radical Islam. Their educations were paid for by the mosque, and their parents received a monthly stipend from the mosque. They were trained and ready to be sent anywhere in the world to perform whatever acts of terrorism that were needed in the struggle for dominance over Christianity and Judaism. They were taught that these religions of the Book had misinterpreted the word of God and only through the revelations of the Prophet Muhammad could God's teachings be revealed. They were taught that the infidels must either convert to Islam or be annihilated. This included women and children as well as noncombatant men. The ancient Islamic teachings of tolerance of and cooperation with other religions had been abandoned by these extremists.

Loretta called Phelps after she returned to her hotel. She informed him of her meetings with Kahn, Ruderman, Goldman, and Capital Investors of America. She said, "Boss, we have enough information to link this hedge fund to Al-Shamir, and I am confident that the other agents will come up with similar information when they investigate the other nine hedge funds. I would like to break into the offices of Capital Investors of America this evening. I need an IT guy from the FBI to hack into their computer. This will give us backup information that will corroborate the testimonies from Sam Kahn and the SEC."

Phelps said, "I will arrange for the assistance you need for tonight. Stay put, and I will get back to you in less than an hour." Loretta decided this was a good time to go to the gym and workout. She changed, grabbed her cell phone, and headed to the workout room of the hotel.

Phelps called his boss in Washington and got the needed assistance for Loretta in NY. He then called Harry in Basalt. "Harry, I need to let you know that the potential for a terrorist attack at Aspen Valley Hospital is very real, along with similar potential attacks at the hospitals in Vail and Steamboat Springs. We will be dispatching agents to your area as well as the other resorts as soon as possible."

Harry said, "I will do everything I can to help. I will call the hospital administrator as well as alert the local police of the potential threat."

Harry called Aspen Valley as soon as he got off the phone with Phelps. He reached Kathy's office and said, "Prudence, I need to speak to Kathy as soon as possible."

"She is presently in a meeting with her staff."

"Can you interrupt her for a moment?"

"Give me a second, Harry."

Harry waited and began planning what needed to be done next. He needed to meet with the Aspen chief of police and the Pitkin County sheriff.

His thoughts were interrupted when Kathy got on the phone and said, "What can I do for you, Harry?"

"I wanted to let you know that this threat is real. I want to set up a meeting with you, the sheriff, and the chief of police for this evening."

Kathy said, "Harry, I'm really nervous about all this. I can't believe this is really happening. This seems so farfetched."

Harry responded, "Try to remain calm. We have time to prepare, and I really trust the help we will be getting."

Kathy then said in a calmer voice, "I will be here at the hospital this evening, and we can use our conference room. Just give me a few minutes' warning before you get here."

"See you soon, Kathy." Harry walked into his boss's office to update him on the most recent events and asked Chief Owens to arrange a meeting at the hospital with the Aspen chief of police and the Pitkin County sheriff for 5 PM.

Chief Owens said, "Harry, I thought you left New York to get away from this sort of thing."

"I guess there is no escaping this problem. Terrorism is a way of life for these radical Islamists, and we will never be free of their tyranny until we stop the flow of money that supports these acts of terrorism. It's publicity they are seeking—it's their way of striking terror. What better place than famous ski resorts to get the press coverage they thrive on? Even though Aspen, Vail, and Steamboat Springs are small towns, they will still serve their purpose."

"You do realize that you will have no jurisdiction in Aspen?"

"I understand that, Chief, but I feel obligated to help them. I am the one person in this area with some experience in terrorism. In addition to that, I am friends with the man running the show from the NCTC."

Chief Owens said, "I will call and set up the meeting for you, Harry. Is there anything else we can do to help?"

"Not that I can think of now."

Phelps was busy arranging for additional NCTC operatives to be flown into the Eagle-Vail Airport to be dispatched to Vail and Steamboat Springs. He decided to take his team to Aspen. Phelps and his operatives packed their gear and headed west on I-70. Jeff Ronson was driving while Phelps was on his cell phone with his boss as well as Loretta and the other teams of operatives. He got everything arranged just as the sun was setting on their drive through Glenwood Canyon. A light snowfall had begun about two hours earlier, leaving a white blanket over the majestic ledges of the canyon and a beautiful white border on the edges of the Colorado River. The road was in good shape, and they made excellent time through the canyon to the exit that led onto Highway 82 at Glenwood Springs.

In the lobby of her hotel, Loretta met with the FBI agent who was going to assist her that evening. His name was Greg Fletcher, and he was a young man in his early thirties, thin, and of medium height. He had a well-trimmed beard and his hair was long, giving him the appearance of a college professor rather than an FBI agent. He was selected for his technological and computer skills, but he had also worked in the field and was familiar with the use of weapons.

They went over the floor plan of the office that Loretta had drawn from memory after her visit with Mitch and Jonathan. They decided to wait until later in the evening to break into the investment offices. They had to time their break-in so that they would avoid traders who may be trading oil contracts on the overseas market exchanges. This was difficult since crude oil not only traded at the NYMEX in NY but also at the ICE in London and most recently at the Dubai Mercantile Exchange. Loretta felt the best chance of going uninterrupted would be in the early evening. They decided to approach the building separately at 8 PM and meet in the main lobby of the building. Loretta had also arranged for backup from the FBI to be present at the office building.

Ed met with Jack, Penny, and Kathy at the hospital at 5 PM, just prior to Kathy's meeting with the police officers. They had decided to hang around at the hospital till Kathy was finished so they would be available if their help was needed. They went down to the cafeteria to get some coffee while they waited for Kathy to finish with her meeting.

Harry, the Aspen chief of police, and the Pitkin County sheriff arrived at the same time and went into the conference room with Kathy. Harry introduced himself to the other officers, and they all took seats around the large, oak conference table. Harry started the meeting with a brief statement of the facts as he understood them.

He said, "We have reason to believe that there is a group of Islamic terrorists heading our way to possibly detonate one or more explosive devices in the hospital. Agents from the NCTC are also on their way here to help. The man in charge is an old friend of mine from New York. We worked together in the aftermath of 9/11, and I can assure you he is the best agent for the job. There is also the possibility that similar attacks could be taking place in Steamboat Springs and Vail."

Kathy asked, "Why the hospital?"

Harry answered, "We don't know their reasons for attacking the hospital, but that is the information that the operatives were able to obtain."

The sheriff then said, "Harry, it makes no sense to try to outguess them. We should be ready for all the possibilities. We have a recently formed bomb squad that has been training for such an occasion. We can have them ready at a moment's notice."

The Aspen police chief then said, "We have a small force and unfortunately nobody has any antiterrorist training, but I will call in all of the shifts and be ready for whatever assistance is needed. We can also mobilize the EMS crew and the ski patrol team since they have training in emergency medical care."

Harry was satisfied that he had gotten their attention. They exchanged cell phone numbers and left the hospital. They each knew what was expected of them and were anxious to get back to their offices to make the necessary arrangements.

Ahmed and the cell members approached the Aspen area just as the sun was setting. It was still snowing lightly as they drove past the turnoff to Snowmass Village and headed toward Aspen on Highway

82. They passed the Aspen Airport and Buttermilk Ski Resort, and just prior to entering the turnabout they all caught a glimpse of the majestic, snow-covered Maroon Bells mountain range. They were all silent and clearly in awe of the area and its beauty.

Ahmed pointed out the turnoff to the hospital as they drove around the turnabout. They pulled up to the real estate office on Hyman Avenue, and Ahmed sent one of the young cell members into the office to get the keys to the condominium. He returned to the car in a few minutes and said, "No problem."

They drove around the town of Aspen for a few minutes prior to heading back to Snowmass Village, where they were planning to spend the next few nights. They passed the Aspen Gondola that carried skiers from the base to the top of Aspen Mountain. They also drove past many of the restaurants and bars, which were filled with people enjoying après ski. Just as they were heading out of town, one of the cell members in the backseat pointed out the Chabad synagogue on Main Street and the high steeple of the church in the same area as the hospital.

They drove on in silence and arrived at the Meadow Ranch complex in twenty minutes. They parked their car on Owl Creek Road and carried their baggage up the outdoor steps to their unit. They were just in time for evening prayers. The Meadow Ranch complex was a group of town houses and single-family homes separated by aspen-lined walkways. There are a lot of full-time residents who resided there as well as people who owned second homes in the development that they used for vacations as well as rental purposes.

Kathy returned to her office after the meeting with Harry, the chief of police, and the sheriff. Prudence was getting ready to leave for the day when Kathy walked into the office.

She said, "Kathy, is there anything I can do for you before I leave for the day?"

"I think we have done all we can for now. Before I leave I will stop by the ER and let them know what is going on and what will be expected of them in case we do have a terrorist attack. I will double check our employee list to see if any names appear suspicious. This whole thing is crazy."

Prudence started to leave, but she stopped next to Kathy and gave her a hug. She said, "It will all work out. I have faith in Harry." "Thanks, Prudence. I feel the same way about him. Why don't you go home and get some rest. I will call you later if we need you back here."

Just as Prudence was leaving the office, Penny, Jack, and Ed walked through the door with sandwiches and coffee.

Ed said, "We figured it will be a long night." Kathy looked at Ed and just smiled.

Phelps and his team arrived in Basalt at 6 PM and went directly to the police station to meet with Harry. Chief Owens and most of the staff had already left for the day, and the station was quiet. Phelps looked around and said, "Not exactly like your old precinct in Manhattan, is it, Harry?"

Harry smiled and said, "Not exactly. It certainly has been a lot safer, but now that you guys are here all that may change." They all nodded and smiled. Harry then said, "I got you rooms at the Inn at Aspen, which is located at the foot of Buttermilk Mountain and close to the airport. It is also located between Snowmass Village and Aspen and is within five minutes of the hospital. I assume you still think the hospital is the main target."

Phelps nodded in the affirmative and said, "That was the plan we got from their computer. However, they probably know that we have that information and know we have been interrogating the captured cell members, so I guess anything is possible. We are hoping that maybe they have given up the idea of a terrorist mission in this area. How did your meeting go with the local authorities?"

"They will be cooperative, and because of the nature of the area we have a lot of paramedics and ski patrol personnel who are all trained in rescue operations and acute medical care. They are being informed this evening of the potential threat. The hospital administrator and her staff have not been able to identify anybody that could be associated with this group of terrorists. There are two questions that we have not addressed. First, should we warn the public? Second, should we evacuate the hospital?"

Phelps looked at each member of his team and said, "I think I can speak for my entire team. We feel our best chance of putting this terrorist cell away is to be ready for them if they choose to come here. If we inform the locals and tourists, it could cause more fear and panic than an actual attack. Evacuation of the hospitalized patients also carries some risk. Let's face the facts. We have an open society, and a terrorist organization can attack at any time and anywhere with minimal effort, especially if they have no regard for their own lives. My team and our superiors feel we should try to anticipate their move and not inform the public."

Harry said, "If that's the case, then let's get started with your plan."

Chapter 41

March 2008

LORETTA AND GREG met in the lobby of the office building which housed the offices of Capital Investors of America. They were both dressed in black pants, black turtleneck shirts, and black jackets. The evening-shift guard was sitting behind his desk in front of a bank of screens which gave him access to the array of cameras located throughout the building. He was a young man in his late twenties, tall, and very muscular. He had the look of someone who had recently been in the military.

He rose when they approached and said, "The building is closed to visitors in the evening."

Loretta showed her credentials and said, "We need to get into the offices of Capital Investors of America. We have the authority and appropriate search warrant with us." She then took out the search warrant that Greg had obtained earlier in the day from a federal judge in Manhattan.

The guard then said, "It seems very unorthodox to enter a business office at night. I'm afraid I will need to call my supervisor before letting you into their offices."

Greg stepped up to the guard and said through gritted teeth, "Do it fast or we will take you in for obstruction of justice. Do you understand?"

The guard looked at both of them and after a few seconds agreed to let them up. He then said grudgingly, "There isn't anybody present in the offices at this time, so you will have to let yourself in by whatever means are at your disposal. That's the best I can do for you."

Loretta said, "That will not be a problem, and we can assure you that we will leave the place in the same shape that we found it." The guard pointed them to the elevator bank on the far side of the lobby.

Greg and Loretta went up to the seventh floor and without any difficulty picked the lock and entered the offices. Loretta directed Greg to the set of computers in the accountant's office. He sat down and began hacking into the needed files that would divulge the fund's economic data and the names and addresses of the investors. They left the lights off in all the other offices while Greg worked in the accountant's office.

The guard began to have second thoughts about how easily he had allowed Loretta and Greg to enter the offices of Capital investors of America. He called his supervisor, who said that he really had no choice since they had a search warrant. The supervisor then said he would call the renters and let them know what was happening.

Within a few minutes Jonathan was notified, and he immediately called Ahmed on his international cell phone. Ahmed was just finishing evening prayers with his group of cell members in Snowmass. He said that he would dispatch people from the Manhattan cell to address the situation. He advised Jonathan and Mitch to go to the office and see what they could do to delay the operatives. Jonathan then called Mitch, and they decided to meet in front of their building in a few minutes.

Loretta entered Mitch's private office and opened his computer. She was surprised to find out that his computer didn't need a password to initiate his desktop. She thought that this was just a manifestation of his arrogance. His desktop had multiple icons related to futures trading, such as eSignal and an RJO Vantage trading platform. He also had a few popular futures-trading newsletters as well as the Hightower report. She found a folder that contained a list of clients with information concerning their percent of ownership in the fund as well as profit-and-loss data for each investor. She was downloading the client folder onto a flash drive when she thought she heard a noise coming from the outer office.

While she was completing the download, she whispered into her wrist microphone for Greg to be careful because she thought she heard a noise in the outer office. She finished the download and shut off the desk lamp. She then shut down the computer and drew her Glock 23 pistol. She crawled along the floor to get a better view of the outer office, and then all of a sudden her gun was kicked out of her hand. She looked up to find two men standing over her and smiling. They were of obvious Arab descent and of medium build, and they were dressed in jeans, long-sleeved shirts, and leather jackets. They did not appear armed, but they certainly had a menacing appearance. Loretta did not see Greg, but she assumed he had not been seen since the accountant's office was located on the other side of the suite of offices. The larger of the two men reached down and pulled Loretta to her feet by her hair. She did not scream out or make a sound, which surprised both of the men. The one who had pulled her up now spun her around so he could have her in a stranglehold.

He then spoke into her ear with a British accent, "What do you think you are doing invading the privacy of this company?" She did not answer right away so he tightened his grip around her neck, causing her to gasp. Just then Greg turned on the office lights and came around the corner with his Walther P99 pistol drawn and aimed at the assailants. He put a round right in the kneecap of the man standing next to the one holding Loretta. He dropped to the floor in agony.

The man with the stranglehold on Loretta suddenly pulled out and opened a switchblade and placed it over the jugular vein in Loretta's neck. She moved without hesitation, planting the heel of her shoe on his toes and at the same time raising her head and striking him firmly on the chin. She then grabbed the hand that was gripping her neck and spun the man around and to the floor in a hammerlock position. He yelled out in pain and dropped his knife. She quickly handcuffed him. Greg came over, cuffed the other assailant, and used the man's belt as a tourniquet to stop the bleeding from his gunshot wound. Loretta then spoke into her wrist microphone for the backup FBI agents to call 9–1–1 for paramedics and local police.

Mitch and Jonathan saw the lights flick on in their office from their position across the street from their building. They entered the building and went directly to the elevators leading to their offices. They both noticed that the night guard was not at his desk.

Just as the elevator doors were about to close, two FBI agents stepped into the elevator. They had been watching Mitch and Jonathan from the shadows down the street. They smiled, and one of the agents said, "Can we join you boys?" They all exited the elevator together and went into the office waiting room, where Loretta and Greg had the two Arab assailants handcuffed with their arms behind their backs.

Mitch and Jonathan were noticeably surprised when they recognized Loretta. Jonathan said, "What is the meaning of this invasion of our privacy?"

Loretta ignored him at first and motioned for the agents to cuff both Jonathan and Mitch. She then called for transportation to transfer her captives to the FBI field office located at 26 Federal Plaza in Manhattan.

She then went up to Mitch and got close to his face and said, "Have you ever heard of the Patriot Act?" He didn't answer, so she said, "As controversial as the Patriot Act may be, it allows us to hold you and Jonathan because we have reason to believe that you are helping fund Islamic terrorism and doing it by taking advantage of information provided by an insider from an oil-producing Arab country. In addition, these two Arab buddies of yours just assaulted an officer of the law who had a warrant to search this office." Mitch and Jonathan didn't respond, but it was obvious that they were shocked they had actually been caught when they had always assumed that they had covered their tracks.

Phelps was happy to hear from Loretta and get her report of the events that took place in New York. He said, "I only hope that the agents in the other nine cities will be just as successful. As soon as you wrap things up there, I need you back here in Colorado."

The snow continued to fall throughout the early evening as Ahmed sat alone in front of the fireplace in the condominium at Meadow Ranch. He had sent the cell members out to get dinner and familiarize themselves with the area. He could feel the pressure that was mounting on him to accomplish an act of terrorism that could bring him back into a favorable position with Al-Shamir and his financial accomplices. He knew that this was the place that could bring a sufficient amount of media coverage and publicity to strike fear into the minds of wealthy American citizens. There were even a significant number of European and South American tourists in Aspen at this time since the U.S. dollar was weak against most foreign currencies. He was also confident that the cell members assigned to him would not hesitate to give their lives to please Allah and the Islamic fundamentalist movement. He decided to spend the next twenty-four hours devising a plot that would create the most havoc in the Aspen area.

Penny, Jack, Ed, and Kathy finished their sandwiches and coffee in the hospital cafeteria. They had decided to inform those physicians who had patients in the hospital of the potential threat. Those physicians would act in the best interest of their patients in deciding on the risk of continued hospitalization verses the risk of early discharge and outpatient care. Penny would take on the task of reviewing the disaster protocol with the nurses in the emergency room and the shift supervisors in the intensive care unit as well as the medical and surgical wards.

Kathy and Ed decided to take one last look at the employee list in hopes of spotting a recently hired suspicious person who may be connected to the terrorists. They finished around 9 PM and were obviously exhausted and frustrated.

Ed said, "Let's get out of here and go over to my place to relax for a while."

"Let me call my mother and be sure everything is okay with Laura."

Ed said, "I'm going to take a look around the hospital and get familiar with the layout while you make your phone call." When he returned he found Kathy ready to go with her coat, gloves, and hat already on. Ed grabbed his leather jacket and gloves, and they both exited through the rear exit to the employee parking lot. Ed had parked his rental car close to Kathy's Jeep Wrangler, and they followed each other to Ed's condo in Meadow Ranch.

It was still snowing lightly when they got out of their vehicles. Ed loved the feel and sound of the snow crunching under his boots. They held hands as they walked up the walkway to the condominium. Ed noticed that the lights were on in the unit further up the walkway and commented to Kathy that his neighbor must have gotten a renter for this week since it had been empty earlier. They entered through the lower-level entrance and took off their coats, gloves, and boots. The condo was dark as they climbed the stairs to the upper-level living room and kitchen. Ed put on some classical music and opened a bottle of chardonnay. He started a fire in the wood-burning fireplace. They toasted to good health.

Ed said, "Kathy, it's snowing and you're exhausted. Stay here tonight and I'll drive with you to the hospital in the morning. I'm not comfortable with you being there alone until this craziness is over."

"You're right. I just need to get some things out of my Jeep. I'm so glad you're here. Quite frankly, I'm terrified. This is no longer about somewhere else in the world."

As she was returning from her Jeep, she saw the village shuttle stop in front of the condominium complex and watched three men exit. They were all of medium build, wore dark clothing, and had on knitted ski caps. Kathy could not make out their faces. As they walked passed her, she said, "Good evening," but they continued up the steps to the next level of condominiums without answering her. She shrugged and entered Ed's condo. The two of them spent the rest of the evening relaxing by the fire and listening to classical music. They went to bed around eleven and fell asleep in each other's arms.

Chapter 42

March 2008

IT WAS FRIDAY morning, and the sky was only partly cloudy. It looked as if the weather would remain clear for the next twenty-four hours. Harry reasoned that if the terrorists were coming to Aspen it would probably take them a few days to get familiar with the area and plan their attack. He decided to call the Aspen chief of police and have his men begin calling all of the real estate brokers and hotel managers in the Aspen-Snowmass area to try to get information on recent short-term rentals in the area, especially if rented by those of Arab descent. The Aspen chief was agreeable, and Harry did the same for the area from Glenwood Springs to Basalt. It took most of the morning to complete his inquiries. There were no promising leads, but each of the real estate agencies and hotel managers he called took his cell phone number and promised to call if anyone suspicious turned up.

Harry left the police station around 8:30 AM and headed to Aspen to see what progress was being made by James Phelps and his operatives. When he arrived at the Inn of Aspen at the foot of Buttermilk Mountain, he located Phelps and his team in the conference room on the first floor of the inn. They had maps of Aspen and Snowmass spread out on a table and were planning to use an approach of patrol and containment of the area using an operative teamed up with a local police officer.

Phelps said, "We are planning to be dressed in plain clothes and take shifts watching potential targets. Fortunately Aspen is a small town where tourists and strangers are easily spotted. The local police chief and sheriff's office were informed of the plan and felt this was the only way to preempt an attack. They had already arranged for the use of the Aspen High School gym and the Snowmass Recreation Center for medical triage and acute care by EMS personnel in case of mass casualties in the area."

Harry said, "Sounds like you guys have a good plan. I wanted to let you know that we have called all the rental offices and hotels to hopefully come up with the location of the terrorists, since we must assume they will need housing for a few days while they get familiar with the area."

Phelps said, "It's a long shot, but good thinking, Harry. What preparations have been made at the hospital to protect the staff and inpatients?"

"It was decided that we would leave it up to the physicians to discharge their patients on a risk-reward basis. We intend to patrol the hospital grounds and entrances for potential terrorist threats."

Leslie Rosario overheard their conversation and said, "We can use the local police for that job and in addition utilize bomb-sniffing dogs to guard the hospital entrances and exits. I will work on the arrangements to bring in several dogs with their handlers, and they can be accompanied by local police officers."

Jeff Ronson then said, "What do you think about closing the airport for the next few days?"

Phelps responded, "That will cause a lot of concern and panic unless some weather comes in to give us the appropriate excuse to close the airport."

Andy Regalto opened his computer to get the latest weather forecast. After a few minutes he said, "There is a front coming in tonight. However, as you know during this time of year these fronts can dissipate very quickly."

Harry then said, "What targets are you planning to concentrate most of your efforts on protecting?"

"We were thinking that the hospital, the airport, and the most congested shopping area in Aspen around Mill Street, Hyman, and Cooper Avenues."

Harry said, "I would also worry about the new base village in Snowmass." As Harry was getting ready to leave he added, "Well, you guys have a lot of work to do. I'm heading back to Basalt. Good luck."

Ed and Kathy awoke in each other's arms. They took a shower together, got dressed, and Ed made some coffee. They both had some cereal and headed out the door. There was four inches of fresh powder on the ground. Though they both would really have enjoyed a day of skiing, neither made a comment on the snow conditions, but each knew what the other was thinking. They headed toward the hospital along Owl Creek Road, and they both silently marveled at the beauty of the fresh snow covering the aspen and evergreen trees on the way, as well as the pure white, unruffled and smooth snow covering the large horse ranch property that occupied about one quarter of a mile of Owl Creek Road.

Ahmed and his accomplices were getting ready for morning prayers. They had performed Wudu by washing their bodies, and then they completed the recitation of the Kalima-Shahadah. They all faced east and completed their prayers simultaneously. They all had the feeling that they were joined together by the grace of Allah to complete the most important mission of their lives. After morning prayers, they had a small breakfast and then Ahmed sat them down at the dining room table and outlined his plan. He sent two of them to the village mall to get ski clothes and rental ski equipment. He then instructed the other two to make four suicide bomb vests and an improvised explosive device, or IED, with a radio-controlled triggering mechanism. Ahmed then left the condo and drove into Aspen to investigate the areas that would most suit his needs as targets.

Loretta arrived at LaGuardia Airport in Queens at noon and was accompanied by three FBI agents she had borrowed from the New York office. She left her original two operatives to continue guarding Sam and Evelyn Kahn. She briefed the other agents in the first-class lounge while they were waiting for their Continental flight to begin boarding. This flight would take them directly into the Eagle-Vail airport. She had maps of Aspen and Snowmass that she had downloaded and printed from her computer and also gave them some insight into the personalities of the team in Aspen that they would be working with.

After they had taken off, she took out her computer and organized her files that held all the information concerning the legal case against the hedge funds involved with Al-Shamir. She knew they had enough information to close down the ten hedge funds, and she was also confident that they were going to deal directly with the man named Al-Shamir. They now knew where he lived in Dubai, and they had information that also linked each of the hedge funds to a mosque in each of their respective cities.

Chapter 43

———◆◈◆———

March 2008

IT WAS 5 AM on Saturday when the snow began to fall, at first lightly, but then it gathered steam as the front moved in from Utah. Ahmed was awake for most of the night after his conversation with Al-Shamir at 2 AM Colorado time. He had outlined his plan of attack in Aspen. He also pleaded with Al-Shamir to leave his family unharmed and to assist them financially. He waited until 6 AM to awaken the cell members for morning prayers and final instructions. They would perform Fajr, or the predawn prayer, after a thorough cleansing of their bodies. This would be their final prayer before their mission began.

Ahmed was pleased when he observed their calmness and attention to the details of the plan. He was grateful to the imam at the Denver mosque for his skill in the training and indoctrination of these particular cell members. He could envision a growing number of dedicated young Islamic extremists throughout the United States being prepared at mosques in every major city getting ready to carry out similar acts of terrorism.

Ed arose at 7 AM, showered, shaved, and got dressed in jeans and a turtleneck shirt. He and Kathy had decided last evening after working in the hospital all day that it would be best for Kathy to spend the night at home with Laura and her mother. They had planned to meet

240

at the hospital at 8 AM, and he would help in any way he could if an attack materialized.

The Aspen airport was closed to incoming and outgoing flights as of 7 AM because of "weather conditions." All private jets were also placed on hold, and only a skeleton crew was present at the airport. Security personnel, however, were present in full force.

Phelps and his operatives were teamed up with officers from the local police and the Pitkin County sheriff's office. They were expecting the DSS bomb dogs with their handlers to arrive in the early AM to patrol the hospital and airport.

Harry and Phelps met for breakfast at 8 AM at the Main Street Bakery. They both had the feeling that today would be the day for the attack if indeed it was going to occur in Aspen. They went over the defense plans together and were convinced that their plan was as good as any under the circumstances.

They were just getting ready to leave when Harry got a call on his cell phone. It was the Aspen chief of police. He said, "Harry, I may have a lead on the location of a group of renters of Arab descent."

Harry asked, "When did they arrive and where are they located?"

"They rented from Joshua and Company, and they are staying in Meadow Ranch on Owl Creek Road in Snowmass Village. They checked in two nights ago."

Harry got the address of the unit from the sheriff and said, "Thanks, Chief. We will send over some operatives right away to investigate the rental unit."

Phelps immediately called Leslie Rosario and Andy Regalto and instructed them to head over to the Snowmass Village firehouse, which was across the street from the Meadow Ranch Condominiums, and wait for him there. He would be there by 9 AM. Harry followed Phelps in his own car.

It was 8:55 and still snowing when they all arrived at the firehouse. They went inside the fire truck bay accompanied by the EMS officer of the day.

Phelps explained, "Harry and I have just received information that leads us to believe that there may be a group of terrorists located across the street in the Meadow Ranch complex. Everybody should be wearing their bulletproof vests. Andy, you will take the lead and

Leslie will follow behind with her equipment to disarm a bomb if one is located. Harry and I will follow behind the two of you. We will approach from the upper-level parking area so we can come in through their back door. Are there any questions?"

They were checking their weapons as Phelps was talking, and they all indicated that they were ready to go. They all got into Phelps's Ford Explorer and drove up Meadow Ranch Drive off of Owl Creek Road. They exited the Explorer, approached the condo in crouched positions, and remained silent, only using hand signals for purposes of communication. There were no signs of activity coming from the condo as they approached. Andy Regalto tried the rear door that led into the kitchen on the top floor of the unit. The door was unlocked.

Andy entered the kitchen, staying in a crouched position. He made his way into the dining and living room area and was surprised to see that the wood-burning fireplace was still ablaze. Phelps entered next and was followed by Harry and Rosario. They quickly went through the unit. The unit was empty—however, there was still food in the refrigerator and the occupants still had clothes and other belongings scattered throughout the condominium. Harry noticed some copper wiring that was left on the floor in the dining room area as well as an empty container labeled "Nitric Acid." He also found an empty box in the trash that contained a single detonator. They continued to search the place but found no other materials needed for manufacturing a bomb.

They were getting ready to leave when they realized that there were four unmade beds but only street clothes for two people. They found prayer rugs and Qur'ans for four people as well.

Phelps and his operatives left the condominium to resume their patrolling duties in Aspen and the hospital. Harry stayed behind and waited for the officers from the sheriff's department to arrive to perform the crime scene investigation.

Harry called Kathy at the hospital. Prudence picked up the phone in her office and said, "Administrator's office, may I help you?"

Harry said, "Prudence, this is Harry McNally, and I need to speak to Kathy ASAP." "She's right here, Harry, hold on."

"Hi, Harry, I hope you have good news for us."

"I'm afraid not, Kathy. We located a condo right here in Snowmass where we think the terrorists have been staying. We found materials that suggest they have been making explosive devices. I wanted to let you know that we believe the attack will occur today, but we have the hospital well guarded and as I'm sure you have noticed there are trained, bomb-sniffing dogs with their handlers at all the entrances to the hospital."

"I appreciate all the help, Harry, and frankly this whole thing has me pretty rattled. I am such a wreck. I'm tired of looking at each employee as if they are accomplices, and now I find myself suspicious of the physicians I have known for years. I know you have been through this before, but I'm not sure how much longer I can put up with this kind of stress, with not knowing what to expect. I just keep picturing the scenes of 9/11, and I find myself wondering what Aspen will look like after a terrorist attack. Why here, and why us?"

Harry said, "At least we have the advantage of a warning and time to prepare. We never knew what hit us during 9/11. I wish I had more that I could say to make you feel more secure." "You're so right, Harry; I guess I have no right to complain."

It was 9:35 AM when the crime scene team arrived from the sheriff's office. Harry introduced himself and explained what they had found. He apologized that he and the operatives were not wearing gloves, but they had to approach the condo in attack mode.

The head of the CSI team said, "Don't worry about it, Detective McNally. We will take over from here." Harry walked across the street and got into his Bronco. The snow had finally stopped, and the sun had just begun to shine through the remaining thin cloud cover. As Harry drove toward Aspen on Owl Creek Road, he noticed that the morning crowd of skiers were exiting their parked cars and heading to the Two Creeks quad-speed lift. He thought to himself that today would be a busy day on the mountain since the sun was shining and there was fresh powder on the runs from the evening snowfall. He knew that the locals would be out today as well as the tourists.

It was 9:55 when he arrived at Aspen Valley Hospital. He wanted to be sure that all the preparations he and Phelps had discussed were in place. As he got out of his Bronco in the parking lot, he was immediately greeted by one of the DSS bomb dogs with his handler and one of the local Aspen police officers. The dog came right up to Harry, using his nose to inspect Harry from his boots to his upper torso. He was especially persistent at scratching at the shoulder holster Harry wore under his jacket. Harry identified himself and reached into his back pocket to procure his wallet, which contained his badge.

The Aspen police officer said, "Sir, do not move. Raise your hands in the air immediately!" Harry did as he was told, and the officer then opened Harry's jacket and removed his revolver from its holster. He then said, "Now you can show us your identification." Harry produced his badge and explained that he had been working with James Phelps and the local police.

They all shook hands, and as Harry walked away he had a sense of confidence that it would be really tough to place a bomb near the hospital or enter the hospital as a suicide bomber. The main concern, however, was the fact that there could still be an insider who worked at the hospital and who had already smuggled an explosive device to some unknown location inside the hospital. Harry decided to enter the hospital by way of the ER and again was confronted by a bomb-sniffing K-9 and searched by a local police officer. He took one last walk through the halls, checked out the kitchen and maintenance area, and then stopped by Kathy's office to see how she was doing.

It was 10:15 when Harry reached Kathy's office. Kathy was sitting at her desk dressed in jeans and a long-sleeved jersey. Harry knocked on her inner office door, which was partially open.

She looked up and said, "Hi, Harry, what are you doing here?"

"I just thought I would check on my favorite hospital administrator and see how she was holding up."

Kathy responded, "I must have sounded pretty bad before, but I'm feeling better now. I was working on my staffing and realized that I needed to be prepared for a large number of casualties since it is possible that the hospital may not be the epicenter of the attack, but rather other sites could be involved."

"That's a great idea, Kathy. I wanted to let you know that we have this place really well protected with bomb-sniffing dogs and police at all the entrances and exits."

"That is really reassuring, Harry. We have received a tremendous amount of support from the physicians on staff. They have assured us that they will be available by cell phone for any emergency where their services are needed."

"It sounds like you guys are as ready as you can be. Don't forget—these terrorists thrive on our inner fears and panic for their attacks to reach their maximum potential." Harry said good-bye, turned, and walked down the hall to exit the hospital via the front entrance. He drove out of the hospital grounds and turned onto Highway 82, which would bring him to Main Street.

He had made arrangements to meet Phelps at the Aspen police station on Main Street at ten forty-five. As he made the turn where Highway 82 became Main Street, he noticed that there were several men walking toward the Chabad Jewish Community Center of Aspen. A few of the men were dressed in long, black coats and wore black hats, similar to the dress that Harry remembered seeing in Manhattan at the Hasidic synagogues.

Harry met with Phelps at exactly ten forty-five in the parking lot of the courthouse where the Aspen police station was located.

Harry said, "How did your meeting go with the chief of police?"

James answered, "It went well. These guys are more sophisticated than you would expect for a small tourist town. They have provided all the assistance that we have asked for, and their officers and office staff have been working around the clock in full force."

Harry then said, "I asked the sheriff if he could place some of his men around that condo we raided after the CSI team left just in case they return."

Phelps then said, "I think today is the day. I can feel it in my gut."

Harry responded, "I feel it too. I just hope we have the key areas protected. Let's head back toward the hospital and airport area." They got into their cars and drove out of the parking lot and back onto Main Street.

The time was 10:55 as Harry passed the Chabad synagogue. He noticed that there was a man getting out of his car parked on West Hopkins and Fourth Street. He was dressed in black with a fur head piece. He was relatively short, had a black, short-cropped beard, and wore black leather boots. Harry found it curious that a man who followed the dress code of the Chabad Lubavitch would drive his car on Shabbos, or Saturday. Harry then noticed that the man reached into the trunk of his late-model Cadillac and pulled out a large backpack. Harry decided to circle around the block and come up behind the man's car.

He called Phelps, who was following several car lengths behind, on his cell phone and said, "James, pull over across from the Chabad."

Phelps said, "Why, what's the problem?"

Harry responded, "I see somebody suspicious approaching the synagogue. Something is out of place, and if you think about it, why couldn't this be a target?" Phelps pulled over and parked across the street from the Chabad. He got out of his car and began walking across Main Street toward the Chabad entrance. He could hear the prayer service coming from inside, indicating that the service had already begun. Harry pulled up behind the Cadillac and exited his Ford Bronco. He drew his pistol and quickly walked toward the man who was approaching the Chabad entrance. Harry looked at his watch and noticed that it was 10:59.

The man dressed in black saw Phelps heading toward him and turned to see Harry coming up behind him. He began running toward the entrance and at the same time removed the backpack. Just as he was getting ready to toss the backpack onto the steps of the synagogue, Harry stopped and with a two-handed grip aimed and fired. The bullet hit the man in the thigh, causing him to fall into a pile of snow on the side of the street. He screamed in pain and dropped the backpack, causing its contents to spill onto the snow that had piled up on the side of the road.

While lying face down in the snow, the man reached for a wireless detonator that had landed two feet from the bomb. Phelps saw what had happened and stopped, aimed, and fired. The shot hit the man dressed in black dead center in his forehead. His eyes remained open although lifeless as his body slumped onto the snow-laden street.

At exactly 11:00 AM, there were three explosions that could be heard in a series separated by ten seconds. The first came from the Starwood Estates area. The second came from Snowmass Mountain. The third came from Aspen Mountain.

Chapter 44

———◆◆◆◆———

March 2008

THE FIRST BLAST occurred in Starwood Ranch Estates at the palatial home of Prince Bandar bin Sultan. This estate home was one of the most expensive and lavish in Aspen. It was located on ninety-five acres and was worth in excess of $135 million. Its location afforded views of the entire ski resort area and surrounding mountain range. The blast destroyed most of the 56,000 square feet of living space, leaving only partial sections of steel and brick supporting structures standing amid charred and burning debris. The stables, which contained several very expensive show horses, were also destroyed. All of the horses as well as the stable crew died in the explosion. In retrospect, this site of terrorism should have been obvious since the owner of the estate was an Arab with close financial and political ties with the United States and had never supported the extremist movement financially. All those present in the estate were killed along with the suicide bomber who made his way onto the premises by masquerading as a cousin of the prince.

The second blast came from the Snowmass Mountain ski resort. The explosion originated from one of the new Swiss-made, eight-passenger Poma gondola cabins, causing the destruction of the cable and the collapse of all the cabins from the base to the summit of the mountain, crashing the cabins to the snow-covered terrain. The gondola carried skiers from the base village to the Elk Camp area, covering 1.6 miles in 8.7 minutes. It had been a recent addition to the already very popular ski mountain and added improved access for intermediate and beginner skiers.

The third blast originated from the Silver Queen gondola located at Aspen Mountain, or "Ajax" as the locals called it. This gondola traveled 3,000 vertical feet from the base of Aspen Mountain to the summit at 11,212 feet. The explosion occurred from one of the four passenger gondola cabins approximately halfway to the top and also caused the collapse of the cable and the subsequent destruction of most of the cabins as they crashed to the ground. The terrain crossed by this gondola was much steeper than the one at Snowmass, and additionally the areas below the gondola were more remote and difficult to reach.

The blasts were loud and seemed worse than they actually were because of the reverberation of sound off both Aspen and Snowmass Mountains. There was an initial panic that occurred in both the Snowmass Village area and the town of Aspen. The blasts not only caused the destruction of the gondolas, but glass windows were blown out of many of the magnificent homes that bordered the ski trails in the vicinity of the gondolas. Skiers were knocked to the ground by the blasts and flying debris. The gondola cabins on either side of the ones containing the suicide bombers were also blown up, causing body parts to scatter in multiple directions.

Flying debris caused multiple injuries to those in the path of the gondola cabins. As the cables were severed by the blast, people hung onto or fell from their respective cabins. Cries for help, screaming, and moaning started to be heard everywhere. Skiers, snowboarders, and lift operators were in shock and were fearful that there would be other explosions. The onlookers at the base villages of both Snowmass and Aspen were horrified by the sights and sounds of the injured and frightened people as they made their way to safety. The screams of mothers and fathers could be heard all over the ski mountains as parents tried to locate their children. Friends and loved ones tried to reunite utilizing cell phones and walkie-talkies. Panic was setting in as the reality of the horror became real. The peace and tranquility of these two magnificent ski resorts were now replaced with blood and destruction.

Fear was generated from the television coverage from both of the local channels that were based on Aspen Mountain, warning people to stay indoors except for emergencies. All the ski lifts were shut down, and the ski patrol attempted to evacuate skiers from both mountains. The injured were evacuated first with the use of snowmobiles and litter baskets.

There was an immediate response from both the Aspen and Snowmass fire departments as fire trucks and EMS ambulances streamed out of the East Hopkins Fire Station in Aspen and the Owl Creek location of the Snowmass-Wildcat Fire Department. The added noise and fear that was generated brought back memories and feelings of impotence similar to the feelings that all of America felt during 9/11.

It took over twenty-four hours to evacuate the injured and dead. It was especially difficult as nightfall approached because there was no lighting on the mountain. Only the headlights of the snowmobiles and snowcats could be utilized to supply the needed light. It took the cooperation of the ski patrol, fire departments, and EMS units to coordinate the effort. They were also assisted by the down-valley units in Basalt, Carbondale, and Glenwood Springs.

The two triage areas that had been previously arranged were immediately overwhelmed by the flood of injured and frightened people. Decisions had to be made on the spot by the rescuers on the mountain as to which people needed to be transported to the triage units or to the hospital. The injuries were predominately orthopedic in nature, with fractured legs and spines as the most common form of injury related to the gravitational fall of the gondola cabins. There were several common internal injuries as well, such as lacerations of the liver and spleen and blunt trauma to the chest, causing cardiac contusions and collapsed lungs.

The death toll at both mountains and the estate home in Starwood Ranch totaled 161 persons, of which 40 were children. The list of injured totaled 210, and most of these were serious, requiring surgery. Aspen Valley Hospital and local physicians tried to handle the load of patients in an efficient manner, but even with the help of the down-valley physicians they were overwhelmed. Physicians, nurses, and operating room technicians were flown in by helicopter from the teaching hospital in Denver.

Jack and Ed were instrumental in the organization of the triage areas and emergency room care. They worked without a break for almost forty-eight hours. Kathy and her staff worked tirelessly, being

249

sure that all the needed supplies were readily available to the nurses and physicians. Many of the locals also made themselves available for routine tasks at the hospital, such as maintenance and cafeteria work.

The press came into Aspen from all over the world along with the major television networks and their associated crews. There was not enough housing to handle the crowds at first, but since the skiing areas remained closed, most of the tourists left the area and the housing situation eased quite a bit.

The coverage was, as expected, sensationalized. The media played right into the hands of the terrorists by spreading fear, panic, and terror throughout the civilized world. Most of the headlines falsely stated that this was the first attack on American soil since September 11, 2001. The truth of the matter was that there had not been any massive attacks like this since 9/11, but there had been several other terrorist-related episodes.

The first two involved the use of anthrax in September and October 2001, but these attacks were never clearly related to Islamic terrorists. There was the December 2001 foiled attack by Richard Reid and his shoe bomb on American Airlines flight 63. On July 4, 2002, an Egyptian gunman opened fire at the El Al ticket counter in Los Angeles International Airport, killing three people. In October of 2002, John Allen Muhammad and Lee Boyd Malvo conducted the Beltway Sniper Attacks in the Baltimore and Washington area, killing ten people in various locations from October 2 until they were arrested on October 24. In addition, there were multiple other, less dramatic episodes up to 2008. This attack in Aspen, however, reiterated the vulnerability of the United States' open society to acts of terrorism.

The investigation by the FBI that ensued clearly demonstrated that the explosions occurred by the detonation of suicide bombs at all three locations. They were, however, unable to identify which of the people that entered the gondolas were responsible by reviewing the surveillance tapes, since they were all wearing helmets and goggles when they passed the cameras. They did identify the suicide bomber responsible for destroying the estate home and killing all its occupants. He was traced back to an Arab family in Denver.

The press had a field day with this act of terrorism, as they did in the wake of 9/11. The number of innocent, noncombatant men, women, and children, as well as the destruction of property that occurred, made for especially good headlines. The coverage was worldwide as it had been post-9/11. Some of the headlines read:

MASS MURDER IN ASPEN
HUNDREDS DEAD IN ASPEN
WE ARE STILL AT WAR
TERROR'S TOLL
ANOTHER DAY OF INFAMY
WAR DECLARED ON ASPEN

Chapter 45

April 2008

THE U.S. STOCK market had just completed another failed rally attempt, oil futures were approaching $150 per barrel, and gold was nearing $1,000 per ounce when the news hit the financial world in early April that ten hedge funds were being closed down because of their links to Arab terrorists and violations of insider-trading rules. There was coverage on CNBC, Bloomberg, as well as the *Wall Street Journal*, but what seemed unusual was the fact that the press downplayed the Arab connection and predominately stressed the greed of hedge fund operators. There was no mention of the mosque closures in the ten respective cities where the hedge funds were located except by some of the local reporters, and their articles never even made the front page of the local newspapers.

It was 1 AM United Arab Emirates time when the Navy C-2 Greyhound twin-engine aircraft lifted off from the aircraft carrier in the Gulf of Oman. The aircraft carried the team of James Phelps, Loretta Smyth, Leslie Rosario, Jeff Ronson, and Andy Regalto, along with three Navy Seals who were responsible for the backup and extraction of the team after their mission was complete. They were heading for the Al Dhafra air base in the city of Dubai. The mission was clearly one of **retribution—retribution** for the lives lost and injured in Aspen and at the Eisenhower Tunnel.

252

The agents involved knew better than to believe the popular notion that all of the major players in the Dubai government as well as the wealthy Arab families of Dubai were innocent of involvement with terrorism against the United States. The United Arab Emirates had a record of Al-Qaeda support in the past. They, along with Pakistan and Saudi Arabia, recognized the Taliban as the legitimate government of Afghanistan. Two of the 9/11 hijackers were from the UAE, and the FBI had claimed that the money for the 9/11 hijacking was transferred through the UAE banking system. The agents hoped that some day it would become evident to the world that in order to win the battle against the Islamic terrorists, the Muslim moderates would need to step up to the plate and join the fight in order to stop the killing of innocent noncombatant men, women, and children.

At 3 AM the team left the Al Dhafra base and traveled by truck to the edge of town on Sheikh Zayed Road to an area one hundred yards from the waterfront estate of Al-Shamir. They were dressed in black and were all wearing black Nomex hoods, except for Leslie Rosario and Loretta Smyth, who both wore black jeans and black, tight-fitting jerseys. Their heads were not covered. For all intents and purposes they had the appearance of a couple of tourists.

The team carried an array of weapons and wore bulletproof vests. Each of them had reviewed maps of the estate and the surrounding area during their flight from New York. They each had an assigned responsibility, but their common goal was to put a stop to this one particular Arab who by way of his financial support enabled the continuation of the jihad against the United States and its allies. World domination was not an old idea in world history. However, every attempt in the past had eventually been interrupted, and this team was going to do their small part to see that these radical Islamists would not be successful in their attempt at domination.

It was 4 AM, and the guards at the gate of the estate were caught off guard when Leslie and Loretta approached unescorted, giggling, talking loudly, and walking with a staggering gait as if they were intoxicated. As they got closer to the front gate, the guards began talking to them in Arabic. However, both women kept walking toward the front gate without responding. When they were ten feet away, both Loretta and Leslie pulled out M9 Beretta pistols with silencers from the small of their backs and took out both guards without missing a step. Jeff came out from behind the trees across the street and took out the surveillance cameras at the front gate. He tossed bulletproof vests that he was carrying to Leslie and Loretta, and they scaled the gate to enter the property.

James and Andy approached from the waterfront side of the estate with two of the Navy Seals. They entered by scaling up the rocky cliffs to the pool area, which was unguarded at this time of night. The team so far had gone undetected by the guards, though they knew that the servants would soon be awakening to perform their morning chores. The information that was supplied to them from the diplomatic corps led them to believe that Al-Shamir was home without his family since they were in London on a shopping trip.

James and Andy placed the first set of explosives in the rear of the main house of the sprawling estate. The explosives were spread out every twenty feet.

Leslie and Jeff did the same in the front. Suddenly, the exterior lights came on and two large, barking German Shepherds came at Leslie and Jeff from the front entrance.

Apparently the security system warned the men in the home security office when the surveillance cameras at the front gate failed to function. When they couldn't reach the front gate personnel, they released the dogs. The ferocious guard dogs ran at Leslie and Jeff, barking with teeth bared. Loretta was trailing by a few feet and saw the dogs coming. She kneeled and shot the one coming at Leslie while Jeff got the other as it was prepared to lunge at him.

The entire crew of security personnel was now awake, and the local police had been notified. Two security guards came out of the front entrance just as Leslie approached. They reached for their holstered guns, but Leslie got two quick shots off and both men went down immediately. She put another shot in each of them as she ran past them and entered the house. They both died instantly.

Jeff came in right behind her and took out a guard perched on the second level of the home near the staircase with his shotgun pointing at Leslie. She looked at Jeff and motioned thanks. They both started up the stairs toward the bedrooms, where they presumed they would find Al-Shamir.

James and one of the Navy Seals placed more explosives inside the house, and as they saw the servants they motioned for them to get out of the house.

Andy entered the main security office and found the guards there holding their hands in the air as a gesture of surrender. He knew they had no ability to take prisoners and could not allow these men to go free. He shot them both.

Loretta searched the downstairs area, which housed the media and billiard room as well as the wine cellar.

Leslie and Jeff reached the second floor of the home and found themselves looking down a long, wide hallway with multiple closed doors on each side. There were statues and sculptures lined up along the hallway along with large, magnificent tapestry wall hangings. The floors were covered by beautifully designed Persian rugs, which were obviously handmade and maintained as if they were brand-new. They had no idea in which room Al-Shamir would be hiding, but they were confident that by now he would have his bodyguards with him.

Jeff whispered into his wrist microphone to Phelps, "Boss, have you guys cleared the rest of the house, and have we blocked all possible escape routes for Al-Shamir?"

"We have searched the entire first level and the basement as well as the servant quarters. We have not seen him or his bodyguards."

Leslie then whispered, "I feel we could be walking into a trap up here."

Before Phelps could answer, they heard the sound of sirens approaching. Phelps then said, "Let's blow this place and hope the son of a bitch is hiding up there."

Jeff said in a louder, more emphatic tone, "But we won't be sure we get him." Before Phelps could respond, a door opened from one of the rooms twenty feet down the hall. A large Arab man stepped out, aiming a Colt .45 automatic handgun at Leslie. Before she could dive to the ground, he fired and hit her left shoulder. She fell to the ground in agony.

Jeff, at that moment, was looking down the hallway in the opposite direction. He turned and in one smooth motion aimed and fired two shots, striking the bodyguard in the chest and left side of his face. The Arab dropped to his knees, stared straight ahead for what seemed like an eternity, and then fell face forward in a large heap with blood oozing from his wounds and staining the Persian rug.

Jeff helped Leslie up, and they retreated back down the stairs to the first floor. The sirens were getting louder at this point, and Phelps gave the signal for the team to evacuate the premises. They all left via the rear of the estate, passed the pool area, and at the edge of the property atop of the cliffs they found the rope ladders that had been positioned by the Navy Seals. They made their way down the ladders quickly.

Leslie was carried by one of the Navy Seals who was six foot three and muscular, and he carried her without difficulty. They were on the beach in minutes and boarded a rigid, thirty-foot inflatable boat armed with a 65 mm machine gun. As they cast off, Andy Regalto detonated the explosives, causing a massive explosion which lit up the Dubai sky, adding to the golden glow of the beginning sunrise.

THE END

Epilogue

SUMMER FINALLY ARRIVED in Aspen. The rivers and streams were at the highest level seen for several years because of the extraordinary amount of snowfall that had occurred during the winter months and the late-April snowstorms. The construction crews had already begun to rebuild the gondolas at both Snowmass and Aspen Mountains. The mood of the locals was one of continued fear and depression similar to the effects that 9/11 had on New Yorkers. They not only had to overcome financial losses, but many lost family members in the collapse of the gondolas, and even more sustained serious, life-threatening injuries. Everyone was hoping that the freshness and beauty of summer would reverse the mood that was pervasive in the valley.

The summers in Aspen were glorious with crisp, cool air, deep green evergreens, and wild flowers filling the meadows. The hiking trails were dry by June, and there was a renewed vitality in the air in anticipation of the Aspen Music Festival that was held every summer. Word spread through the community that those responsible for the acts of terrorism were captured and received the retribution that was due to them. This, however, did very little to change the mood of the Aspenites, but with time, hopefully most wounds would be healed.

Sam and Evelyn Kahn's life was beginning to approach normalcy as June approached. Sam had recovered enough to resume a part-time accounting job that Gary Goldman had secured for him from a close friend who had offices in the same building that he occupied. Gary and Sam resumed their routine of having lunch together, discussing politics, and trading jokes they received on the Internet. The Kahns had dropped the lawsuit against the hospital and were trying to put the entire nightmare behind them. Sam was still collecting on his disability policy, and from a financial standpoint he and Evelyn would be comfortable. Evelyn resumed teaching in summer school, and their children visited every weekend now as they realized how close to death their father had come.

Harry and Grace could hardly wait for summer to arrive since they both enjoyed fly fishing in the many beautiful streams and rivers in the Aspen Valley. They had a big decision to make this summer since Harry had an offer to return to New York to work in a newly developed antiterrorism unit that was being formed in Manhattan.

The nightmares that had plagued Harry since 9/11 seem to gradually disappear after James Phelps informed Harry of their final mission in Dubai. Harry had the feeling that at times revenge really was sweet. Harry decided to wait until the end of the summer to make a decision to either return to Manhattan or live his life out in Colorado.

The plane carrying Kathy, Penny, and Jack landed in Fort Lauderdale on time from Denver. Ed met them in the baggage claim, having already checked his bags with the Holland America cruise personnel. The three of them had decided to kick off the summer by getting out of Colorado and joining Ed on a cruise through the Panama Canal. Prior to the trip they vowed not to discuss terrorism, medical malpractice, or the stock market. Jack and Penny could not help but wonder if Ed had an engagement ring tucked away somewhere in his carry-on.

Afternoon prayer services had just been completed in the newly built 10,000 square foot, $2.3 million mosque in Boca Raton, Florida. The mosque was built in an Arabic and Spanish style of architecture with copper domes, a minaret, and a towering spire. It was designed to replicate the Prophet's Mosque in Medina, Saudi Arabia, and had a reputation that linked some of its supporters to Al-Qaeda as well as other jihadist organizations.

The imam slowly walked from the prayer hall along the walkway covered with blue and yellow tiles toward the front entrance, where he was planning to wait for the arrival of his biggest supporter and benefactor. The sun was low in the sky, but the temperature was still in the nineties when the white Mercedes limousine pulled up to the main entrance of the mosque. The driver quickly exited and came around to open the rear door for Al-Shamir.

The imam approached with arms extended and greeted Al-Shamir, kissing him on both cheeks and saying, "Assalamualaikum."

Al-Shamir answered, "God is reckoning over all things." They separated, and just prior to walking into the mosque there was the cracking sound of a sniper rifle. Al-Shamir's head suddenly snapped back from the force of a bullet that struck him dead center in the forehead, and he fell to the ground. A pool of blood accumulated around his body, staining his white robes as he lay lifeless at the entrance to the mosque.

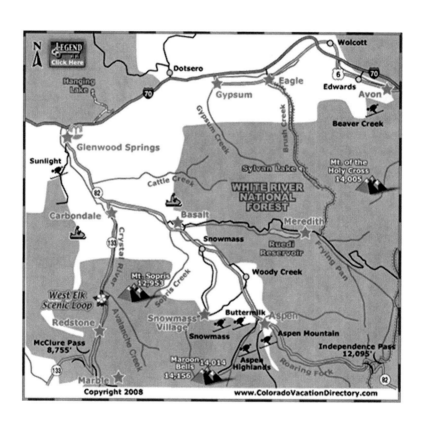

LaVergne, TN USA
13 January 2010
169778LV00001B/1/P